THE POLAR SAGA
BOOK I

THE SPIRIT DRAGON'S KEEPER

CATARINA LILLIEHÖÖK

Published by Book Hub Publishing, An Independent Publishing
House, Ireland. www.bookhubpublishing.com

ISBN: 978-1-0685633-8-6

To Xu Xi

It was my destiny to meet you.
Without you this book would not exist.

THE DRAGON TEMPLE

ARCHIVE HOUSE

TOOL SHED

VEGGIE PATCH

ROOKERY

HEAVENLY EMPEROR'S PALACE HALL

CROUCHING TIGER

SLEEPING BEAR

SIX SAINTS' HALL

SILENT GRASSHOPPER

HOPPING HARE

TEN THOUSAND BUDDHA HALL

PRACTICE HALL NO. 1

WISE PANDA

THE BLOOMING LOTUS FLOWER'S PALACE HALL

PRACTICE HALL NO. 2

SCURRYING MOUSE

ARMORY

UPPER COURTYARD

LOWER COURTYARD

CHAPTER I

I HAVE TWO IMMEDIATE PROBLEMS. THE FIRST IS MY HAIR. It's cut short, like that of a *boy*. The South China sun is bearing down on my neck like a flaming beast.

"Tamen laile!"

Beyond the curtain of swaying bamboo, excited voices announce our arrival. My throat tightens. How old will the boys in there be? And how many? I have dreaded this moment for nine long moons, and this is my second problem. *Long Si*, the Dragon Temple, is not for girls, especially not nine-year-old foreign girls. With twitchy fingers, I follow my master. Curved rooftops dance in my side vision, and tall mountains tower menacingly around us. How did I get from reindeer herder to this? Everything is still unreal. I have not seen a motorcar since we crossed the border; we have no horses, and Master Li's money has dwindled along the way. The long walk has left me bone weary, and fear spikes in my system in front of the imposing gate. We enter, and I nearly stumble into my master as he halts in the lower courtyard. Buildings, mounted stone tablets and sculptures of lions and turtles surround me. My eyes instantly pick out the grand structure beyond the stairs and the upper courtyard: the Blooming Lotus Flower's Palace Hall. I know it from Master Li's drawing. He made me memorize it all.

For a suspended moment, everything in the courtyard stops. Next, a flurry of boys surrounds us, gawking, drawing near in tighter and tighter circles. Five feet away, they stop. Their gazes strip the meat off my bones, making my heart beat wildly. Pressing my lips together, I try to hide the toe peeking from my worn left shoe.

"It is good to have you back, Abbot Superior." An old woman with a laundry basket nods in greeting.

"Ah, Mei. I hope the washing is not too hard on your joints."

A second woman, wearing an apron, hurries across the upper courtyard brushing flour from her arms. "You're back!"

"Cook Ma," Li sharpens his gaze, but at her almost imperceptible headshake, disappointment flits across his face.

The crowd quickly melts away as a man with broad shoulders pushes through. His face has a carved quality, and the ends of his long black moustache nearly dips into the forked beard below.

"Master Li," he nods curtly as he comes to a stop.

"Master Gang." Li offers a tight-lipped smile. "How are your fighting classes?"

"Very good." He puffs up his chest, nodding at a boy with square cheeks and hard eyes. "Yong Da's excelling. As you know, *ta ai chi ku*." The boy eats bitterness like sweets.

Yong Da rakes me with his gaze.

I can tell what will come will not be pleasant, so I bow my burning face. A big cockroach scuttles between the throng of black canvas shoes.

"*Ta shu she.*" The boy spits out my birth year: Snake. Master Li told them? Shock prevents me from glancing at my master. "*She* won't be able to fight any warlords."

Fight warlords? Despite the heat, I shiver to my toes.

Apart from the two boys flanking Yong Da, the others look away, embarrassed. I've learned it's not the Chinese way to be so direct. Yong Da does not care.

"*Nüwu,*" he snorts: witch.

They know I'm a girl. My short hair is fooling no one. Or did Master Li tell them this also? I am not a witch. Anyone born in the year of the Snake can have many good qualities. Master Li taught me about China.

"*Xiao long,*" says a little boy no more than five or six, staring from under somebody's arm. "It's not snake; it's *xiao long.*"

One of the masters pats his head. "That's right, Xiao Wei." He adds the prefix for *little*. "Little dragon is what she is."

In the Chinese zodiac, Snake comes next to Dragon, and to soften unpleasant connotations, Master Li told me that it is common to call oneself small dragon instead of Snake. How can a birth year matter so much? And why did he tell people in the village I'm an orphan? I heard him. *Guer, tai kelian le.* I had bitten my lip in anger. Liar! I am not an orphan. I am Mila. My parents are reindeer herders in the wild lands far above the Polar Circle. Master Li stole me and gave me a new name: Lu Mi La. In China, the surname comes first, and Lu means reindeer, so now I am Mila Reindeer. But that was many moons ago, and my memory is hazy.

"Off you go," the master gives Little Wei a gentle push. "All of you, back to your chores." He turns and smiles. "I am Master Peng, teacher of scripture. I will show you to your room."

My room—as though this is home. Home is so far from here that my throat tightens. Home is Sápmi, the northern part of Fennoscandia, a region stretching over four countries of arctic territory: Norway, Sweden, Finland, and Russia. Temperatures often go below thirty, and the sun in winter does not even reach the horizon. Where it's wild and free, where life moves with the seasons and the migrating herd, and where you learn to observe. I have been here less than five minutes, but already I know three things: Cook Ma bears a secret, Master Li has something Master Gang wants, and Yong Da hates me. Teeth cutting into my lip, I keep my eyes trained on the ground. The cockroach has advanced further into the throng of feet.

Master Peng motions for me to walk, and as I follow, I feel their unkind eyes burn my back in one huge collective protest: *A girl!* But right now, I am grateful. I am allowed my own space. The boys sleep in dormitories.

"Here you won't be disturbed." On the second floor in the Pavilion of the Crouching Tiger, Master Peng opens a door and points inside. "Rest now," he advises. "Supper won't be for another few hours."

I am trying to think of something clever to say, but my heart still pounds too wildly. He retreats, closing the door behind him. The floorboards in the corridor creak faintly as his steps dwindle.

I stare at the cramped quarters; a tiny window sheds light on a narrow bed, a chair, a small table with a water pitcher and a wash basin. Compared to swarms of boys, the silence is deafening, yet I feel like the room is moving around me. What little resolve I have left breaks, and I collapse on the bed and cry. "You're an orphan," Master Li had reminded me right before we entered the gates, his steely grip making my arm throb. *Bie rang wo diu mianzi.*

Lose face. He told me not to embarrass him, but how could I embarrass him? I am his prisoner! My mind still refuses to believe that my life shattered the night those bad men came to my village over nine moons ago. But here I am, and Master Li decides: *Ni ting wode.*

Chinese, or what these people call *Putonghua,* has since invaded my brain, distorting my mother tongue to a blur of indistinct sounds. But sometimes, there is that flash in my head. *Be careful, Mila. Be careful not to show.* My mother, yes, once I was that Mila, but now? And careful not to show what? I can't remember. Her voice is familiar, but did she speak Swedish? Or was it Sámi, the ancient language of the reindeer herders? A mixture? It rolls around and around in my skull but will not give me an answer, and anyway, it doesn't matter. All that was before.

Before, I was blindfolded and taken to the slave market.

The memory chills my skin like an icy hand.

I want to push it away, but the narrow bed draws it back, as though the stale, musty blanket prods me to remember. Curling up, I sob as images pound me. It was horrifying, not seeing, not understanding, knowing only that I was locked into a room that moved and made a terrible noise. I realized I must be inside a motorcar or a truck, which are things I had heard of in Sápmi but had never seen. Before that, I was out on the mountain searching for a lost reindeer when men approached. They wore dark long coats with bearskin collars. Even from afar, I could see the sneer on their sinister faces, and it should have been a warning, but we were too slow. The last I remember is Mother's terrified scream.

"Run, Mila. *Run!*"

She shoved me aside and threw herself at the men.

In a panic, I ran, pushed through snow drifts, pulse roaring in my ears. Then everything went black.

When I came to, everything seemed out of focus, and my blindfold was not torn off until days later. Confused, I looked at crowds of men and women. It took a minute for my eyes to adjust to the light, but slowly, they picked out cages, elevated stands and people in chains. With a chilling realization, I gasped. The slave market at Gorgarath!

This witch's cauldron of evil was rarely mentioned at home. And should any of us children come within earshot, it was quickly extinguished by hushed voices and sharp glances. All I knew was that it was very far away and east as the crow flies.

Rough hands dragged me from the truck, and a sensation pierced my drugged state, pierced the distressing smell of clammy, sweaty bodies mixed with fear. It was the same sensation I'd experienced during my sixth year of calf marking in Lapland, Sápmi, north of the Polar Circle, as though ants were crawling all over my body, as though someone was seeing right through me, into my soul.

Outside the truck, people were shouting, haggling and

gesticulating. "*Seikhar*," someone whispered. "Good price."

I prayed to Ukko, the deity who is the giver of life and the protector of my people.

The memory makes me squirm in hatred and shame on my hard bed. I wanted to struggle, wanted to scream, but how could I struggle against grown-ups? To whom would I scream? I was petrified. My body is wracking in mute sobs, as it is right now.

A knock on the door makes me jolt like a startled rabbit. I quickly dry my eyes and go to open it. Cook Ma.

"I thought you might be hungry." She offers a steaming bowl. "Some broth will do you good."

I take the bowl and close the door. Then I sit on my bed, staring at the clear liquid. Pieces of green float around in it, *bai cai*. I know the broth will taste of ginger, soy, sesame, and vinegar, but those first impressions of Master Li keep assaulting me, making it impossible to eat. How my breath stopped when he appeared after I had been sold and thrown onto the back of a horse cart. Masked, he jumped out of nowhere and pulled me to the ground. In a flash, my two captors were before him, knives palmed.

He ripped a sword from the harness on his back and charged in a rain of strikes. Two against one, but even my untrained eye could tell he was superior. With military efficiency, he disarmed them, knocked them senseless and tossed me back up on the horse cart.

Then he scooted into the driver's seat and whipped the reins, sending the horses bolting. I was still numb. The shock of having lost my family and been abducted twice in a matter of days left me staring mutely as we made our way south through

Russia and along what remains of the ancient Silk Road.

The next day, my new master bought me a pair of pants, found a rusty pair of scissors, and cut off my long, dark hair.

"*Ni shi nan haizi, dong ma?*" No, I didn't understand Chinese, but the villages we passed were grim and poor, and people stared at us. I soon got it. He wanted me to be a boy.

I think of all the boys here and shudder. Too many. I put the soup bowl on the floor, and heat builds behind my eyelids again. Out there, it is too noisy, but here it is too quiet. Suffocating, like my journey. The first week, we traveled in silence. My new master and I did not understand each other, and I did not comprehend if he had rescued me or if he was just a new captor. Was an even worse fate awaiting me?

I wanted to spit in his ugly old face. He must be forty at least, but whenever his thin uniform stretched tight, I could see that his body was pure muscle. I knew he must be terribly, terribly strong.

We could only communicate by simple sign language, and weeks turned into moons. We passed many strange places, and now, thinking back, names get tangled in my mind: Ural Mountains, Caspian Sea, Uzbekistan, Hindu Kush, Tashkent and Samarkand. There was the odd motor car, sometimes a truck, their harsh roaring startling me every time. I felt safest when we joined a caravan and traveled on horses and foot. I walked until my feet bled, smelling the camels' regurgitated half-digested grass, like wet, slimy compost on an overly hot day. I learned to ride, something we never did on the reindeer, and my bony seat ached as though it was one big tender bruise. But more often, we spent our days on the back of some loaded wagon, and Master Li began to teach me *Putonghua*, the everyday speech of the Chinese. He pointed at things and said the word. I repeated. And so we went. There was not much else to do, and I dared not oppose. I dared nothing; even to just ask for the bathroom, I had to muster all my courage, and that part hasn't changed. I must find a privy now.

I slide from the bed and peek carefully out my door. No one is there. One more step, and I am moving weightlessly along the corridor and down the stairs. At the pavilion's opposite end, I see a kitchen. I must go over and ask. But there will be boys. Will they overhear that I need a bathroom? I stand so still that I lock my knees. I have learnt that if my knees are locked and my body stiff, I don't shake.

Then I take a deep breath and walk. But somebody comes rushing out from the kitchen, and I freeze.

It is only Cook Ma, and she seems to read my thoughts. She calls me little friend, *"Xiao pengyou*, do you need the restroom?" She beckons, "Come, I will take you."

I scoot to meet her at the door that is between us and follow her out and around the back. She stops in front of a small shed and points. "Girls only. I'll wait here."

Inside, gloomy light barely reveals a concrete floor with a hole in it. The long, horizontal gap at the top of the walls allows free airflow, yet the place stinks of urine and worse.

I finish my business quickly, and as we return, boys are spilling out from the kitchen, ogling me. My legs go numb.

"Her name is *Reindeer*," somebody whispers, provoking a burst of giggling, and my face goes bright red.

But Cook Ma puts a hand on my shoulder. "Back to work, all of you," she shoos them off and follows me upstairs. "Don't worry, you will get used to it. It's not as bad as it seems."

I sit on the bed and touch my Sámi bracelet of pewter wire sewn onto reindeer hide. It is the traditional armband back home; everyone wears it, and it brings me a morsel of comfort. Away from the Silk Road, my brown hair and dark eyes aren't enough to blend in. There, I was a servant or a slave; no one asked. The crossed swords on Master Li's back probably didn't invite questions, either. Except for a few skirmishes, we were left alone, disappearing into the stream of travelers and merchants along the busy trading route. But I felt watched, and once, in a dilapidated town somewhere in Kyrgyzstan, evil men appeared.

Master Li's knife whizzed through the air, and I rushed into a building and huddled in the shade while he morphed into a blur of moving limbs.

Afterwards, I still trembled. "*Shei?*" I asked in my stammering Chinese. Who were they? "What a bad place!"

"Every place has bad people."

Not Sápmi. Only reindeer and nature.

He retrieved the knife embedded in the chest of one of the attackers. The street had gone eerily quiet, but eyes observed us behind flimsy curtains. With a calm brushing down of his clothing, my master continued our journey, and I scurried.

"Just common thieves," he muttered. "Nothing like the triads."

"What are triads?"

"Nothing."

"But what are they?"

"*Bu yao danxin,*" don't worry.

"No." I stopped under the hot midday sun that had scorched us every day since we began crossing this cursed land.

"Tell me. I want to know."

He motioned forward. "Another time," he said, and I dared not press.

"*Qu nali?*" I wanted to know where we were going.

"*Zhongguo.*" China.

"*Weishenme?*" He never replied to my whys. It was the hundredth time I'd asked and the hundredth time I did not get an answer.

"*Wo yao huijia,*" I said quietly. My request to go home was not new.

"*Bu xing.*" Not possible.

"Says who?"

"Says the oracle bones."

"What are oracle bones?"

He picked up our lessons, language and all things Chinese. I gritted my teeth at his power and authority, balling my small white hands until spasms travelled along my arms. I wanted to kick and scream, but I was afraid. Slowly, the bleeding ache for my family was pushed out by my overfull brain. I struggled with flowing characters that he drew in the dirt, hand signals for numbers and incomprehensible pronunciation drills. My hatred mellowed but never ceased.

"*Si,*" he said with a deliberate lisp, lifting his upper lip to show how his tongue pressed against his teeth. "In Chinese, a word can have many meanings. *Si* can mean the number four, for example. Or seem, think, feed, die, silk. It can mean even more, so which one is it? You have to know."

Die, I mouthed silently.

But not today.

CHAPTER 2

O N THE SECOND DAY, MY TRAINING IN LONG SI BEGINS.
My first session leaves me shattered before it has
even started. Master Li decides to hold off on staff training
because I am too young and inexperienced. This means I will
not yet be studying with Master Gang. His name means steel,
so he is called Steel Master, and he is Head of Fighting. I should
heave a sigh of relief, but all of the disciplines intimidate me. I
have never held a sword or kicked anything higher than a pile
of frozen reindeer dung in winter.

I am put in a group with younger boys, all dressed in gray
fighting uniforms with loose-fitting pants and long white cotton
socks that reach the knee and must be tied with a black ribbon.
The long-sleeved jacket ends halfway down my thigh, held in
place by a wide sash at the waist. No Sámi bracelet.

"Run!" The master yells at us to circle the lower
courtyard.

Everyone takes off, but I have never run fast like this.
From the start, I lag like a cow behind roe deer, and before the

first lap, my crushing defeat is apparent.

Something flashes in my peripheral vision, and from one of the mounted stone tablets, something red comes flying. A tomato. It smacks into my temple with a force that makes me stagger. I keep going, even though it feels like there is a hole in my head. One of the boys turns to look as he runs. It is the one they call Xiao Wei. It feels like he wants to say something, but my head throbs from the impact, and maybe he doesn't dare to speak, and I cannot hear anything anyway.

Heart roaring in my ears, I come around the courtyard on the second lap and see some boys hiding behind the stone tablet. Yong Da. His mouth is twisted like a sneering monkey. He flings his arm, and a small stone hits my neck, and then they all turn and flee. I keep running. I don't feel the sharp sting. I don't feel anything. Only my feet smacking into the flagstones, the beating on the side of my head. I want to go faster, but the distance between me and the leaders keeps growing. I fall behind, further and further, only me, everyone's up there, Xiao Wei, everyone.

Then we stop. I think my heart is going to explode. My numbness fades, and now my temple throbs, and my neck stings. I want to rub the painful spots, but I don't. I don't speak, and I don't cry. We are ushered into one of the training halls, and I feel naked without my bracelet around my wrist. I am given a wooden sword, a small one that fits my size, and the master works us through basic stances, parries and blocks. All too soon, the sword weighs like a rock in my hand, and the footwork makes the breath tear in my throat.

I begin to grasp what Master Li said about *face*. He was away for over a year and a half to bring me here. I am clearly the worst student in their history, even though they are all younger than me. I have failed miserably, and he has already lost face.

It takes me the rest of the day to recover, and I desperately long to retreat to my room. It does not happen because as soon as practice is over, a sinewy old master appears and grips my arm with surprising strength. Long grey hairs spurt from a wart on his chin, and with jerky steps, he drags me like a ragdoll across the upper courtyard. At the Pavilion of the Wise Panda, I freeze as I see the boys' dormitory. He is going to move me there! But as soon as we enter, he steers left instead of up the stairs all the way to the corner. He shoves me into a small, scruffy room and pushes me down on a stool. I yell like a stuck pig when he grabs a fistful of my hair and a knife.

"*Zemmele ni ah?*" He starts anew before I have replied, not really wanting to know what's wrong.

"No, no," I don't want to, "*Bu yao.*"

"*Anjing, sha haizi.*" He snaps at this stupid child to be silent. "Everyone must shave their head."

"Cook Ma," I squeal. She is all I can think of. Then, "Ah Mei," the laundry lady. "They don't have shaved heads."

"That's because they work here, not being trained as monks...nuns," he amends as though the idea of a female monk is terrifying. Again, he grips my hair.

"Stop! Stop!"

Through my screaming, I detect movement. Master Li flows in like a cool breeze.

"*Deng yixia,*" he commands, and the man stops.

Cook Ma is right on his heels.

"*Zenmele?*" growls the old man. What now?

"Perhaps you can just...cut it," Master Li says. "No shaving."

"No!" Cook Ma hisses under her breath. "Leave her be. Hasn't she been through enough already?"

When they see that I watch them, they step back, some unseen communication passing between them.

Master Li nods; nothing needs to be done.

The master mutters at Li to suit himself, scratches his wart and walks away.

I scramble from the chair and out to freedom, clutching at my unwashed tufts of hair. But in my distress, I run the wrong way, straight into Yong Da and his bully friends. Terrified, I stop, staring wildly and still clutching my hair.

"No shaving?" Yong Da glares suspiciously. His face morphs into nasty smugness. "That just proves it. Her name is Reindeer. She's born a snake, and besides a witch."

"Not like us," says the stocky boy beside him.

"Definitely not," agrees the one on his other side.

"Mi La, come this way," Cook Ma arrives at my side, again saving me from unknown horror.

I do not need to attend the second fighting practice on this first day. As we reach the Six Saint's Hall, Cook Ma says I am allowed to go to my room, and that is when I see it. In her eyes, something that mirrors my distress? I do not know. I only want to walk away as fast as I can without drawing attention.

I slip inside the Pavilion of the Crouching Tiger and up the stairs. On the bed, I curl up and cry. They want me to look like one of them. I am not a boy! And I don't belong in a stupid temple. This is all Master Li's doing.

The freedom calms me, but by supper, my anxiety

returns. As I step into the refectory, everything stops. Everyone in the hall looks up, and my face grows so hot I think my ears will catch on fire.

I drop my gaze and steer toward the food line, navigating the piercing stares. With my bowl of steaming rice and vegetables and one *baozi*, the plain flour buns found everywhere, I glide like a ghost through the room, lowering myself onto a chair at an empty table. I bow my head and eat.

After a while, I hear another chair being pulled out. Somebody is sitting across from me, two seats down. I dare not breathe. A fast glance. It is Wei Wan, the younger boy again, who said I was a small dragon instead of a snake. For a moment, our eyes meet. Then we both look at our food. After evening meditation, I will be allowed back into my small room. I pray I make it.

"Eight moons," I hear Master Li in my mind.

Memory pulls me back to when we crossed the border from Kyrgyzstan to China. I never kept track of time. I had not dreamed that I would one day be so far from home, looking like a boy, grimy, disheveled. My nails were so packed with dirt it was enough to plant a flower. Though in the old trading hub of Kashgar, in the western province of Xinjiang, I fit right in. Staying on my master's tail, I jostled through the bustling bazaar crammed with spices, nuts, musical instruments, pashminas, dried snakes, weapons, and fur caps. He purchased several daggers and small bags of spices, or were they poisons?

I remembered now that he'd never answered my question.

"What are triads?"

He muttered in displeasure. "A Chinese organized crime syndicate."

"What is a syndicate?"

"A gang. A mob."

"Is this a triad?"

"No, this is a market, and we must leave. Head south."

"What waits there?"

"*Nide mingyun.*" My destiny?

His reply surprised me, but then we passed the livestock market, where stomping and mooing filled the air. Smells of damp fur and steaming dung hit my nostrils. Nervous animals, dust, things that fired me oddly as if something long shuttered in my heart were now awakened. *Máttaráhkká*, Earth Mother. Oh, how I missed home. Suddenly, I was flooded with pictures: Mother, Father, my sister Maddji, and my little brother Olli. Our *lávvu*, the traditional Sámi tepee that can be taken down and put up again to follow the migrating herd. The calves, the bulls, the *vajans*—the mother reindeer who cared so much for their little ones, I grew up calling all mothers *vajans*.

Master Li eyed me curiously. I looked away. My native Scandinavia, the reindeer, he wouldn't understand.

Yet, I made an effort. "*Jia, ni you jia ren ma?*" I stuttered with all the wrong intonations, trying to ask if he had family.

He touched the strange scar on the underside of his forearm. "*You yige didi.*" One younger brother.

Olli appeared in my mind. Then my sister. Then mother, and out of nowhere, a word popped into my head—*Seikhar*. A vast green light covered the heavens above. It swirled and shivered as though the gods were dancing. Aurora borealis, the northern lights of Sápmi, sometimes occurring during winter nights. And suddenly, I am home again, looking down at my upturned palms. The snow was cold and the night dark, but the lines of my palms shimmered. Thin red streaks crisscrossed my skin, flowing like tiny rivulets.

Mother saw it. "The northern lights," she inhaled sharply. "It set them off!" She grabbed my hands and folded them against my tummy. "Has it happened before?" she whispered, face pale.

I shook my head. Her gaze darted to Father, who stood shocked, holding the stray reindeer we had gone out to find.

"If it happens again, Mila, you must hide your hands. Remember. Hide your hands; it's important and never say the word."

Seikhar.

I snapped out of my odd vision. Master Li was still observing me. "*Hao ma?*" Are you okay? His gaze went to my closed fists.

"*Hao,*" I replied bravely, resisting the impulse to hide my hands. Nothing had happened, no red shimmer; everything was fine. Except that it wasn't. I was eight years old, I had been abducted twice, and I was far away from home.

It is the third day at Long Si, my first day of chores, and I am in the worship house of Ten Thousand Buddhas. In the faint light of candles, I crawl between statues of deities with a small hand broom and dustpan, sweeping up ashes from all the joss sticks. Damp concrete presses through my silk pants, scraping at my knees, but I am glad to be away from the stares. I would spend all day in here if I could.

Footsteps make me perk up. I recognize Master Li's voice. He is talking to someone.

It's Cook Ma. "You've been away for a long time. Are you sure you're right?" From around the corner of the massive statue I am hunkering behind, I can just see Master Li taking a joss stick.

He lights it in the nearest candle. "I followed the signs."

"They took you all the way to Scandinavia?" Ma lights a joss stick of her own. For a second, it goes quiet as they close their eyes and bow before a deity.

Li opens his eyes. "No, only as far as the slave market."

"And how can you be sure you didn't go wrong in a place like that? The *feng shui is* terrible." She refers to the ancient system of laws that are considered to influence land and buildings through the flow of energy.

"The oracle bones told me clearly. And besides..." He places his stick in one of the holders. "The Nefarious got to her first."

Ma's eyes fly wide. "Are you sure?" She lowers her voice to a whisper. "Are you sure it was them?"

"Trust me, I had to free her an hour east of Gorgarath."

Her indrawn breath is clear. Gorgarath. As though that just explained something. "Does anyone know?"

Li shakes his head. "Master Gang must not find out." He gives her a stern look. "You know how hard I had to fight for this."

"Of course not. But..." She looks distressed again, that vague curtain of darkness. "Year of the Snake—that doesn't match."

"No." Master Li rubs his chin. "There is that, I know. But I spoke to the traders. Maybe she can still be compatible."

Ma quiets for a moment. "Do you know for certain that now is the right time? Did the bones speak of a year?"

"They said the wood earth cycle between Dog and Ox. 1936 is close enough."

Behind the statue, my hands are stiff and cold. The concrete is grinding into my knees, but I dare not move.

"Anyway," says Li. "It is too early to tell. She is not of that age yet. Pray it all gets sorted before the warlords."

What age? Warlords again! And why did Cook Ma react so strongly to Gorgarath?

Suddenly, a scene appears in my mind. Back home in Sápmi, the tool shed. I had come to return a shovel, but someone was already in there, and I heard, "Gorgarath." The forbidden word.

Nimbly, I dropped down behind a sled.

"Stop fussing about the slave market," Father told Mother sternly. "It's too far away. We're all safe from it."

Mother quieted, but I saw the glance that passed between her and Grandma Koini. From my safe spot, I furtively observed them. But still, I couldn't tell if their silence was only obedience or if it masked something else, like a secret. What kind of secret? And if Father said we were all safe from the slave market, then how could I end up there anyway?

And then from there to here?

Goosebumps race up my arms.

CHAPTER 3

THE JOURNEY HERE WAS HOT, DIRTY, UNCOMFORTABLE, and frightening. But trying to blend into Long Si proves an even greater challenge. I am stared at, glared at, or seen through like I do not exist at all. I am a Peruvian llama dropped in the middle of a reindeer herd. On the journey, at least I had Master Li by my side. As much as I hated him, I was never alone. Now I don't see him much. He is the Abbot Superior, the ruler of Long Si, and not one to approach lightly.

I know what oracle bones are, pieces of ox shoulder used for divination, but I still don't know why I'm here. And no one is likely to tell me, so instead, I spend time with the temple cats. My favorite is a white female I have named after her colour and pure vibration: *Habllek*; in my language, it means powdery snow. Father tried to teach me all the two hundred words we have for snow, each one describing different aspects of the snow's quality and condition, but I only remember a few. If I were home, I would learn more, and Father would teach me while allowing me to play in the snow at the same time. That's how we learn in Sápmi. Right now, I miss it terribly.

I scratch Habllek's neck. She looks so peaceful. She reminds me of my own reindeer that Father gave to me as a calf two springs ago. She had lost her *vajan,* and I bottle-fed her every day until we managed to convince another *vajan* to care for her. But by then, she and I had already formed a long-life bond.

A lump pushes painfully in my throat. The idea of home vanishes a little more with each passing day, and several weeks have already passed. Thank Ukko that Grandma Koini and her stories by the fire, which kept me and my siblings awake and wide-eyed until late, remain clear in my head. I can see her bronze eyes reflecting the flames, still hear her slow, gravelly voice as she fed us tales of *edelhjort,* the magic deer; the fulcrum hare, the harbinger of doom; and of what dwelled beyond Treriksrøysa—that mythical Northern tripoint of Norway, Sweden and Finland, where strong geopathic powers merge.

"Enough, Koini," Mother would order. "We don't want them stuffed with your stories."

But Grandma stirred the pot that hung on a chain beneath the *lávvu's* smoke hole and continued in a whisper. Only when Mother returned, finding us still awake, and gave another sharp reprimand, would she finally stop and go to rest. But not me. It was in that time between waking and sleep, when reality begins to warp and conscious thought dissolves, that my mind would weave her words into pictures. A hazy pattern of untethered notions that etched themselves into my mind.

"One day, I will tell you," I whisper in Habllek's ear.

"What're you doing?"

I jump up at Yong Da's ambush. Habllek flies from my arms, twists in the air and shoots off. Behind Yong Da, two of his bully friends draw near.

"What?" says the one that reminds me of a bulldog.

"Talking to the cat!" Yong Da sneers. "I knew you were a witch!"

"I'm not a witch."

"Anyone who talks to animals is, and a white one at that. Are you so ignorant you don't know what that means? *Sha yatou*," he spits.

No, I'm not ignorant. You just called me a stupid girl, and white in China is the color of death. "I'm not a witch."

"I heard you. You used a secret language."

Yes, it's called Sámi. "I'm not a witch."

He draws close and nails me with a gaze that sets my heart pounding. He is two years older than I am and much bigger and stronger. Ukko save me.

"Yong Da, what are you doing?" Cook Ma glares as she comes around the corner with a big basket of corn.

I scurry off as fast as Habllek did, trying not to let my fear show. Yong Da saunters off, sneering about uselessness and warlords, but I don't care. Silently, I send gratitude to Cook Ma for saving me once again. Or was it Ukko, the lord of the clouds, who protects people from evil spirits? How many evil souls dwell in this foreign prison?

Less than one moon, and I am already exhausted. The gong sounding at four thirty and being at the first chanting at five is not a problem. Nor is the breakfast of eight-treasure soup with rice and beans, lily slices, and lotus seeds. The chanting reminds me of the *joiking* we have back in Sápmi, but we never did it twice a day, before and after breaking fast. And then, right after the second chanting, the first *gong fu*, three hours of hard physical training.

In my group, with the youngest boys, some are only four or five years old, I can hear my brother Olli laughing at me. If I wasn't numb with fear, I would be embarrassed, but I'm too busy trying to grasp the traits of animals.

"You must study hard," says our master. "The snake, the crane, the tiger, the leopard, and the dragon."

I want to say that dragons don't exist, and why don't we study reindeer to learn from their compassion and wisdom? But this teaching stems from the Ming Dynasty, our teacher says, and has had a huge impact on *gong fu*, Chinese martial arts.

"The animals offer insights."

I could have told him that.

"You must watch their habits. How they move, how they rest, how they gather and release their *qi*." He glances at me and reluctantly adds, "internal energy."

Silence falls over the group as he takes a few steps with utter stealth. He feints, blocks an imaginary opponent with arm and kick. Then jumps and lands without a sound.

Slowly, he straightens and looks around. His wandering gaze stops on me. "You, at the back."

With clammy hands, I walk to the front. Numbly, I move into the starting position and try to perform foot moves, punches, strikes and blocks as our master calls them out. Sweat is pouring down my temples, and fear of making a mistake makes me concentrate so hard I scarcely breathe. Stolen glances rain down on me, and I cannot wait until we chant mantras again; at least then, we sit with our eyes closed.

At eleven o'clock, we have lunch, and once more, curious eyes crawl like spiders along my body. I stare stubbornly into my vegetables and tofu. And rice. So much rice.

After lunch, we have a break. That's when I retreat to my tiny chamber to take a nap, but I can't really sleep, not at night, either. My room is so tiny, so different from the wide mountains and plains of Sápmi. I look at the ceiling and wish it were a sky.

Or I go and find Habllek. During the first bleak weeks, Habllek is my only friend.

No. That's not true.

"Are you ready? It's nearly three o'clock." Wei Wan stands before me, wooden sword in hand.

Second *gong fu* session awaits, and he's gotten his sword out from the armory again, even though we're not supposed to.

I nod, unsure whether to be grateful for the company or embarrassed. He is only six, younger than me by *three years*. But he is kind, and when I take the lead toward Practice Hall Number Two, he trails after me.

"I'm going to nail them," he jabs the wooden sword in the air.

"Who's them?"

"The warlords."

"Why?"

"That's why we're here, to fight the warlords. Everyone is. You too."

Warlords again! Why am I never properly told what that means? A rush of pleasurable anger fills me at this new reason to hate Master Li.

"We take a vow; everyone does. I'm going to kill them."

I pat him on the shoulder. "You're going to try to avoid

getting slugged to pieces, and you're going to learn."

"I know the Rabbit sequence."

"So does every three-year-old in the neighbourhood." That is not entirely true, and I instantly regret saying it. But he doesn't seem to take offence; instead, he puts on a determined look.

"I know Bear and Hopping Heron too. Almost."

I want to say something encouraging, but I don't know how. "Just try to stay out of trouble, all right?"

I cannot hear the reply because, just then, Yong Da and his followers come along on their way to the other practice hall.

He stops right in front of me. "So, *witch*," he sneers, elongating the word. "I see you have found yourself a champion." Wei Wan shrinks behind me. "And you're still here, a whole moon. That's surprising, what with so much change and all. What's it like for you to live in a real house?"

A few people stop and listen.

"That's right." Yong Da looks around the small crowd that's now gathering. "Where she comes from, they live in yurts, like those poor bastards in Mongolia. Together with the pigs and all. Isn't that right?"

We don't have pigs, but he doesn't wait for me to correct him because he knows I won't. Instead, he puts his hands on his hips.

"I'm not sure you people can even read and write? Perhaps you do cave painting?" That earns him a burst of laughter, and he puffs out his chest.

Deimatic behavior, Father taught me, means bluffing, such as making oneself look bigger. It's very common in any animal that lacks strong defences.

"Frozen tundra," he snorts. "Not like our China. We've had civilization for five thousand years."

"Right," someone says.

"Dynasties," someone else adds.

"Emperors," comes a third.

"See, this is what's worrying," Yong Da drones on. "How can someone like that be supposed to keep up traditions? What if we get bad blood into our sacred space?"

"Yeah, bad blood," a boy agrees.

"Only selected acolytes are supposed to make it here," says a new voice.

"Just my point. But what do we know about her?" Yong Da spreads his hands in mock confusion. "Who built those frozen fields of nothing? They don't even have trees."

Much of Sápmi is above the tree line, which means trees cannot grow there. It has to do with temperature and altitude.

"Was it King Reindeer Horn?"

A new burst of laughter.

Yong Da raises his eyes to the crowd around him and calls them friends. "*Pengyoumen*, I just don't know that someone from such a place can contribute to our community; how can she know anything?" He turns to me. "I mean, where's your history?"

"History," someone mumbles. "Important."

"Right." Another concurs. "Heroes."

"No heroes," says Yong Da. "No, nothing."

He doesn't wait for me to say anything, and I am not going to either. He is too scary. "Your country just appeared on a map from out of nowhere?"

"Like, when?" someone queries.

"Exactly." Yong Da talks as though he is delivering a speech. "When? She doesn't even know herself."

"Ice age," I blurt.

Everyone is startled.

"What did you say?" Yong Da leans in.

"We didn't appear out of nowhere." My voice is too quiet. "Sápmi's landscape is primeval. It was molded through repeated advancing and withdrawal of ice sheets during the last ice age."

My answer has them all go quiet. For about five seconds. Then Yong Da laughs. "Ice age! Oh, that's so *primitive.*" He laughs so hard he slaps his knees. He laughs so hard that he tumbles into his ugly bulldog friend. Laughs so hard everyone else laughs, too. "No wonder you need a six-year-old to hold your hand!"

I want to say that he does not know my land. That Earth Mother is timeless, and our world consists of three levels: the Netherworld, the Middle World and the Upper World. The Netherworld is for the deceased and the gnomes. The Middle World is for people and earth spirits, and the Upper World is for the gods. Our *noaidi*, the shaman, is the keeper of order; he's in contact with the beyond. He heals and predicts, secures good hunting, and takes care of the natural resources. With the shamanic drum and its mythical images, he can fall into a trance and travel to faraway places.

But now, both fighting masters emerge from their respective halls, calling sharply to *gong fu* and disrupting the commotion. The word witch clings to my throat, and soon it will not be Wei Wan who must work or stay out of trouble, but me.

"*Yao shi li!*" The master barks to push harder.

We are ten minutes into sword practice, and heat punches through my body. I desperately lunge and retreat, sneaking glances at feet and arms around me. Wei Wan is one row ahead. I focus on him. He is not very strong, but he is good with technique. The afternoon practice drains me, but it means two hours away from Yong Da and his minions. That alone is worth it.

After we finish, Wei Wan asks, "Are you hungry?"

I am so drained and frustrated I cannot even respond. Is it a good idea to be seen with him again? Yong Da will taunt me for it. But Yong Da will taunt me for anything. I wipe my brow with my sleeve and nod a yes. I hate Yong Da. And I hate Master Li, who brought me here. *Hate*.

At five thirty, we make it over to the refectory in the Pavilion of the Crouching Tiger, where we eat noodles and *baozi*. Despite the early time, I am ready to go to bed, but I must stay awake for evening meditation. It takes place in the same room as the chanting, Pavilion of the Silent Grasshopper, right next to this one, my own pavilion. The temple grounds house many buildings. It has four main halls on the axis and eight other halls around. Several are worship houses that I am not sure how to use, but they are supposed to give comfort. I think that maybe they're just the place to bring that feeling I cannot name. That is something that makes me want to blink, blink again, every time, hoping for the world to right itself. But it doesn't, and the sensation is still here; to be taunted, stared at, yet remain unseen.

Except for Steel Master. Whenever his hard gaze fixates on me, I get an odd sensation, as though he's saying: "*I'm watching you. Remember that.*"

CHAPTER 4

I HAVE BEGUN TO ADJUST TO THE RHYTHMS OF LONG SI. Every day, all of the nearly one hundred students here must do schoolwork. This includes history, reading, writing, and, of course, Confucius: the ancient philosopher who spoke of social values, morality, and the correctness of relationships. It is China's most important moral ethic because the family is the building block of society. Authority follows an upward flow, younger obeys older, wife obeys husband, and husband obeys chieftain, leading ultimately to the ruler.

This morning in scripture, I am called on. "What does *xiaoshun* mean, Lu Mi La?" asks Master Peng. The subject mainly covers reading, writing and calligraphy, but our master weaves in a smatter of common knowledge, legends and mythology.

"Filial piety," I reply obediently. After my first few arduous moons, I know at least that much.

"And what does that mean?"

"To have a strong loyalty to your parents."

"Hey, mule herder," Yong Da whispers as he pokes me in the back. "How much loyalty in your family? Not so much, huh? They left you."

I ignore him and push my parents out of my head. In Sápmi, we work hard together; we must protect and care for our herd. We are bound to them, and they are bound to us. But here I have no herd. Instead, the temple slowly molds me into its shape. I learn its sounds, its rhythms. I am woken every morning. I eat, I chant, I train, and I work. The same masters shout at me, and the same students flood the space around me. And so, time passes, sometimes without me noticing. Spring is long gone. I have been here five moons already.

And I've learned to cling to Cook Ma, hoping she doesn't notice my desperation. She is called Cook Ma because she is like a mother to all the acolytes; compassionate with suffering, hard on disobedience, and I like her because she is the same age as my own mother, thirty-one. Every week, I go with her to the market in the village, and once, she even took me there in the evening so I could see the electric lights. I did not like them. In Sápmi, we had only fire and candles. Mother said the soft light is good for our eyes.

In the village, I feel liberated. Cook Ma resolutely kills any curious speculations by saying, *"Ta shi Xinjiang de."* She comes from Xinjiang.

Even though the people around us can tell I am not a local ethnic minority, they quickly settle for a distant one, from China's far West. Xinjiang works well, and my fluent *Putonghua* seals my freedom. Out here, I am not an oddity. Out here, I am Chinese. Out here, I do what they do: smile at unpleasant topics, the way out of embarrassment, take what I am offered even if I do not like it, know that a no thank you carries little weight, and even if I really mean it, they will still think I am just being polite. And give me what I don't want.

Today is market day, and we are shopping for vegetables, which is what we mostly buy. And rice and candles.

"*Tai gui*," says Cook Ma as the man selling corn demands two yuan for a pound. She scrutinizes each piece, appears uninterested and, with a look of despondency, agrees on two-thirds of the price. "*Hao ba*."

We stroll around, looking for cinnamon and star anise, before we head over to Cook Ma's friend. Old Xi Qi has invited us to her home, where she serves us a meal. The simple table is set with old crockery, chopsticks worn shiny, and a host of local foods.

"I really couldn't," I smile at the piece of fried snake dangling in front of my face. The old lady tightens her grip on the chopsticks, giving a light shake. "I ate *so* many lotus roots," I assure her. "Very good."

"*Lai ba, lai ba*," insists Xi Qi,

The chopsticks' trembling increases. Whether from sincere attempts to awaken my taste buds or because Xi Qi's arm is tiring, I can't tell. A bead of sweat forms on my forehead.

Cook Ma saves me. "*Bu xing. Ta chi su.*"

"*Ayiya*," the lady waves a hand. She forgot, at the temple, we are all vegetarians. I sigh with relief, and Xi Qi promptly pops the piece in her mouth. Nothing goes to waste. "*Tade mingyun bu hao.*" Its destiny wasn't good, she says of the Snake.

Destiny.

"What is my destiny?" I ask Cook Ma as we head back to

the temple.

She stops mid-stride and raises her brows. "Now, that's a big question for a nine-year-old."

"Nine and a half."

"Why do you want to know about your destiny?"

"Master Li said it was here."

"Did he now?"

"Am I going to fight warlords? Do I have to take a vow?"

Cook Ma chews the inside of her lip, looking tense. "Yes," she says after a while. "Everyone here takes a vow to live a monastic life, to serve and protect."

"Against the warlords?"

"Well, yes, actually, that is the threat we are facing. But let's not worry about that. It may take many years before anything happens."

"So, you don't know about my destiny?"

She smiles kindly. "Patience, Mi La. Later, Master Li will teach you all you need to know about the warlords. For now, your destiny is to study hard, to learn."

And survive, I think grimly as we enter the temple gates. Yong Da is the first person I see, and barely has Cook Ma gone off to the kitchen before he and his ugly minions approach.

Yong Da bumps hard into my shoulder. "The warlords will squash this one like a bug under a boot."

"I can hear the crunch," jeers the boy by his side, a wicked grin on his face.

"Squish," says the third one.

Even after six moons, there are still moments when this new existence makes my courage flee like the rapid rivers of my homeland.

Territorial is a word I learned as a child for animals who defend their space against intruders of their own species. Before I met Yong Da, I had never thought to apply it to humans.

First, the animal marks the territory, and then, if an intruder persists, it will move on to ritualized aggression. A power display such as inflating size, threatening gestures or vocalization. The behaviour most often ends with one of the animals fleeing, usually the intruder. If that does not happen, the situation develops into a fight.

In the animal world, the intruder is free to leave at any time.

Father would have counseled me: Mila, you know how to wrestle a calf to the ground (they're a lot stronger than they look), you know how to rope a reindeer bull, you know how to build a fire, you know how to build shelter, you know how to run, and you have instinct. Listen to *Máttaráhkká*, Earth Mother; do not get distracted by this child tyrant. He is nothing but a lost soul.

And Grandma Koini? She would have damned him to the Netherworld and sent him on a glowing spear to rot with the deceased and the gnomes.

Then she would have laughed.

She would also have laughed at the idea of everything being so closed in: roofs, walls, stone barriers. Where is the openness? Here, stern-looking deities watch from murky corners. Secrets are carved into stone tablets, buried in layered sediments of cumbersome history. Complicated. Grandma Koini was the girl who paddled her canoe and hiked across mountains to get to school. Who simply noticed the world and moved on. She pointed out things she thought I needed to see and, for the most part, without lengthy explanations. *There*. The clean bones of an animal. *There*. Tiny leaves whispering of cloudberries coming into season. The bonding with the land made her walk with light steps, listening. Whether it was the wind, the whisper of a tree or a wolf's howl; "listen," she said. "Listen because it makes you strong."

In my room, I stare at the Sámi bracelet, but it feels as though it is diminishing day by day. As moons pass and my first year comes to its end, my focus has long since narrowed from a world of mountains, reindeer, northern lights, snow, freedom and laughter, to grueling practice and endless chores. I have buried my family in the deepest recess of my heart, thanking Ukko for Wei Wan. And Habllek. They fill my body with weight enough to take another step. Make me believe I can go one more day.

"Lu Mi La." Cook Ma speaks my Chinese name cheerfully, not derisively like Yong Da, yet I pick up a faint glumness underneath. "Do you want to help me feed the birds?"

I look up from Habllek, comfortably spread in my lap.

"I know it is still your break time, but as you're so attuned to animals, I thought maybe..."

I put down the cat and quickly rise. "I would love to." Apart from the regular messenger birds, I've been told there is a trained hunting falcon. I can't wait to see it. In Sápmi, we have osprey, golden eagle, peregrine and goshawk, but I have never seen one up close.

When we get near the rookery, behind the Heavenly

Emperor's Palace Hall, the last of the four main halls on the temple axis, I hear a low cooing. Instantly, vibrations from the animal kingdom resonate through my being.

Cook Ma opens the door, and as I follow her inside, an acrid stench hits my nostrils. The sun that streams through the open-air window falls on a wall of square holes. In each one sits a pigeon, and below is a carpet of fluffy down and feathers.

"I'll show you how to feed them." Cook Ma opens a closet and fills a big scoop with seeds, and then she goes out into the mesh-fenced backyard.

She scatters seeds and calls the birds. I hear a flurry of wingbeats as they fly out and land on the ground, where they start feeding.

Back inside, I see it in the farthest corner, a large bird of prey perching on a rack in a cage. She pulls on a leather gauntlet and walks close.

"Why is it hooded?" I ask.

"Birds of prey are not used to sudden movements or changes in light, like when a door opens. It can startle them. When the hood is on, they think they are safe, and it calms them."

Cook Ma holds out her leather-clad arm, and even with its hood on, the bird steps confidently onto it. "It comes all the way from Jilin, the northeast corner of China. From the famous falcon village where Manchus have kept the tradition alive since the Qing Dynasty." Her attention is fixed on the bird as though it has some strange hold on her.

"That is a long way from home. How did it end up here?" I ask.

"It came with its master, the proud Manchu." A faint tint

of red flushes her cheeks. "He captured it very young and trained it ever since. Once the training is over, the relationship between master and falcon is unbreakable."

"Can I touch it?"

"Of course you can. Come here, reach out carefully." Her gaze turns distant.

I let the tips of my fingers graze the silky feathers. The falcon turns its head as though it can see me, and it feels like all the rivers in the world rush through me. It's always been like this: I connect with animals. "Where is he now, the proud Manchu?"

But Cook Ma doesn't respond. "The best-trained falcons develop an extra sense. As long as they are pointed in the right direction, they can find their master no matter what."

"And where is the master?" I repeat. "Does he belong here at Long Si?"

"He does, very much, and he will return." She puts it back on the perch. "I best head back. Close up, will you?"

There are things I want to ask. I have not forgotten the conversation I overheard on my second day so long ago now. She questioned if it was wise to bring me here, being born in the year of the Snake and all. Yet it feels like she is looking out for me, but there is a tightness in her shoulders as she walks out the door, and I do not dare to disturb her.

I don't know how I know it, but somewhere in this bird's existence lies the key to Cook Ma's unhappiness.

CHAPTER 5

*C*LANK, *CLANK, CLANK,* GOES MY WOODEN SWORD. IT IS the first time I manage a series of parries without letting my opponent in even an inch. Lately, I have noticed a shift in my teacher. It's like he's started to *see* me. It makes me clamp my teeth and pluck out my grit.

He ends the sparring, and we bow. "Eight moons in my group, Lu Mi La," he says, and the corner of his lip twitches at my dropped jaw. I have lost count of the time. He looks stern, but his eyes smile. "Soon, you have been here for two years and are now ready." He brings something from behind his back.

I suppress a gasp. A small steel sword, single-edged and curved, as they have been since the Song dynasty.

A huge knot in my belly releases. Perhaps I will fight warlords after all. "Really?"

"Yes, really. Here, take it. I will personally keep sparring with you for the next few weeks."

I can hardly breathe. I thank my master, slide the sword into a free spot in the armoury and bounce out on light feet. The first I see is Habllek, and I rush over, lift her up and hug her. It is the first glimmer of happiness I have experienced in this foreign place where Master Li has imprisoned me. Master Li, who never speaks to me anymore. Does he hate me as much as I hate him? Then why did he take me?

"Don't disappoint Master Bai," Cook Ma says, meaning my new fighting master. I am about to leave the refectory to prepare for the afternoon session. Three more weeks have passed, and Wei Wan and I have just been moved to a new group, one with bigger boys. I stare at her dumbfounded; how did she know I was worrying?

She gives me a wink. "I just know."

Cook Ma is good with *feng shui* and things like that, energies. Everything is made of energy, she tells me. *Qi*—life force. It just takes different forms: solid, soft, fluid, but it's all the same.

"Your sword is your arm. If you see it that way, you won't have to think so hard."

"Right."

"You'll be fine." She winks again. "You're ten years old, gaining on eleven. Big girl."

I feel comforted by her words. I *will* be alright. I may not have had fighting experience, but I have carried, I have walked. And I have run. Father always said I was a mountain goat. Now I just need to be a little bit more like a tiger.

I feel a different vibration as soon as I step into the practice room. Is this what Cook Ma means when she says that everything is energy? It's not just the life force in our bodies; *qi* is the force that makes up and binds together all things in the universe.

Right now, it feels like it is binding me to the nearest boy in the front row. He glares like an angry rooster. No, *don't let him scare you.* Energies can be directed, that is what I have learned. I force my head high and proceed to the back of the room. Outwardly, no one pays me any attention, but I know they are all watching me in secret. Wei Wan is in the corner. We dare not look at each other.

After the warm-up, we start with standing sequences. Our master orders us to parry, thrust, and block. Soon, our joints and muscles move more smoothly, and I begin to feel prepared for the first sequence, a series of interconnected drills. We lunge, step back, whirl and thrust. By the time we are paired up for free-fighting, I feel confident. But I am not paired with Wei Wan; I am paired with the glaring boy.

The master orders the two of us to the front of the group, throws a quick glance around and snaps, "*Kaishi.*"

It takes me no more than a second to feel the boy's anger. His face twists as he comes at me, sword raised and a silent scream on his lips. I manage to whip up my weapon and parry, but he strikes with such force that I am thrown to the ground, slamming hard into the floor. My head rings and my mouth is dry as I drag myself up and back into opening stance.

"*Zai lai,*" our master shouts.

Once more, he whacks me like a falling rock. He is bigger than me, and my slim arms lack strength. He retires with a few swift steps, lowering his hands in resting pose, waiting for me to get up.

When our master calls out to start anew for the third time, the tips of my ears tingle with heat, and my palms sweat from more than tiredness. Strengthened by his easy victories, my opponent smirks, and several of the other boys do the same.

I grip my sword in both hands, bracing myself for the impact. But just then, I glance at Wei Wan. He makes an almost imperceptible move with his fingers, as when a person is walking. It takes me a second to get his meaning. *Move*. One moment before the boy is about to hit my sword, and I retrieve my parry and step sideways.

The diminished resistance makes him career across the room and crash into the wall. Face crumpled in shock, he shoots up and advances fast, flicking his sword in a sequence of feints and thrusts. This time, I am prepared.

I take a quick step and duck sideways. And again. And again. With swift footwork, I manage to dodge him two more times. He is faster the third time, and I receive a heavy blow to my upturned sword. But instead of wasting precious energy on engaging, I pull out and step back, side, other side, whirl. Sweat trickles down my forehead, but all I can think of is Cook Ma. "Your sword is your arm." It's an extension of me, a limb. I try to let go, to trust it to know what it's doing.

"*Goule*," the master yells, and we stop. Look each other in the eyes and salute.

The boy tightens his lips and manages another glare. But the smirk is gone.

As I step out of the practice hall, I am so relieved I could cry. I *did* it. I lived through the first practice with boys my age, all bigger and stronger than me. And it was because of Wei Wan. I must thank him for helping me. And Cook Ma.

41

From time to time, the conversation between Cook Ma and Master Li still plays out in my head. What is the Nefarious? And what is it that Master Gang—Steel Master—must not know? What is too early to tell, and what age is it that I must reach? Sometimes, when Master Li passes me out in the courtyard, I sneak a glance at him. He barely acknowledges me, yet the air around him seems thick with unspoken things.

The moons pass unevenly. Somewhere along the way, I turn eleven, but that is irrelevant. Nobody here celebrates birthdays. A year's passing brings only the promise of harder work. And more Confucius. With every lesson learnt, I understand a bit more and grasp the core values better, and it all works rather well, as long as I don't ask too many questions.

I like it best when Master Peng tells us famous legends, like the one from the Song Dynasty, which tells of the Monkey King, who was born from a stone. The stone developed a magic womb, and a stone egg appeared when it burst opened. When the wind blew on the egg, it turned into a monkey that grew big and powerful and acquired supernatural powers.

But most often, we spend our time working on the never-ending challenge of reading and writing Chinese.

"Who can tell me about the character for house?" Master Peng asks, and after more than two years of studying, I have at least a basic understanding. The written characters are often poetic and can give helpful insight into the Chinese mind. They each consist of a radical, a key that is a graphical component that offers a clue to its meaning. The second part is phonetic and lets us know how it could be pronounced. Most of the time, anyway.

I raise my hand. "It has the roof radical on top, and below, the symbols for rice and woman."

"And why is that?"

Yong Da says, "Because what do you want under your roof?" He smirks. "Rice and women, of course."

I cringe. Only Yong Da can make his lips form a slim, tight line and still manage to snigger; only he has scorn etched into his forehead so that darkness pools around his eyes.

"*Hen hao*," very good, says Master Peng.

I stare at my desk, heat rising. I want to shout that it's an old-fashioned language built by men for men. But I must contain myself. My Scandinavian outspokenness has done me little good in Long Si. "So, women are useful but not complete on their own? Is that it? Otherwise, how can the character for good consist of woman and son?" I try to keep my voice measured. "Shouldn't it be woman and daughter?"

Yong Da smirks again.

"It's not ridiculous," I snap before he can interrupt. "The character for strength is man and field. What does that mean? That women are not strong? Are the fields around us not full of hard-working women?"

Master Peng smiles, the embarrassed smile used to cover an unpleasant situation. Even holding my temper, I have offended him. You must not question a teacher or use a confrontational tone. Especially not a male one who is much older than you.

Yong Da raises his hand. "I think Lu Mi La is perhaps not clear on the characters *xun* and *xun*." One is spoken with an upgoing tone, and the other with a sharp, down-going tone. A subtle difference with big consequences. He plays Master Peng so well he could be the Monkey King himself, already established as the powerful, sneaky demon. The Chinese language has four tones, and by switching from fourth to second, he changes the word's meaning. The first one means tame, and the word for reindeer is tame deer, though omitting the tame also works. It's like the name given to me, Lu Mi La, Mila Reindeer. The second *xun* Yong Da refers to the means to adhere, to follow.

"For a tame deer to survive," he finishes. "It must follow the herd."

A girl should know her place.

Master Peng produces a second smile, and Yong Da a third smirk. For some reason, locking eyes with him brings me right back to the annual reindeer marking in Sápmi. The calves are marked during the summer when all the reindeer are herded together, and the calves are separated from their mothers. I was six, and Father had just roped a calf and wrestled it down. Right now, I wish it were Yong Da struggling on the ground like the calf I held as my father was about to carve our family marking into its left ear.

The calf was fighting wildly, and I lost my grip.

"Hold him!" Father shouted.

I fought to keep the calf in position. The sharp knife glinted, and as he cut the ear, something hit me like a whiplash. Gasping, I turned my head and lost my grip again.

"Mila!" Father bellowed as the calf mooed and struggled. "What is wrong with you? Concentrate!"

I felt hot and flustered. Nothing was behind me, yet for a

moment, I had felt a sharp pain. I looked around but saw only other members of my village and *vajans*, the reindeer mothers, running around, calling desperately for their young ones.

Sitting on top of our calf, Father shifted his weight to mark the other ear, and I pushed down with all my might. But I couldn't shake the idea that something was wrong, as though someone was observing me.

My brother Olli came running.

"Take Mila's place," Father ordered.

Usually, I would be angry. To be replaced by my younger brother was an insult. But not that day. Scrunching my brow, I rose and walked away. In the disarray of people and distressed animals, I couldn't find anything out of the ordinary. Yet I felt unseen eyes nibbling at my heart with teeth of worry.

In this classroom, it feels just like it did then, like insects are crawling over me. It's Yong Da, his gaze; I can feel it invading my body. My anger merges with the stickiness of my skin, and suddenly, I am beset with sensations. Like the ones that followed me during the moons before my abduction.

"*Shijian daole.*" Master Peng brings me back to the present. Time is up.

I gather my writing materials and rise, wanting to hug myself against an invisible chill. As I leave the classroom, I remember: *Hexfinder.*

I did not know what it was at the time, but now I do. The person I did not see but felt at the calf marking was a Hexfinder—one sent to find children with special gifts. They came back in my eighth year—it was they who took me in the night and abducted me.

It had been a long time since one had come to our village,

a long time since any such child had been born. No wonder we weren't prepared.

CHAPTER 6

SHORTLY AFTER WE FINISH THE SECOND CHANTING WITH A soft, long *om*—the primal cosmic sound of creation, I, Wei Wan, and two other boys carry trays loaded with fruits and flowers to place at the altars in each worship hall. From the Pavilion of the Sleeping Bear, the administrative quarters, Master Li comes walking toward us.

"How are you doing, Mi La?" he asks as he nears.

I stop, and the others melt away. So long has passed without him paying me attention, except in history class, that I am confused.

"*Hai hao,*" I say, I am okay. For the most part. *You still owe me explanations.* Cook Ma said to be patient, still I drum up my courage to speak. "You never told me about my destiny." I ignore his surprise. "You said it was here."

He observes me for a while. "Would you like to come running in the forest with me?"

Now, it is my turn to be baffled. He is offering me to run free, melt into *Máttaráhkká's* open arms? After all this mind-

47

numbing silence? I give him an uncertain look, but his eyes tell me it is true. Despite the familiar whisper of resentment trailing up my spine, I nod in agreement. And so we go, every week, until my heart pounds and my breath thunders in my ears. I like it, no, I treasure it, and I realize, to my consternation, that I am allowing Master Li to be a tiny bit closer to each breathtaking run. Master Li, my rescuer and captor. When will he tell me about my destiny? When will he tell me why he took me? Will I see my family again? And then there's the question only I can answer: Do I still hate him?

Something smolders deep inside when I think of it. But only then.

Slowly, week after week, our running together collects into moons. Meanwhile, I build my strength, I work diligently on my *gong fu*, I follow Cook Ma to the market, and eventually, I chat with the villagers like I have lived here all my life. We talk about this and that. Xinjiang, for example, is my supposed home province. Thank Ukko, I have been there to make up some good lies. When I die, I wonder if I will ever reach what the Buddhists talk about, the Pure Lands Beyond—I lie too easily. Yes, I was an orphan; my parents were poor and had no choice; yes, the good-hearted Master Li saved me. Best to go with the flow as far as my mysterious background, or they might really start asking questions. The Chinese are very curious.

Most of my free time I spend with Habllek, my truest sister. Other than that, I do what every acolyte of Long Si does: I sweep, I clean, I chant, and I meditate. For the past year, I have done little else, and at twelve, I am a lot bigger than when I came, but no matter how I grow, boys are stronger than girls. Though I am light and nimble, my stealth is not bad. When we practice furtiveness, I don't get yelled at. Once or twice, I have caught Master Li observing us, or is it *me?* I chew my lower lip, determined to one day master perfect stealth and be able to sneak unseen away from probing gazes. Pray Ukko the day will come.

And that I will be as silent as Wei Wan.

"Where are you going?" He steals up so close I suspect he meant to take my hand, but he doesn't. Perhaps at the last moment, some subconscious thought nudged him. We don't do that here.

"I'm going to the Ten Thousand Buddha Hall." I smile down at his sweet face. How old was he when he came here? Four? Five?

"Why?"

"To light a joss stick for Guan Yin."

"Goddess of Mercy."

"That's right. Very good."

"But it's dark."

"That's all right."

"And cold."

"I wouldn't exactly call it cold." I think of the winters north of the Polar Circle. That was dark. And cold.

"Can I come with you?"

"Of course you can. Do you know what Guan Yin is associated with?"

"Compassion."

"You're clever."

He nods at that. "But I don't like the dark. Remember when we used to come out from supper and it was still light?"

"That's right."

"Now it's just dark," he says with a sigh.

"It's not."

"It is."

I want to tell him it's not that simple. That the earth tilts and rotates around its own axis at the same time. Explain that another place is getting our light right now, but soon it will change. I want to tell him about stars and snow and the northern lights. But something makes my throat tighten. His parents should be teaching him these basic things—as mine taught me.

"The light will come back," I say.

We step into the Ten Thousand Buddha Hall, and I light a joss stick and bow to the statue of Guan Yin. Cook Ma says many temples are dedicated to Guan Yin, and when you depart from this world, she places you in the heart of a lotus flower—that is how you are sent to the Pure Lands Beyond.

"Compassion," Wei Wan mumbles as he bows beside me. I wonder whom he prays for. His mother? Father?

Briefly, I think of my own family. But these days, less and less. I have fallen into the solid rhythm of Long Si, letting it shield me, forcing me to raise my gaze and watch my step when my heart would instead push my vision to the ground.

I lift my head and push my joss stick into the big holder filled with sand and ash so it can keep burning, keep my prayers going and send a smoky haze over the alarming fact that I do not miss them anymore. A sickly wave of guilt hits me, and I turn to leave.

Wei Wan is like a shadow by my side. Despite all this, his small hand finds its way into mine, and I squeeze it. He squeezes back, and together, we step out into the dark. The dark is where no one can see us. The dark is where I am strong enough to admit that this is where I live now. Long Si, the Dragon Temple.

In my new life, there is no family, no reindeer except me, Lu Mi La. In my new life, other things matter. My muscles are getting toned, my mind is getting sharper, and yet it is a hard journey. Sometimes, I still battle wanting to hate Master Li; he *stole* me. But he is not like Master Gang; Steel Master, —or Yong Da, both of whom I loathe. He is never mean to me. He is calm and fair, and he takes me running.

We have reached the last spot of darkness before the meditation hall, where large red lanterns light up the entrance, not ugly electric bulbs like in the village. Wei Wan's hand slips out of mine, and without a word, he glides forward and into the crowd of boys. I hesitate only long enough to build some distance between us. The touch of his warm skin lingers in my palm, and I am hit by a burning desire to protect him. Does he need it? Or is it me I must protect? All I know is that I must train hard. For one day, I will be in the same group as Yong Da, and I must be prepared.

"Name seminal moments in China's past," says Master Li in history class.

"The Warring States," says Ya Li Shan Da. The boy I fought my first day in the new group. His name is a transcription of sounds like mine, and he looks more Eurasian than Chinese, but he is bigger than me, and I have never dared to ask. "It was strongly characterized by warfare. And bureaucratic and military reforms. And consolidation."

"Name one of the bloodiest periods in China's history."

Wei Wan slips in a quiet answer. "The Three Kingdoms."

"Why?"

"It..." he stutters a little. "It was marked by chaotic fighting between warlords. From all over China."

"Exactly," says Master Li and turns to me. Wei Wan looks relieved. "And what, Lu Mi La, is it that we are doing here at Long Si?"

It is not the first time he's asked this question, but he always seems to direct it to me. Or at least, that's how it feels.

"We are fighting the remnants of it," I say, though I don't really believe it.

A long time ago, Master Li taught us that this vast land consisted of many kingdoms where regional emperors fought for military, political, economic and social control. The boundaries were constantly changing. Through inter-kingdom warfare, temporary alliances were set up and broken. The 1912 revolution of Xinhai ended two thousand years of imperial rule, but even though over two decades have passed, the land is still racked with unrest. Modern warlords ruled various parts of the country until the late 1920s when the nationalist Kuomintang Party officially unified China. It is now 1939—back in Sápmi I never paid attention to what year it was. Earth Mother does not care. But legend has it that small pockets of the original, ancient clans have survived till this day. Hiding deep in the misty mountains in Shaanxi Province, they bide their time.

"And why is Long Si key in the resistance?"

"We possess a special weapon," I say, though I don't really believe that either. But at least these days I have some idea about all that talk of fighting warlords.

What weapon? The reply is always the same whenever anyone asks: It is a secret and will be revealed at the right time.

Master Li raises his brows and gives me a meaningful look as though he can read my thoughts and is reproaching me.

"A very mighty weapon," I add.

When class finishes, I stride outside and pass by Master Gang; Steel Master. He glares at me, then nods at Yong Da and keeps walking. Yong Da follows him. I glance after them as they disappear down the hallway. Yong Da is Steel Master's protégé, and everyone knows it, even though masters are not supposed to have favorites. It's unfair. If I were in charge, I would stop it.

But I am not.

CHAPTER 7

TIREDNESS CRAWLS LIKE A DISEASE THROUGH MY SYSTEM. It has been one moon since I got switched to Group Three: Master Gang's group. I have managed to pull myself up another rung of the ladder. The price I have to pay is more pain and, worse yet, more of Yong Da. The students in this lot are brutal, and he is their self-proclaimed emperor.

In the new group, both Wei Wan and I now practice three kinds of *gong fu,* empty hand, which means no weapons, short swords, and staffs.

On our master's orders, we have been warming up since the first minute of morning practice. Now, the entire group sets off as one, running out of the practice yard, to the hills behind the temple, up steep stairs, onto the goat trails and around. Yong Da takes the lead, of course. Then comes the squinty-eyed boy, who is strong and silent. Ping Guo follows; I call him Apple because his name is pronounced like the fruit but has different characters. Then two more boys, then me. Sixth place. I must get better.

I clench my fists and push on, breath roaring in my chest. The light is still faint, and it's hard to see properly in the forest.

I am so focused I don't hear him, but a sharp shove in my back sends me tumbling.

"*Witch-snake*," Yong Da hisses and sprints past as I crash into the ground. He has doubled back to hurt and humiliate me without our master seeing, catching me off-guard.

Wincing, I sit up, trying to rub away the excruciating pain in my knee. Teeth clamped, I stand up and hobble on. I refuse to cry. Enough of that. But the humiliation stings so that tears of anger fight for space at the corners of my eyes.

The other boys stream past. They don't push me or say mean things. They don't say nice things, either. They don't say anything. But one hand touches briefly on my shoulder. It is Wei Wan. His kind eyes glimmer with silent wisdom. I want to say thank you, but he puts a finger to his lips, and I know to keep quiet. If we are openly friends in this group, it will worsen for us both.

He jerks his head forward, and we run again until we return to Long Si. Panting, I step into Practice Hall Number One, every muscle tensed. Steel Master walks back and forth, inspecting us like mice to be crushed in his merciless claws. I am in the front row, suppressing my breath and trying to ignore my throbbing knee.

"Staff," he roars. "Today, we pair up unevenly. Hazel, hickory, hardwood. No matter."

My heart flips. I am still a beginner in this discipline, and my present staff is made from hazelwood. This staff will break if hit violently enough by harder wood. I pray I will not be paired with Yong Da. And not Wei Wan, either.

I suppress a gasp—a shimmering orb floats in front of Steel Master! In the bleak morning light streaming through the windows, the orange-sized ball reflects a heavy grey-blue. It trembles faintly, embracing the darker field inside. It feels unpleasant and sacred all at once, as though I am looking at something I should not be privy to.

I glance sideways, but no one else reacts. Am I the only one who can see it? What is it? A spirit? A ghost?

A word nudges my mind, hovering at the edge of my perception. What? I concentrate, but it will not come.

Instead, a staff whacks me on the back of my head, making my ears ring.

"*You wenti ma, Xiao Mi?*" Steel Master roars so loud that his forked beard quivers. "*Shenme wenti?*"

I stagger from the blow, his question booming in my head: Do I have a problem? "*Mei wenti*," I reply. No problem. The skin at the back of my head burns like fire. I have to exert all my self-control not to touch it.

"*Zhuyi.*" Pay attention.

"Yes, Master."

"Have you heard what I said?"

My heart thumps in fright. I cannot repeat what Steel Master has just said. He rests both hands on his staff, and I look down. *Not Yong Da.* The practice hall has grown quiet. *Not Yong Da.*

"Perhaps Lu Mi La would like to demonstrate what we're practising today."

Not Yong Da.

"Yong Da," he snaps. "Here."

My heart plummets, and my sweaty hands slide on the

hazelnut staff.

Yong Da walks to the front, shining with delight, juggling his staff from hand to hand. Hickory. Denser, stiffer, and stronger than white oak or hard maple, renowned for strength and shock resistance.

His first hit is so brutal I gasp from sheer terror. I duck my upper body sideways. Backwards, sideways again.

I can't help but grimace as I take a blow to my shoulder. I whirl and do a low sweep, but Yong Da is already airborne. With a soft landing, he takes one velvet step forward and swings his staff.

I parry, but not fast enough. My fingers claw my staff to stop myself from screaming as the blow lands on my right thigh. Limping, I throw myself back and sideways, striking a knee and hip sequence as I retreat. There. One hit. A drop of confidence lands in my gut but is quickly gone as Yong Da charges with a roar.

The blow finds my mid-section, arm and neck in three clean strikes.

The pain is blinding. I collapse to the ground.

"*Goule.*" Enough.

Steel Master is already pointing at two new students, and I am left to my own on the hard, cold floor. I dare not brush against my ribs as I slowly make my way up. My eye is a swollen, bruised mess. Blood trickles down my nose. I do not look at Wei Wan. I do not look at anyone.

I inspect the day's damage by the paltry flame of the candle in my room. Just below my ribs is a dark area, and I feather my fingers across it. Waves of sharp pain shoot along my side, and again, I see Yong Da's disgusting smirk before me.

If he were in one of Grandma Koini's stories, I would ask for her to tell it again and again. Each time, he would grow in my mind from a naughty boy to an evil man, a vile spirit, and finally, a black demon, and so would his punishments because that's how all of Grandma's stories ended, with the villain getting their just desserts. A smack on the bottom, ten whip lashes, thrown into a witches' cauldron and boiled to soup. Or penetrated by one hundred swords. Strangled by the darkness of the Netherworld.

Today was an unjust match, yet I remind myself I held out longer than I would have done a moon before. I press my hand softly against my tender skin. I hurt, *but I did not break.* My bones are intact, my skin unbroken. Father used to say that what doesn't break you makes you stronger.

I must be tough enough to face Yong Da's anger. I don't know why he hates me. He did from the very beginning. Because I am a girl? Before I arrived, only boys were here, as is the tradition of every fighting temple in China. But somehow, Master Li convinced the others that I must stay. Managed to upset an order established millennia earlier. Managed to push through some secret agenda that I cannot figure out. I have tried to ask him about my destiny, but his lips are sealed. All I know is that the more I think of it, the more my mood shifts. Soon, the sob that wanted to break from my mouth subsides, and the urge to cry is gone.

If I find it dreary pushing through Master Peng's endless characters and stroke order, a character must be written in a particular sequence, then history lessons are even worse. We are learning about the early dynasties. Master Li wants to know which one is most noticeable. Several hands rise. He points at Ming Pi, a boy who is also in Group Three.

"Qin," slurs Ming Pi, who seems half asleep regardless of time. "He was the first emperor to unify China."

"And?" Master Li looks stern.

"It was he who started building the Great Wall."

"Just so."

Unification of the legal code is mentioned. As is the creation of units of measurement, the invention of currency, and the development of the written language. Ming Pi recounts most of it.

"What else, Lu Mi La?"

Ukko, I should have paid attention. Now what? I take a chance. "He came up with the concept of a centralized government." I hold my breath.

"Correct."

I heave a sigh of relief.

"And how did he ensure that the chieftains in the provinces behaved the way he ordained?"

"Spies, of course," says Yong Da.

"And who," says Master Li, "came up with the idea to spy in the first place?"

Yong Da's ugly smirk widens. "Well, that was Sun Tzu, the famous theorist who influenced military thinking."

"And what did he say?"

"One who knows the enemy and knows himself will not

be endangered in a hundred engagements," Yong Da quotes the famous strategist perfectly.

"Very good," says Master Li, but he looks at me.

Yong Da seems unstoppable. "It was he who stressed the need to understand yourself and your foe. He identified spy roles, and had great influence on Chinese espionage."

I feel my face tighten. He excels at everything. Ukko take him. The art of espionage? Seriously?

After class, I go to lunch with Wei Wan, who goes on to find San Dun, the Head Archivist's apprentice, and I am left with Ming Pi, whom I can't tell if he's just tired or actually managing to eat in his sleep. I go and search for Habllek. She gives me comfort, as always, yet I can't shake the feeling that started in class with Master Li. It is like he silently interrogates me by acting like a swooping hawk as soon as I relax. He doesn't yell or anything. It's just that...look.

It brings me back in time...to when he left me outside that tavern on the Silk Road. We hadn't eaten since early morning, and my stomach was rumbling for the food he went to order, yet a mad impulse hit me. I looked over my shoulder; no one was watching. *Escape*.

Heart racing, I walked away. Faster and faster and faster until I broke into a run. Past the stall with lemons, past the stall with spices, on and on. Until I stopped, this wasn't the way we had come. I spun around on the spot, confused, and suddenly, everyone was staring at me. My eyes cast around in desperation. But in every direction, it seemed a menacing person had already pinpointed me and was about to block my way or reach out and grab me. Big people, grownups.

A man approached me. He spoke words I could not

understand, and though he smiled, his eyes held ill intent. For a second, I stood paralyzed—what if I couldn't find my way back to the tavern?

I turned and ran. The man called after me, making me run faster. I wove through streets at random, panic building with every frantic heartbeat. A thousand thoughts battled my frightened brain, and I nearly cried in terror.

And then I saw it, the tavern. Outside stood Master Li, feet apart, arms crossed.

I slowed to a walk. My shoulders slumped, neck bent, and I was shaking. He looked at me like I was the dog he had beaten into submission but knew would return. He never beat me physically, but emotionally I was as bruised as a plum transported the entire way of the Silk Road in a wooden crate.

I stopped in front of Master Li.

His gaze was like ice, and I cringed at his remoteness. The usual bustle was happening all around us, but all I could hear were my rapid breaths.

Then he laced his fingers together in front of him. "Welcome back, Mila."

"Master," I whispered.

"What did you have in mind? A little extra exercise before supper?" He could have been yelling, but he didn't. He was careful, controlled, using that voice of low authority. And disappointment.

I snort loudly into my sweeping, ignoring Wei Wan's sideway glance as we work our way across the upper courtyard. This is my favourite chore as I don't have to talk to anyone. I push the long, heavy bamboo handle in broad swipes until I feel the burn in my muscles. If I am here to fight warlords, I'd best be strong.

"What do you think?" says Wei Wan, who is mirroring my moves. "About the warlords?"

Has he read my mind?

"I mean, Master Li goes on and on about the threat, but do they really still exist? Like in the olden days, raiding with swords and hatchets?"

"Hmm..." I draw out the answer. "I don't know. But we're here to be trained in the fighting arts."

"And other things." To my surprise, he says, "Herblore, I mean, you know what it is, right?"

"Learning about herbs for healing. And maybe sharpening the senses," I add because of his look.

He snorts. "You really don't know?"

"Know what?"

"I shouldn't tell you."

"Tell me what?"

"I shouldn't."

"*Tell me.*"

His brow furrows like something fermenting in his mind, a soundless protest he cannot heed. Then, a breath of regret slips across his lips. "They learn to use poison."

I stop sweeping. "What? To kill?"

"That's usually what poison's for." He raises a hand at my widened eyes. "You can't tell *anyone*. Only a select few get picked, and they are sworn to secrecy. It wouldn't sound good if it came out. We have a history of teaching honorable arts, not how to murder people."

"But how, I mean, when would they use it?"

"On missions."

"Missions? What missions?"

"The ones people get sent on if they're skilled enough. Warlords, defend the nation and all that."

I quickly recover from my shock. "I'd like to learn."

"Ha! You'd never get picked. *Ni mei you shaqi.*" He says I don't have a murderous spirit.

"Huh," I grunt, annoyed. "I know who does."

"Yong Da is a fighting machine. I hate to say it, but he's likely to get picked. Though if trouble comes, he'll be useful here too. He'll kill off the intruders faster than anyone."

"He is mostly intent on killing me."

A shade darkens Wei Wan's face. "Don't pick fights with him, Mi *jie*," he calls me Sister Mi. "He's dangerous."

Sudden irritation fills me. I'm sick and tired of being the meek little girl. "So am I," I say. "Could be," I amend, sweeping again.

"Could you?"

"I could learn. I'm stronger now."

"You are," Wei Wan dips his head, and angst pricks me. I am not the only one being pushed around. Wei Wan struggles too, but for a different reason. While I am singled out for being a girl and a foreigner, Wei Wan is just not very strong. He is skinny, fast, and silent. Good qualities in anyone's class but Steel Master's.

This is ridiculous and unfair. I grip my broom harder, sweeping forcefully, feeding my building resentment. If *I* were the Master of Long Si...when suddenly it dawns on me. An idea so simple yet so enticing that I stop sweeping from sheer surprise.

I drop my broom and step close to Wei Wan. Cupping my

hands around his ear, I tell him: "In our spare time, we must work extra. When no one sees us, practice all the skills we need."

He looks perplexed. I know what he means to say: That is not allowed. Neither is stealing a child, I think. But I don't say that.

I resume my sweeping, but I look his way and know we have an agreement. And this is when it starts, already in that silent moment of consent. A risk, a chance to learn, a breaking of rules. A strange blend of terror and exhilaration rushes through me, not new to the world but new to me.

The days get strangely busy. We slip away whenever we can. One at a time so as not to be discovered, reuniting in any prearranged spot. Never speaking, always furtive. And we work hard: sneaking, blocking, punching, tricking.

Focus. Quiet.

I almost forget about my hatred for Master Li.

CHAPTER 8

"**S**TOP," WEI WAN SAYS SOFTLY IN THE DIM ROOM. "You're five yards to my left, slightly behind. Eight o'clock."

"Ukko take you," I mutter and walk up to him. "Your turn."

We are playing stalk the cat, a game I invented to practice stealth. One of us sits in the middle of the big practice hall with eyes closed. That's the cat and the other person, the stalker, has to sneak up unnoticed. You only win if you're close enough to touch the cat. And the cat will practice, too, sharpening senses such as hearing, or feeling a presence.

After five rounds on the treacherously squeaky floor, I am weary. It takes energy to tread softly. Yet I feel content as we split and leave through separate exits. Moons of secret games have sharpened our skills. I haven't yet decided whether to forgive him for slipping bitter melon juice into my soup. My dish was nearly inedible, but I was so hungry I had no choice. The sleeping draft I pilfered from Potion Master's workshop and dumped into his tea made him nod off so many times in class that Master Peng nearly rapped his knuckles for it. I could hardly keep from laughing. He was furious, but I said you have to pay attention, little one, and next, I found a three-inch grasshopper in my bed.

After a few weeks of surprises, neither of us was easily tricked, and now I wait a minute under the eaves, spying out in the dark before I slink out.

And there stands Master Li.

"Master!" I draw a sharp breath. "I didn't see you."

"I should hope not. I was practicing stealth."

My eyes find the ground.

"What do you know about stealth, Mi La? Tell me."

Ukko, what does he want? Punish me for disobedience, no doubt. I reply, "There are different ways; you must read the situation. Crawling brings you close to the floor. If your hands are light enough, they can find the creaks and avoid them. Your knees simply follow your hands. If you stand up, you must bend your legs, walk very softly, and always touch your toes down first. That's how you find the creaks with your feet."

"And did your master teach you to roll carefully from the toes down onto the foot? And to use your belly muscles to distribute the weight evenly?"

"He did." I wait for the onslaught. I broke the rules and snuck into the practice hall after hours.

But instead, Master Li says, "Walk with me." Stunned, I take my place by his side and from the dark comes his calm voice. "How are you feeling?"

I think it is the first time he's ever asked me that question. I am so shocked that all I can manage is, "Fine."

"You have been here four years now, Lu Mi La. Are you happy?" Happy? I work, I eat, I sleep. "Or are you angry?" he finishes.

I can't think of a reply, but at his next question, "Do you have a goal?" I am faster.

"Beat Yong Da."

"And why is that?"

"He's mean."

"Anyone you would defend?"

"Wei Wan."

"Why him?"

"He's weak."

"Is he?"

"No," I correct myself. "I meant small. Small*er*."

"I see. And which one do you think takes the most courage?"

I think carefully. "Defending someone."

I see his silhouette nod slightly, but I can't tell if it's because he approves or just some silent musing.

"Keep practicing, Lu Mi La." He walks off, soon merging with the sheen of red lanterns by the Ten Thousand Buddha Hall.

Not until much later does it strike me that he never gave me a reprimand. And for some reason, it makes me think of those people being sent on missions. I bet this is what they do, forge ahead, break rules and get away with it. I could be wrong, but this is what I think.

67

"Shou laji! Shou laji!"

It's Lao Bai again, Old Bai; I hear him from across the temple walls. Once a moon, he comes by with his rickety cart to collect whatever we might not need. It seems he can find use for almost anything. I put down my tray of offerings for the worship houses and go to the grand entrance.

"Mi La," he beams. He's been very talkative since he got over the terrible shock that I am a girl, which took him slightly over a year. *"You laji ma?"*

I tell him to wait, and there just might be something. After a quick tour to Ah Mei and the laundry room, I bring back a pair of the black canvas shoes we all wear. These have seen better times, and if not even Ah Mei deems them worthy of fixing, then I don't see how anyone can.

"Only these," I tell him as I return.

"Hai hao, hai hao." He nods appreciatively and takes them without hesitation. I am reminded of how resilient the Chinese can be.

He points at the shoes in his hand and gives a toothless smile. *"Xi shui chang liu."*

I nod; it is true. A thin stream flows longer, or; if you are frugal, you can make things last. He thanks me profusely and calls me a good girl. *Hao guniang*, even though that specific term refers to a very young girl. It has been a long time since I thought of myself in that way. And I realize at afternoon practice that it was equally long since Steel Master did. At least judging from his growing disdain every time he sees me. No little girl could be deserving of that.

Luckily, I am not so little anymore.

In morning *gong fu,* we're practicing blocking spear hand and knife hand, focusing on defence. I have worked hard on my blocks in the last moon, not the least in Wei Wan's and my secret practice. I do quite well as long as I am not paired with Yong Da or anyone else twice my size.

After half an hour, Wei Wan is the only one who fails in blocking the spear hand. He keeps getting hit, even though the other boy doesn't hit hard.

The next time he misses, Steel Master strides right up to him, black brows narrowed. "How slow are you? Do I have to bring out the *mu ren zhuang?*"

Steel Master's suggestion to use the wooden dummy makes Wei Wan's face go bright red.

Then, our master throws an unexpected punch, and Wei Wan gets so scared he dodges instead of blocks.

Steel Master leans his stony face close. "*What* did you just do?"

I dig my nails into my palms. This is bad.

"I—I wasn't prepared," Wei Wan stutters.

"Prepared? Who in *gong fu* is prepared for anything? Why do you think we practice multiple blockings at all times?" Steel Master scans the room where everything has stilled. "Have I told you to stop?"

At once comes a hurried bout of thuds and grunts of punching and blocking.

"Yong Da," Steel Master calls. "Help the boy out, will you?" My movements slow. When would Steel Master ask Yong Da to help anyone? "He needs an extra set of hands to attack this slow student so we can help him learn."

I feel myself go pale. He meant the *other* boy—not Wei

Wan.

"What?" Wei Wan's eyes widen. "But that's two against one."

"You're a sharp one," Steel Master sneers.

"That will be...a lot." Wei Wan's words trail off.

Steel Master adds, "I'll tell them not to hit *too* hard. Let's see how you react under a morsel of pressure. If you have any reactions."

Wei Wan never objects to a master. Wei Wan never objects to anyone. "...but," he says.

"What?" Steel Master fixes his hard eyes on him. "Are you afraid?"

Wei Wan says nothing, which is an answer. And a mistake.

"Cease training!" bellows Steel Master.

Everything stops, and a pit of dread opens in my chest.

"Clear the space." Steel Master looks at Wei Wan. "Not you."

My fellow students back away to make a ring around Wei Wan and the other boy and Yong Da. Only as far as needed, but near enough to spot any possible gore. My stomach turns.

"To be prepared, you must be equally ready and unafraid. You will stand here," Steel Master points, "while a fighter feint attacks you, and you must *not* react."

Wei Wan trembles.

"And you will stay until you learn not to flinch. Is that clear?"

In the silence that again falls over the room, Wei Wan stands like a pale statue.

"Wait!," Master Li's authoritative voice booms behind

us. Everyone turns as he strides across the hall. What's he doing here? Observing again? "Is this really necessary?"

My throat dries. That question alone is a loss of face for Steel Master. Li would not do it lightly.

Steel Master replies with a shrewd look, "Ah, Master Li, how kind of you to visit...*my* class. Perhaps you would like to assist? It would be an honor."

Master Li displays a quick, faint lowering of his eyes. In here, he has no authority. A master has the right to lecture his students. And there is no way out of the offer to assist. Annoyance flashes across his face while Steel Master plays an innocent waiting game.

Wei Wan looks frail and tiny between brutal giants. My gaze flicks from him to Steel Master to Li's balled fists, and anger gushes up, bursting from my mouth.

"Stop," I say. "You're scaring him."

Steel Master's expression freezes somewhere between melting and imploding while Master Li gives me such a hard look that his six feet of stony authority nearly knocks me over. I just defied a master. No, two.

I am too angry to mind either of them. "Anyone can stand in front of a feint attack," I say. "It doesn't prove anything."

"I see." Steel Master masks his fury under a tight, evil smile. "Then perhaps you can demonstrate instead?"

In the crowd, I see Ming Pi, eyes wide. He backs away, like everyone else, opening the way I cannot refuse. Once again, Steel Master has proved his method's backbone. Cruel, but to the point. I am left with no choice. Biting the inside of my cheek, I tread hesitantly forward. Ugly Bulldog bumps my shoulder so hard I want to rub it. But I don't. I push through and walk out into the center of the ring.

Yong Da looks at me hungrily, like I am an especially tempting morsel, but Steel Master pushes him aside. "Master Li, it is a privilege to get your aid. I trust you can perform the most lethal kicks and punches without actually hitting your target." Yong Da clamps his jaws in irritation. "Coming as close as possible, I mean. Of course, it's hard to stave off a full-force move so very close to a body. Sometimes a millimeter can make all the difference."

My throat is dry. An unblocked kick could snap my neck. I remind myself Master Li is an expert. He won't hit me. I straighten my back and lower my shoulders. I will not flinch. I cannot flinch. If I do, I prove Steel Master right: this is hard.

"If you wince," Steel Master says in a deliberate voice. "You have forfeited the right to replace Wei Wan."

"Yes, Master Gang."

Li steps close, then grows impossibly still. I am reminded of a viper before it strikes. To not instinctively protect myself will take every ounce of effort I possess. He shifts into fighting stance, and I grip my pants to keep my hands from fluttering. Then he throws a spear hand so fast my eyes slam shut on reflex.

"Again," says Steel Master. "Eyes open."

An upward hook followed by a backfist strike and tiger mouth strike flash by my face so rapidly that my gasp freezes in my throat. I focus on his eyebrows. Shut my brain to what would happen if he hit me with that force.

He relaxes for a moment, but I know it's pretend. I hold my breath, and a spinning lotus kick whirls by my face. A wisp of air chills my skin for a split second before a double-tap sidekick comes near. Too near.

Burning pain flares in my cheek. It's so strong my skin goes numb.

He did it on purpose! I grit my teeth, looking after him as he bows and walks away. Still clasping my pant legs in a tight, sweaty grip, I manage not to touch the burning spot.

"*Gai jieshule.*" Without another word, Steel Master finishes the practice. Though the stern look he gives me sends shivers down my back. As though I surprised him, and it infuriates him. Not to mention making him lose face.

My heart beats so hard it hurts. Through my stinging skin, I feel every muscle, every nerve, every cell. Anger, fear and adrenaline rush through me like a torrent.

I storm out of the hall and run after Master Li.

"How could you?" I say as I burst into his workroom, knowing full well I have no right to tell a master off. But my anger is exploding. "You did that on purpose! And you could have chosen easier moves."

He scoffs. "Would you have preferred Yong Da as your opponent? What do you think *he* would have done on purpose?"

"I can't believe—"

"You are twelve years old, Mi La. I find your ignorance a bit tiring."

"Ignorance?"

"If I meant to hurt you, do you not think I would have done so already? Now get out."

This time, his stern eyes defeat me. He points at the door, and I walk out, fervently rubbing my cheek.

The vibration of his kicks still lingers, lethal force millimeters from my face. My fear is racing, as is my anger, my screaming skin. Two boys from my group come out from practice; one nods appreciatively, and the other makes a subtle thumbs-up.

What? What did they just do? A hundred armoured boots march through my skull, and I run into the kitchen.

"*Jie*," Wei Wan shouts. "You saved me!"

Beside him stands Cook Ma. "I heard what you did." She looks serious. "You shouldn't defy a master," she scolds, but a smile is leaking through. "That's the spirit," she whispers, mostly to herself.

Spirit. I am not entirely sure what it signifies, but it sounds like something good. Did she mean brave?

San Dun, the archivist apprentice, comes hurrying, excited and terrified all at once. "You stood up for Wei Wan, Mi La. That's so courageous!"

"I saw you grasp your pant legs and focus on his forehead," says Ming Pi, who looks more awake than he's been in four years. "That was clever."

"You should have seen Yong Da," quips a boy who has never spoken to me before. "He looked like an angry monkey. I've never seen him so ugly."

"What, you mean today?" asks Ming Pi.

There is a moment of belated reaction before we all burst out laughing. Wei Wan does a monkey dance, copying Yong Da, and then he adds an ugly grimace, and I laugh harder. Ming Pi copies Steel Master, and now I laugh so hard I can't remember when I did it last.

I feel like I just fell from a building, and somebody caught me. The kind of scare that makes you feel alive, makes your insides shiver and sing at the same time. I realize this is what I want, that satisfaction of helping, *daring*. Strength and courage. Here and there, a hearty guffaw. And it strikes me that I can have that.

All I have to do is get picked for a mission.

CHAPTER 9

MY LIFE CHANGED ON THE NINTH DAY OF THE FOURTH moon, my second year of the Dragon. That was the day I stood up for Wei Wan, when haze turned to clarity and fear turned to strength. It gave me a goal, and time flowed differently after that.

"Tell me again, the missions. What are they really?" I press Wei Wan.

"Now: How many times have I told you, Mi *jie?* We never know how or when they pick someone with special skills or who is sent to perform a task."

"I'm going to do it."

"And what exactly makes you think a reindeer girl from the Polar North would get picked?"

I was prepared for this.

"I'm going to study him," I say grimly.

And so, I spy on Yong Da. Well, not exactly, but I steal glances more often than I should. I notice his clean strikes with perfect knuckle alignment, how he spreads his toes schoolbook-wide to get flawless contact surface in the front kick, and how he pushes out his heel so strongly it makes his drop-axe kick lethal. He is a fighting monster, and I am not. That is why I watch him. And keep practicing stealth. And dream about missions.

And so I am sucked into an existence where time blurs into one long, endless carousel of training, eating, sleeping, and repeating. This is not new, but now it happens at a different level. Wei Wan and I sneak off on our secret training at all godforsaken hours, constantly challenging each other to take one step further. Just one step. This is when Wei Wan comes up with the idea that we should learn to climb the rooftops. And so, we do. Often at the break of dawn, a thrill of forbidden before first chanting, melding into our normal routines. Life is fleeting as time passes; a brief speech from a teacher, a glimpse of mist-ridden bamboo outside the temple walls, a yawning cat, a tempting smell. Train. Eat. Sleep.

Year of the Dragon.

Year of the Snake.

Year of the Horse.

And so, three years disappear.

And then that night. I slump on the narrow bed in my cramped quarters. It's an effort to lean forward to untie the bindings around my calves. I begin to pull off my pants, but a smear of red on the inside of my thigh startles me. I rise and grab the candle on my nightstand and put it close, staring. Then I pull down my undergarment. A big dark blotch stains the cotton material, and I almost yelp out loud. My moon bleeding has started! A horror close to panic rushes up my chest. No, no. Not yet! I want to turn back time and delay it. Stop it. But it's not possible. I am stuck with it forever. And pain, there will be pain; some get it less than others, but every moon I will suffer, be weak and fatigued, Mother told me. And what do I do now? How do I hide it?

Mother, *vajan,* where are you? Being surrounded by only boys can still make me feel brutally alone, even after all this time. Before I know it, sobs are wracking my body. But then I stiffen, dry my tears. Silent, I must be silent. Cook Ma and Ah Mei have their sleeping quarters at the other end of my corridor.

I put my pants back on. I have to get protection. The only place I can think of is the scullery. Towels, thin towels. And I must go now.

Carefully, I push up the door. It is not very light in my chamber, but still, it takes a moment for my eyes to adjust. Then I sneak on silent feet across the corridor and down the stairs. My mind races. I am fourteen years old. It is the year of the Horse. Is that a good year to start your moon bleeding?

I slide into the scullery and find my way to the corner where, behind a curtain, shelves line the wall. I feel my way there: towels, coarse, mid, thin. Cook Ma is as organized as the Head Archivist. I grab a thin one and test it between my fingers. This should do; I'll tear it into smaller pieces. Best take two. Cook Ma won't notice.

A sound freezes me.

What was that? A mouse? One of the cats? No, there are footsteps. Footsteps...of someone who knows stealth but has gotten lazy. Who knows their way around and is counting on not getting caught. Heart pounding, I reach out a shivering finger and nudge the curtain aside. Somebody is walking past, not three feet away. I stand frozen, peering into the moonlit space, seeing only his back as he enters the cool room. A moment later, he returns with something in his hands. *Baozi*. I teeter between keeping hidden or giving myself away. In the end, I can't resist.

"What a surprise."

With a shriek, Yong Da drops the buns. "*You*," he snarls. "What're you doing here? Sneaking in the dark like a two-faced witch. I'm going to report you. That's what you get for being a snake!"

"I came to get something to wipe the water I spilled from my wash basin." I hold up the towels. "What are *you* doing here?" I raise my brows. "Stealing food, it looks like. Cook Ma will be interested."

He raises his arm to hit me.

"As she will be in a black eye."

Trembling with anger, his fist stops mid-air.

I square my shoulders and walk out of the scullery.

For the next three days, I am scared witless of my new fate. I am sure it must show because Cook Ma looks at me strangely, and when Master Li takes me on his run, I can't find my rhythm. I keep looking down, touching the thighs of my gray fighting uniform, checking for red spots.

He stops. "You're distracted."

"I'm not." Yet every minute of every hour, I am thinking

of what will happen if someone finds out that my bleeding has started. Or worse, if all find out. The thought makes me want to vomit. I tell my master no. I am not distracted.

"Is it dreams that are troubling you?"

My dream world has changed dramatically. I see myself. I am a girl but also a woman, and I feel confident yet scared. Twice I have had a falling dream where I am somewhere in a higher realm but know I must come down. To reality. As soon as I materialize on earth, I am back at Long Si. I stand in a puddle of red. I can feel the blood streaming down my legs, colouring my pants, making me damp and sticky. In front of me is Yong Da, pointing and jeering. All the boys gather around, laughing and taunting. They draw nearer and nearer, laughing louder and louder. Just when they're about to start pushing me, I wake up in a sweat. Eyes staring wide, breathless.

"No," I say. "No bad dreams."

"Are you going to tell on him?" Wei Wan glances up from his soup bowl, a hopeful glint in his eyes. "Please do."

Four days of my moon bleeding have passed, and nothing has happened. I have a dull, aching pain in my lower abdomen, but no lightning bolt has struck me down from a clear sky, and no blood has stained my clothing. I decided telling Wei Wan about Yong Da in the kitchen was safe. Of course, I have not told him why I really went there so late, sticking to the same version I gave Yong Da. That's all he needs to know.

I shake my head. "No, let him suffer. This way, he'll be nervous. I obviously haven't told anyone, or he would already have had Cook Ma on his back. But he can't be sure I'm not going to."

Having the upper hand on Yong Da feels ridiculously good. I hope his nerves jump every time he spots Cook Ma. Guan Yin's compassion, which we are all supposed to be cultivating, seems long gone at this moment, but I decide it's worth it. Maybe she will understand my feelings and forgive me if she has so much compassion.

Apart from my moon bleeding, nothing has changed. My plan to practise hard and learn all that I can, remains. At supper, our fellow students linger at the table, and Ming Pi describes a new dog he saw at the gates this morning. Although his detailed description surprises me, I am not interested.

Wei Wan and I glance at each other. *Stalk the cat.* As we finish eating, we look at each other in the busy refectory. My look says: *Same place.* His look replies: *Agreed.*

One after another, we leave the crowds and step out into the dark.

Never speaking, always furtive. Sneaking, blocking, punching, tricking.

Focus. Quiet.

As though my dark glee from distressing Yong Da has left a trail, Steel Master comes searching for me during chores. I am clearing rubble and crumbled mortar in the corners of the lower courtyard, and now, in my side vision, I see him approach. What have I done? What lie has Yong Da poisoned him with?

Praying I am not his target, I sweep with my hand brush

and pluck invisible pieces of rubbish. Sweep. Sweep, sweep, sweep. *Go away*, I will him. *Go away*. My *gong fu* has improved noticeably, but it's the sixth day of my bleeding, and my aching abdomen has left me weak and tired. And the secret training with Wei Wan last night exhausted me. I cannot take more beating or bruising.

His purposeful strides near, and my body shrinks.

But just then, Cook Ma calls: "Lu Mi La, there you are. I need you to help me in the kitchens."

Steel Master stops sharp, face twisting in irritation. "*I* need her," he snaps.

"Oh, how unfortunate." Cook Ma comes down the stone stairs from the upper courtyard. "*Bu hao yisi*," she smiles, claiming to be sorry for the inconvenience. She is clever. You do not want to challenge a master and make him lose face in front of others. You can get away with almost anything if you profess to this subtle fake embarrassment.

She steps past him and orders me up. "I need help in the scullery. A whole container of stinky tofu broke. The stench is dreadful."

I am already standing.

Steel Master glowers and stalks off. My palms are sweating. She really went out on a limb for me.

In the kitchen doorway, she leans in close. "You must learn to stay out of trouble, girl. You don't want Master Gang as your enemy."

Dread returns like a weight in my gut, and I want to say that Steel Master is already my enemy, but she narrows her eyes. "Your *yin* is very strong today."

Yin and *yang*, the principle of inseparable opposites, rests on the balance between *yin*; the force associated with shadows, moon and femininity, and *yang*; the bright, sun and masculinity. I should know by now that Cook Ma sniffs up energies like a dog on a chase.

"Ah," she yelps with a startled look. "You got your first moon bleeding! That's why two of my thin linen towels were missing!"

Scarlet floods my face, but she lowers her voice. "Not to worry, girl. You have me and Ah Mei." She puts a hand on my shoulder. "We're here for you."

A wave of emotion floods me. I have to curb myself so as not to throw my arms around her neck. I am a world away from home; I don't know whether my family is dead or alive. I am torn between missing and not missing them. And I am irrevocably surrounded by boys.

"Don't worry," Cook Ma whispers. "I will get you linen and show you how to tie your breasts, too. You're a woman now. They need support."

She takes me to a chopping board to peel onions, the one vegetable we hardly ever eat. They stimulate the senses and are unsuitable for those in the early stages of cultivating the mind. I can't stand onions, can't stand how they sting my eyes, but compared to Steel Master, this is a dream. It's also a clever way to hide tears.

"What about the container?" I ask.

"What container?"

"The broken one. With stinky tofu."

"Oh, that." She waves a hand and walks away. "Don't worry about it."

I look around, but nowhere is there a broken container.

CHAPTER 10

THAT FIRST TERRIFYING MOON BLEEDING SEEMS FAR away. All through the year of the Goat, I was still concerned. But then came the year of the Monkey, and I figured enough was enough. I can't be sixteen and worry about some spot on my pants. I am gaining on Yong Da. Lately, he hasn't been able to beat me so easily. However, this monthly affliction can still leave me weak and tired. I am falling back in the ranks again.

"Care to inform me how many times you have been bested in staffs, Lu Mi La?" Steel Master towers over me like a raging lion. "Perhaps you should train a little harder?"

I despise the sound, the blaring trumpet of his reprimand—so sharp it makes my bones vibrate as I recoil on the hard ground.

I have been in this group for two years now. But if I am sixteen, it means Yong Da is eighteen. It is only three days since he last took out his frustration on me, and today my ribs hurt like broken glass before we even started. I want to protest, say that it's not fair. These boys have all been practicing this discipline far longer than I have, except for Wei Wan and three others who are also younger, but I never get paired with any of them.

"Detention," he snaps. "Perhaps an evening sorting scrolls in Second Archive will help motivate you."

Second Archive. My heart sinks. The cold, deserted basement is so full of spiderwebs, dust and cockroaches that no one ever goes there.

"Without food," Steel Master intonates.

But I do not hear. The orb! It's back, which once hovered in front of his chest. And like last time, it is suspended in mid-air, giving off a sinister feeling. Perhaps it *is* a ghost? Or an evil spirit that has attached itself to him?

Why can I see it? *Be careful, Mila. Be careful not to show.* As I recall Mother's words, something clicks loudly in my brain. This is what she meant! It's all coming back to me now; she told me that one day I would be able to see people's hearts, the spirit core of their being, but I mustn't let anyone know.

The orb trembles in the air, shimmering in dark grey-blue, and Grandma Koini's words surface. *There are different kinds of hearts.* The memory is strangely hazy, as though she told me when I was half asleep or we met in a dreamscape. Like Mother, she knew but never spoke openly about it. I think I understand why; it was too dangerous. No one must know, or the Hexfinder might learn of it and come to take me away.

An orb, I remember now, may change depending on emotion, but each person has a base heart. What I'm seeing in this moment, I innately know, is a Metal Heart.

"Up!" Steel Master kicks my leg. "Move!"

I scramble to my feet, shaking from his harsh voice and my internal revelation.

"You will spend the rest of the day sweeping the upper courtyard."

"But we have scripture next. Master Peng will be waiting."

"Not for you. Animals are best kept outside." He scoffs. "Pig, reindeer, what's the difference."

Yong Da smirks at his crumpled victim. He knows he has hurt me again; he thinks he is consistently winning. But he is *not*.

I am a grown-up now. Practically speaking, I could run away with a little bit of stolen money. But every time I entertain that thought, memories from the Silk Road flood me. Somewhere near the Caspian Sea, I think, the first time I refused, really refused, to take one more step. When I, in my inept attempt to defy authority, took that one stride across a chasm I almost couldn't return from.

It was not the first time I simply stopped and not the first time Master Li tried to persuade me to go on. But I sat down under the burning sun and did not move. Until he said, "Very well, Mi La. In that case, you are on your own," and he walked away.

By the time I realized he was not coming back, my belly ached from fear. I ran along the dusty road, ran until my lungs burned and ice filled my every vein. As daylight rapidly fled, the next village appeared: stalls, eateries, market. But no Master Li.

I was so exhausted I had to slow down, and then they came. Men, boys, the whites of their eyes gleaming in the semi-darkness, prowling around me until they were near enough to touch me, and tears streamed down my cheeks. I stood surrounded by bodies, pressing closer, whispering, speaking in tongues I did not understand. My hands shook so badly that I had to clutch the hem of my dirty shirt. I'm *a boy*, my mind screeched. Can't you see? It did not matter. They were hungry; a boy, a girl, a victim, it was all the same. I felt their sticky hands on me, and my throat locked.

A sword flashed through my veil of tears. Somewhere in the turmoil, Master Li grabbed my wrist, and we ran to a waiting horse. I made no protest as he threw me onto the saddle and jumped up after me.

For days afterwards, I was a pitiful creature. I did not speak; I did not eat. And every time Master Li looked at me, I saw disappointment again. But the guilt was drowned by the horror of almost being left to a pack of preying hyenas.

Here, the hyenas are Steel Master and Yong Da, and they know I will not leave. So, I must learn to handle them.

After a midday meal of stir-fried *bai cai* and noodles, I am outside again, pushing the huge old broom that weighs my tired arms. Numb from the cold, I keep sweeping, but my mind is stuck on the heart orb. If I can see people's hearts, what does it mean? And can I see them at will, or does it depend on the other person?

My punishment looms like a shadow over my head for the rest of the day. Alone in the dark chill of Second Archive, and nothing to eat. As darkness falls, my stomach rumbles, and when a tall, broad person carrying a lantern strides across the upper courtyard, my belly tightens in a knot. Steel Master stops by the Blooming Lotus Flower's Palace Hall, the grandest of the four worship houses. All he offers is a long, cold stare.

Without a word, he leads me across the grounds and into the furthest pavilion, the Crouching Tiger. As we pass the refectory, steamed broccoli with ginger wafts into my nostrils. My stomach clenches.

"This way." He makes sure I pass the seating area so that everyone can see.

I don't look up, but I know Wei Wan is watching me. Everyone in Long Si is; a silent host of stunned onlookers. Even Yong Da keeps his mean monkey mouth shut, but I feel his cutting glare like shards of glass.

At the end of the pavilion, Steel Master forces up the rusty bolt of the cellar door and picks up a second lantern before stepping through.

The lanterns' light dances across the walls and trapped air swirls like a damp shawl around me. Down the trodden stairs we go, onto flat ground and along the first corridor, all the way to Second Archive, this dusty mess of forgotten history. In the next room, row upon row of ceramic canisters are awaiting to be once again filled with soy sauce and set to ferment. Second Archive has honeycomb walls to allow regular air flow, but it is too dark to see anything through the holes.

Steel Master enters, places the lanterns on a table and walks up to the nearest shelf. "Sort them according to subject." He points to a heap of scrolls, half-ruined by wormholes and moisture. "Chronological order."

Then he takes one lantern and stomps off, steps receding

as he walks along the corridor until complete silence envelopes me. Beyond the lantern's meager glow, the darkness is compact. I pull the top of my worn fighting uniform tighter, but chilly air leaks into my body.

Reluctantly, I grab the top scroll. The dust comes off in a big cloud, making me cough as I shake it. First Archive, on the second floor of the adjacent building, is where all the principal books and scrolls are kept. I have been sent there, too, for punishment many times, but the Head Archivist is nice. So is San Dun, his apprentice. That is probably why I am not sent there anymore.

I open the scroll and glance at the context. It is an accounting of the money spent on restoring the temple a very long time ago. Long Si is nearly one thousand four hundred years old and must have undergone many changes. I pull out a new scroll, similarly motheaten. For about an hour or so, I can still make out muffled sounds from upstairs, but just barely. Then, all the footsteps and voices die. I focus on my task, but the stillness is unnerving. I sort the documents by date and subject: fiscal, maintenance, inventory, letters, and personal notes from former masters. Most I can categorize, but not all.

The Three Masters of Long Si. I move my lantern closer to better see the parchment I have just unrolled. *Long Si was founded in the year of the Rooster, 625, seven years into the Tang Dynasty.* I think for a moment where to catalogue it... General records? Then I read some more. *It is said that the three brothers who founded it were destined to save the future Middle Kingdom.* I hesitate. It doesn't sound like a recounting of facts but a story. *They all succumbed to different afflictions; Master Fu Pan, the oldest, died of lung rot. The middle brother, Master*

Song, was slaughtered by invaders, and the youngest, Master Zheng, died of unknown causes. They had, however, fulfilled the mission to establish their temple on the most powerful spot in all of China. Because of the expertly hidden secret of... A spot of mold blotches the yellowed parchment, but I can read the following few words; *Feng shui jixiang.*

Feng shui, the idea of energy flow influencing houses and land, has played great importance throughout China's history. And here, at Long Si, the scroll claims, it is most auspicious. I scrunch my brow. Why would that be? I read some more. *It is no coincidence that during the Tang Dynasty, they first appeared in the emperor's robe as a symbol of power.* That what appeared?

I continue. *Since fated to save the nation's future, the three brothers are predicted to be reborn. They will reunite in the same place, their souls knowingly or unknowingly drawn by the power of their original discovery. They will all bear marks pointing to flowing water inspired by their leader and lodestar, the...* Here comes another obscured word. All I can make out is something within brackets: *For more information, see* The River God's Chronicles.

I put the document aside. That will be the pile for miscellaneous. My hands are stiff, and hunger pangs plague my empty belly. What time is it? How much longer must I endure this godforsaken pit?

A hissing.

I whisk around. Heart thumping, I stare at the honeycomb wall. But only ringing silence and gaping black holes return my stare. I lick my lips and stand for a long while, but nothing happens. Before grabbing the next scroll, I position myself at an angle so I can look toward the corridor outside. Then; the hissing again!

"Who's there?" I keep my voice steady.

Grabbing the lantern, I push the door wide open and peer out. I am met by intense blackness. There is not even a torch at the end of the corridor. No one could come down here without me noticing; the trellis-like wall reveals everything. But this is Long Si, where students and masters alike can fight like warriors and sneak like cats. I look right, and there it is: another hissing!

Chills race up my spine.

"State your name," I demand.

No reply.

Lantern raised, I take two shivering steps, letting the sheen fall on the next room's ceramic urns. I sneak past, holding my breath. A few more steps, but nothing. I continue to the end of the corridor and peek down the next one. Just as I decide to go back, the hissing returns. I nearly choke on my own breath, but still, I am alone.

I am anxious to get out, but I dare not leave before Steel Master allows it. And if he comes now, he will be furious that I have left Second Archive. I hurry back, clutching the lantern and my open jacket. I slide through the open door and take a scroll, shaking it vigorously to free it from dust and make some noise. This place is too eerie.

"Is that all?"

With a shriek, I drop the scroll. Steel Master steps into the archive.

He sweeps his hand at the table. "This is the total of what you've accomplished?"

"Yes."

"If it were up to me, I'd make you stay the night," he sneers. "But since I'm not one of the *founding* masters, I presume I don't have the right." His two tufts of beard vibrate as he angrily turns around. "Off. I want to go to bed."

Trembling, I trudge after him as he storms along the black corridor. Before he passed, I saw the shimmering orb of his heart. Cold, ominous, angry. Metal.

CHAPTER 11

S TEEL MASTER'S METAL HEART GETS ME NOWHERE, AND right now, I am soaked from both heavy rains pounding down on the South Asian tropical monsoon zone and from standing in the river, scrubbing uniforms against a flat stone.

Like in Sápmi, there is water. The land there is covered by brooks, rivers and lakes and I recall being told that water is my element. *Remember, the birthmark* prompts an inner voice. What birthmark? I don't recall, but I am happy to help Old Ah Mei with the laundry. Every now and then she gives me a wrinkled smile which is worth more than any words, and sometimes she tells me stories. I like the one about the Triple Goddess, and Ah Mei explains, as long as I don't ask the wrong questions. No one here likes too many questions.

In history class this morning when I asked how Han Gan, the famous painter in the Tang Dynasty, could not only catch the horse's image but also its spirit, Master Li said, "Yes, that's correct."

"Yes," I replied. "I know, but how did he do it?"

"He studied with Cao Ba, the court painter."

"But he surpassed him because of exactly this ability. How?"

Lines appeared between his eyebrows. "*Jiu zhe yang.*"

The conversation was over. Never mind how the painter did it, like so many other things: Done, established, decided—it's just how it is.

I pull a new garment from the small pool formed by rocks. Asking when or what may work, but never the how or the why. I scrub the garment harder, even though I know it's only the Confucian thinking shining through. Master Li cannot defy the norms of his society any more than I can. Respect for authority means you swallow facts but do not question.

We have slowly worked through the dynasties: Xia, Shang, Chou, Qin, Han, Six, Sui, Tang, Five, Song, Yuan, Ming, Qing. Eras of family rule that dominated China for over three thousand years. I have pored over texts, old photos and illustrations of emperors, court ladies, luxurious palaces and embroidered gowns. It has piqued my curiosity about China and myself. *Destiny.* How can fate possibly bring a reindeer herder to China? Questions still flood me, but I know my curiosity is a mistake, a betrayal of the values. It is not my task to confront a master; in China, it is no one's task. Master Li and I never once talked about what happened. The rescue, the long travel, my family. Again, that smoldering in me never really dies.

I soak the scrubbed piece, ridding it of soap, and then I wring. Harder and harder, willing away the rising pain that threatens to close my throat. Frustration. And that old rotten guilt. I never tried to run away, not really. Throughout the entire journey, I only made a few half-hearted attempts. I was too little, too scared, and yet guilt claws at me day and night. I push it away, let it fade, and pretend I have forgotten.

But I haven't.

Only a few days have passed since I was sent to Second Archive, and I can't get that scroll out of my head. I try my hardest to remember. The Three Masters of Long Si were brothers, born over a thousand years ago, and will return to save the nation. And then, the chronicles.

There are no answers as I sweep the yard with Wei Wan. The River God has invaded my mind. How could some brothers be connected to a god? My hands involuntarily jerk when I see San Dun. I shoot a quick glance around. Over by the Hopping Hare Pavilion, some boys are cleaning windows. The old gardener is digging around in the rows of planted bamboo, skeletal face aimed downward. His thick glasses make him look like an insect, and I wonder if they really help his eyesight. No one is looking.

"Just wait a minute," I say to Wei Wan. With my big broom, I walk fast to the second north-western building, the Pavilion of the Silent Grasshopper.

San Dun smiles nervously as I catch up. I don't think he's ever spoken to a girl before I came, except for his mother. And Cook Ma. He places his hands on his generous girth, and I ask if he knows about *The River God's Chronicles?*

"No, I can't seem to recall..." At my disappointed look, he quickly adds, "But I could probably find out."

"Really?" A frisson of hope races up my chest. "That

would be kind."

He offers another smile, his round face making him look younger than eighteen. "Well then, I should be off. Ten Thousand Buddha Hall awaits my prayer."

"Wait." His words make me remember that first day of chores, so long ago, when I overheard Master Li and Cook Ma. "Do you know what the Nefarious is?"

"Oh, yes. The Nefarious, that's just another name for the witch triads."

"The witch triads? What's that?"

"It's a branch of the regular triads. They specialize in abducting people with paranormal skills, you know, magic and things."

"Magic?" I startle as though he just smacked my head. The Nefarious stole me for my magic? Through the Hexfinder?

San Dun's eyes go big; he thinks he has frightened me. "Anything metaphysical, really," he hurries. "Preternatural things can have very logical explanations once you grasp a bit of physics."

"But for what?" I stammer. "For ransom?"

"Oh, you mean the Nefarious? No, they take people to use them. Apparently, it was really big a few decades ago. Many successful people went missing, then later they resurfaced in new positions, usually influential ones, local or national governments, large corporations."

"And?"

"Well, you see, it looks as if they're there of their own making, but they're actually planted by the witch triads and forced to do their bidding."

I hear the call of a bamboo partridge. The warning signal

Wei Wan and I decided on long ago. Someone is approaching.

"Thank you, San Dun. I must go."

I turn back and see him half-hidden in the shade behind the pavilion's bottom corner. Master Li. Am I imagining things, or has he appeared more often lately? I am stuck between wanting to approach him and returning to my task. But what would I say to Master Li? I can't make myself ask about my destiny one more time. Can I?

I tighten my grip on the broom and walk back to Wei Wan. Why can I never make Master Li happy, even long after I had stopped flouting his rules on the Silk Road? Like that time we passed the turquoise mines, I think they were near a place called Nishapur. All I did was gaze longingly at the mines, the bright shining stones from the market we had passed the day before still fresh in my mind. But I didn't beg for a turquoise. I didn't cry or say a word, yet he looked at me disappointedly.

I catch up with Wei Wan, who stops talking to Ming Pi, and Ming Pi looks at me as though he knows of my frustration. As though his sleepy mind has picked up on things that he wishes to be a part of. Did he see my silent encounter with Master Li? Does Master Li frighten him too?

I turn my back and sweep with hard, rapid strokes. Sweep until my muscles ache and my fingers cramp from holding tight.

CHAPTER 12

T HE HISSING QUICKENS MY PULSE. I FIGURED IT WAS A blessing in disguise to be sent back to Second Archive because I wanted to search for *The River God's Chronicles*. But it seems the god has other plans.

I look at the open door, but nothing stirs. Quickly, I calculate the time. It will be a good while before Steel Master returns.

Ignoring his last warning that if I didn't do a better job this time, he would make me spend the night, I sneak out from the archive and into the corridor. I got beaten again, by Yong Da. His best bully friend cheered him on, the ugly bulldog one. I crashed to the ground so many times I am sure they still laugh about it, but they don't know that I had a reason. I saw Yong Da's heart, an orb black as pitch. Ink Heart. The sight stunned me, so I lost my concentration, and I don't recall what happened after the fall. I can't remember the impact, the pain or the stinging humiliation. I only remember seeing the heart. In that second of onslaught, a mysterious power flashed through me.

But next, I was flat on the ground. One separate memory for each attack, so overwhelming I felt weightless.

Steel Master's shouting that followed was less subtle, and here I am again.

I raise my lantern and pass the room with soy sauce urns. I must keep my body compact and in a light crouch to distribute the weight evenly. I lift a foot and listen for each step, then lower my toes and gently roll down. *Stalk the cat.* Ukko knows I have practised it.

At the end of the corridor, I take a left. Every now and then, I hear the faint hissing. It must be some animal. But what kind of animal could be trapped down here without making a racket? I circulate the winding walkways, but the hissing gets fainter and eventually peters out. I am stiff and cold. The idea of getting lost in this black labyrinth sends a shiver down my back. Steel Master wouldn't mourn my disappearance. Would anyone?

Something catches my eye just as I flick my lantern to inspect the last room. A murky wall hanging. I stride over and pull it aside. Behind is a circle, three feet high. A miniature moon door. I try pushing it, but it does not budge. The harder I push, the more I want to know what's behind it. Something with the round shape...it reminds me of the top of a *lávvu*, the round hole that opens to the skies.

I put down the lantern and drop to my knees. This has to do with Sápmi, I just know it. I think of cold winter nights, searching my mind, and I see the northern lights through my imaginary smoke hole. Mother was scared of my glimmering hands. And Koini, too, was so cautious of my ability to see hearts that she never mentioned it, save for that time she whispered about the various categories when I was half asleep. There are different kinds, she said. Emotion can affect the orb, but the foundation of a heart will always be the same.

San Dun said the Nefarious abduct people with magic skills. They bought me at the slave market. I remember it because the seller said, "*Seikhar.* Good price." And suddenly, I realize why the word is familiar, why it popped into my head on the Silk Road. It was because I'd heard it before. Grandma Koini murmured about it one night by our fire: *Seikhar. Children of the Northern Lights.*

Suddenly, I recall a heated discussion from long ago.

"It's impossible," father snapped. "None of us are."

"Yet she is; you have seen it yourself," my mother replied.

"The hands could be..." his words trailed off. "Something else. None of that is true; it's just a legend."

"It is not."

"They're a cult."

"A tribe. Real, not a mad leader with delusional followers."

"A cult."

"Call it what you will," Mother said, her voice tired. "It exists, and she belongs there."

Father had a menacing look in his eyes. "How?" he demanded. "How is it possible? It doesn't run in our family, no matter how far back you go. If it would, I would never have fathered children."

"You are forgetting something."

Father grumbled. Then he raised his head, confusion bleeding into worry. "You mean..."

Mother nodded. "Yes," she said quietly. "The ceremony. Remember what the *noaidi* said. This reindeer sacrificed itself for her."

A cloud of memories swamps my head. Eyes closed, I sink against the moon door. Like all children from my lineage, I was initiated with a ceremony. When I was four years old, a reindeer was slaughtered. To honor the animal, every part must be used. Eaten or turned into hide or sinewy string, even glue made of the hooves. Everything except the heart.

I recall the words of the *noaidi*, the mediator between the human world and the underworld, who performed the ceremony.

"You have a very special daughter, *Beaivi*." Out of respect for my mother, he called her 'goddess of the sun', also meaning 'mother of humankind'. "This reindeer has given its heart to her. She must complete the ceremony by consuming it."

I see father again, back in the conversation with mother. His eyes bulged. "The heart," he whispered. "You mean it happened when she ate the heart?"

Mother nodded again. "I see now," she said in a low voice. "Why the *noaidi* suggested he perform our ceremony separately. He knew all along. She is *Seikhar*."

"But," father spluttered. "They left, whatever existed or was left of the cult—tribe," he corrects himself. "It was too dangerous for them, even up in the High Country; they fled."

"It doesn't mean they no longer exist."

In the dark underground of Long Si, I sit upright and stare at my upturned hands. My palms are glimmering. The lines in my skin pulsate and flow like miniature rivers. Red, vibrant, like the reindeer's heart dripping with blood.

Now I understand. At the ceremony with the *noaidi*, this ability, what ability exactly I don't know, was activated when I ate the reindeer's heart. The animal knew what my spirit held, knew that I was born *Seikhar—Seikharinne*, the suffix; *inne,* denoting female: Girl-Child of the Northern Lights. When I consumed its heart, it transferred part of its spirit to me, and my being fused with it. Reindeer Heart.

But why is all this happening now? The recollection, my shining hands?

For the remaining hours, I foggily sort papers and old documents. My memory is dancing like a dog chasing its own tail. I am *Seikhar*, one of the legendary Children of the Northern Lights! How can it be possible? I have never met any. Only heard rumors. Grandma Koini. Of course. Alone in the cold cellar, I try to recall forgotten stories amongst piles of crumpling parchments. Not really forgotten, never. With Grandma Koini, tales and legends spun their way into your mind like creeping ivy.

A baleful feeling seeps in, and a scene flashes before me of twilight wrapped in black nights. And cold, icy cold, as though light and dark are wrestling, and I am somehow part of it.

I see Koini by the fire, her leathery skin, the glint in her eyes veiled in riddles and secrets. Her words always riveted me to the reindeer pelt I sat on, and even here, deep down in Second Archive, the memory is so vivid my lips part slightly, my breath comes heavier and my body leans forward. *Dangerous*, Koini intoned in a lilting whisper. But what is dangerous? My memory dog dances ever more wildly, chasing its tail around and around. Remembering the Children of the Northern Lights is the bait it has been waiting for, the temptation to trigger a wild and reckless hunt.

In my mind, Grandma Koini gives a slight but satisfied nod. She liked to see the effect of her words; it was the power she held over us children, that ability to exert some dominance and at the same time know she was doing the right thing. She notified, gave advice, and helped people steer clear of hazards.

A chunk of her tale organizes itself into sentences and drops into my head.

The only thing that can stop them is Seikhar, Children of the Northern Lights. But they must be united, that's why they had to flee. Nowhere is safe for them.

My grimy hand pauses on the parchments. Can stop what? What was it that was so dangerous they had to flee? Is there danger here, for me, now?

My thoughts tumble in an endless churn.

When Steel Master finally comes to get me, no doubt only because he wants to go to bed himself, he throws a derisive look at my work. "Is this all?"

"Yes." I feel his sneer.

"I can't hear you."

"Yes, Master."

"That's a shame."

He doesn't wait for me to say anything because he knows I won't.

"You might have to come back then. Finish what you never manage to finish."

I know what he is going to say next.

"Since you're so slow. And utterly useless." He strongly emphasizes the last word before he raises the lantern to leave. "Not that I'm surprised."

Steel Master belittles me, as is his habit.

Yet, inside of me, there are whispers of strength, victory, and unknown skills.

As he walks ahead along the musty black corridor, he holds his lantern perfectly still so it doesn't swing.

I hold mine loosely so it swings, and this I know: I am *Seikhar*.

It has been three days since my last detention, and it's a miracle Steel Master has not yet put me back in. His irritation over my less-than-impressive work still lingers like a shadow around me. For a second, I thought he was going to make me stay the night. But that could indicate that he had lost his temper, and that would mean face loss.

I had planned to tell Wei Wan about the moon door, and that I am *Seikhar*, but I can't find him. Instead, I bump into Ming Pi, who hardly looks asleep.

"Detention," he says. "So brave."

I am so into my newly found magic I just look at him. "What?"

"It usually means you've annoyed Steel Master," he goes on. "That is brave." I hadn't really thought of it that way. "And bravery leads to things," he finishes.

"That's a clever way to think," I say. "Are you brave?"

Ming Pi gives an embarrassed smile. Two years younger than me, that's a big difference. "I'm sure you are." Something wipes the smile off his lips, and I turn to see Yong Da approach, bullies in tow. "You just have to remember to practice it," I add.

"Loser." Yong Da steers toward Ming Pi, but I step in front of him. "Oooh," he sneers. "Loser helps loser."

His wicked-looking friend approaches on the other side, but from the corner of my eye, I see Ming Pi square his shoulders and not back away. I turn to him and continue our conversation. "Practice makes perfect, right?" I give an encouraging smile.

"Right," he stutters out the word as Yong Da's bully pal knocks his shoulder.

"And you will practise," I say firmly. "Because I know you have a very good memory. That's how you can recall details, like describing a certain dog very clearly or recounting facts in history class."

Now, his smile is less hesitant. I have landed on something he takes pride in. "Well, tell me," I say, "what will you do next time they come?"

"Not back away."

"That's right."

His gaze clears, and when his friend comes to get him for chores, I imagine he walks a little straighter.

I head off to clean out the rookery, which is my task for the afternoon. On the way, I steal a few moments with Habllek, who headbutts my leg and purrs when I scratch her. Inside the shed, I am glad to see Cook Ma. Despite her sad eyes, she always lifts my spirits.

"Lu Mi La, how are you today?" She asks as she enters

from the meshed yard where she's been feeding the messenger pigeons.

"*Hai hao*," I say, okay. I wish my exciting news didn't have to be a secret: that I'm *Seikhar* and can see people's hearts! But then, she won't know what I'm talking about.

By the hunting falcon, Cook Ma opens the cage. Carefully, she reaches in and strokes the feathers of the mighty bird.

"Does it have a name?" I ask.

"It does, but we do not lightly reveal it. In a name rests power. Sometimes, no name is as good as any name."

I start to scoop droppings and feathers into a wooden bucket. "I understand." I don't really, but her words have a certain ring to them. I guess it's connected to energies and invisible forces.

Ma is absorbed in the bird, which is large and still and beautiful.

"So where is he?"

She redirects her attention to me. "Who?"

"The proud Manchu, the one you said is its master."

It's ever so light and ever so quick, but a glow dashes across her face. "He...left for a while."

"And do you think the falcon misses him?"

"We all miss him."

I walk over to the furthest corner to sweep there. "When will he come back?"

"Soon," she says and walks away. "Soon."

But somehow, I get a feeling she doesn't really believe it.

CHAPTER 13

"A HISSING? WHAT HISSING?" WEI WAN LOOKS AT me from under the bangs he doesn't have because his head is shaved. But I always imagine him with thick black hair, straight and shiny bangs, all the way to his kind eyes.

"I told you, I don't know," I mumble so no one can hear in the busy refectory. "But something. And then a miniature moon door, hidden behind a hanging. I couldn't open it."

"Isn't it scary down there?"

"Definitely."

"So why do I feel you can't wait to go back?"

"Wouldn't you want to know if a hideous beast lived right under your feet?"

"No."

"But a *secret door*?"

"What if you disappear and never find your way out?"

I don't tell Wei Wan my new secrets either. I hardly understand them myself, but what if they can help me get sent on a mission?

"What about *The River God's Chronicles?*" Wei Wan asks. "That you told me about earlier."

"Why is that more exciting than mysterious sounds in dark dungeons?"

"Because you can explore them in broad daylight. And it's not a dungeon, just the basement of a pavilion."

"Aren't you a smart one?" I break my *baozi* in half. "Here, take it."

He looks longingly. They don't give us too much food at Long Si. "No, it's okay."

"Take it."

Yong Da passes by. "Did you spit on it?"

Ugly Bulldog grins. "Freaky."

Ignore, Wei Wan mouths at me.

"Maybe she bewitched it," says mean bully friend number two.

Chopsticks clatter onto our table. "Make a cross, kid," Yong Da sneers over his shoulder. "Pray for protection. That's what they do in witch countries."

"Ew," Wei Wan pushes the chopsticks away with his tray. "Yong Da germs."

"Definitely." I agree. "Don't touch; risk of ugliness and stupidity."

We both burst out laughing. Wei Wan must be my very own Guan Yin, a constant source of *baozi*-eating kindness and compassion. And he is right about *The River God's Chronicles.* They've pulled at some unseen string in me for too long now, but a whole week passes before I get a chance to go and look for San Dun. I find him bent over the big table in the main room of First Archive, studying something with a magnifying glass.

"Oh, Lu Mi La." He looks up but forgets to put down the magnifying glass. For a second, I see only one huge eye staring at me. "Head Archivist has gone to midday meal."

"I know."

"Ah, of course you do." He puts down the magnifying glass. "You're clever." He points to the table where a lantern is lit. "I'm afraid I haven't been able to dig up much. They were written so long ago. But I managed to find some scraps."

A terrifying grief-stricken relief washes over me. I don't know why. "You found some, really? What—" I breathe. "What does it say?"

"Have a look." He collects some half-withered parchments and pushes them over.

My breath catches. These I have to have.

I word the following sentence carefully. "It would be of great help if I could...take them with me."

San Dun's gaze flattens, and he looks away. I feel bad. I shouldn't make him do things that aren't right. But something sings and flares inside. As if a once-told story turned nearly to dust but was saved in the nick of time.

I smile. "I promise to bring them back."

His lips twitch. "Uh, okay, then. But...don't tell anybody. And in the same shape."

"Of course." I take the bundle and scoot out before he changes his mind.

The rest of the day crawls, and by evening, I am sorely tempted to try and escape the meditation, but I dare not.

Finally, by the sheen of a candle, I am on my bed, musty blanket over my knees, letting my fingers gingerly traipse across the ancient parchments. A scent of drafty old cellar lingers around them, and my pulse thickens.

THE RIVER GOD'S CHRONICLES

Recorded: Before time.
Location: The Birthing Place of Dragons

Dragons? I curb my urge to gulp up the information, forcing myself to browse the moth-eaten papers until I find a rather intact one. Carefully, I dip into history line by line, as though reading too fast would somehow overwhelm this bygone relic.

In many belief systems, dragons are connected to water and weather. Pictured as the rulers of fluid bodies such as lakes, rivers, waterfalls or seas, they had great influence on humankind. It comes as little surprise, then, that the God of Water is a dragon. Some have called him River God. He is the bringer of life, giving rain and the representative of yang, the masculine power of generation.

The rest of the paper has almost disintegrated, but excitement trails along my limbs. Eagerly, I extricate another page, where only the bottom part is intact enough to read.

Initially, the River God was thought to be ruling alone. Still, according to ancient oracle scriptures, spirit-walkers (one who can walk with spirits, see appendix 3.4) have reported encounters with a lesser deity connected to the River God, a— a what? The parchment is stained by mold. It's impossible to see in the meagre light. I hold it closer to the candle. *Exists in...form. This...creature is said to have appeared on this earth with a purpose (to help its descendants). (Regarding the definition of esoteric descendants, see Appendix 2.6).*

As the page ends, I move on to a new one.

For this to happen... Here, someone has spilled candle wax. Frustrated, I jump a few lines. *The strong yang trait demands a yin power. Thus, the one destined to work...must be... It is also only possible if...* More spilled wax.

Enough. I cannot decipher anymore until I have a knife sharp enough to remove the wax. But still, I can't wait to tell Wei Wan of this ancient treasure, bursting with song and fire.

During the following midday break, I got my chance to recount my findings in as much detail as I could. "I was touching something from thousands of years ago. Can you believe it?"

"But what did you actually find out?"

"What do you mean?" I snap, flustered at the lack of interest.

"Well, what is it that exists, and in what form? You mention a creature, but what creature? What is the purpose mentioned, and who is destined to do what?"

For a thirteen-year-old, he is sharp. Still, there's a bite in my tone. "It's *ancient*."

"Doesn't matter if it doesn't tell us anything."

"You're annoying."

"You're ungracious."

"Ungracious? Where did that come from?"

"From my incessant repository of strange and puzzling knowledge."

He is so funny I almost laugh out loud. But I don't, because I'm angry and he doesn't get it. Even though, actually, he gets everything. All the time.

The next day, after morning practice, I slip into the weapons' cache. Sneaking glances and practicing stealth, I pretend the knife I need is for a more exciting purpose than scraping wax off an old scroll. Selected students in group four have knife throwing on their regular schedule, but nothing here is ever locked away. As it is, we are all walking deadly weapons anyway.

Quietly, I shut the door behind me. As I reach the second door, I angle sideways, release a breath and slip through. Three more soundless steps, and I am at the knife rack. The top brand, Skyhawk, is lined up in a glassed case, but I'm fine with just the nearest one. Swiftly, I close my fingers around a hilt and put the knife in my pocket. I turn to leave this small annexe through the building it is connected to, Practice Hall Number Two. A simple smoke screen in case anyone saw me enter. But just as I tip-toe through the door, I bump into someone and squeal in surprise.

"Wei Wan!"

We stare at each other like two bulls before a fight.

"What're you doing here?" I demand.

"What are *you* doing here?" he retorts.

"I asked first."

"Nothing." He avoids my gaze. "You?"

"Nothing."

We glare at each other. "I'm older. You should respect me by answering my question."

"I'm younger. You should care for me by not harassing me."

Since my conscience isn't crystal clear, I don't press my case.

"Suit yourself," I say and leave.

"*Hao ba.*" He goes the other way.

This is weird. I have never felt that Wei Wan is lying to me, and yet, at this moment, he is clearly holding something back. Well, I guess so am I. I didn't tell him I was stealing a knife.

I didn't see it coming, though I admit that the chronicles might have influenced me slightly. I realize it when Yong Da bests me in the opening sequence of staff class. We stand seven feet apart, sides toward one another. I hold my staff in my right hand, the bottom part on the floor but pressing against my right foot. Yong Da's position is identical but mirrored. We turn our heads forward; this is when you look into your opponent's soul, but it feels more like a staring contest.

At Steel Master's command, I kick the bottom end of my staff up into my left hand, drop my right foot in rotation and thrust up both arms. My grip is solid, and I resist Yong Da's downward strike. He swings the bottom of his staff up, but I block low.

We both rock back to one-legged toe-touch, use the momentum to surge forward and slam our staffs in a crackingly loud cross. He draws back to make room for a forward thrust, but I retreat and twist, knocking away his strike. Face tight, he comes at me with a four-spin. I can only back up, twisting my staff fast as he advances. As I hit the wall behind me, I bounce forward, and again, our staffs clash in a second cross. But Yong Da is stronger and I see his heart.

A shiny black orb floats in front of his chest, vibrating with strength and emotion. It stuns me for the second he needs. He brings my weapon to the floor with one lethal push, and I nearly lose balance. A strike to my back knocks me clean off my feet, and I crash to the ground.

Steel Master gives me such a furious glare I register no pain. I only know that I see his heart; steely blue, cold, angry. Then my eyes fasten on it strangely. I feel his power for a moment, as though I'm sipping a strong liquor and feeling its effect.

I explode up from the floor.

Yong Da strikes. I can hear his staff whistle through the air, and reflexively I swing sideways and throw an axe kick that hits the end of his staff. It slips from his hands in an end-over-end rotation, flying across the room to Steel Master—and thwacking him hard.

He staggers, and for a stunned second, my brain is empty. Then I have just enough time to think *I beat them both* before Steel Master roars, "Detention!"

He stands with fists balled, fury spouting like hot steam from his face.

I briefly consider apologizing a thousand times over. Hitting a master is unthinkable, and half of me picks up the shocked looks of my fellow fighters, standing around the hall like pillars of salt. But the chill in my heart can't suppress the elation I feel. My brain buzzes something with his shimmering orb, whispering of...*heart power*. I am frantically fumbling for, for...a key? I know I am close. Beneath my stressed-out head, my heart whoops and twirls. *A key to Seikhar.*

I quickly drop my gaze and turn to leave. My body will break out in pain once the adrenaline is gone, and right now, being alone in Second Archive doesn't seem all that bad.

"But first," Steel Master snarls. "Master Li's office."

I can't stop the heat that rushes into my cheeks. I still haven't forgiven Li for hitting me on purpose that time when I stood up for Wei Wan, even though it's so long ago. I haven't forgiven him for a lot of things.

Without a word, I leave and make my way to the Pavilion of the Sleeping Bear. I try to think of whether I am sent here for almost losing, ending up winning or hitting Steel Master in the head.

Li sits at the desk in his workroom on the ground floor. Parchment and ink before him, lit candles in holders along the walls.

His face is locked in grim lines. "Another detention?"

"I hit Steel Master in the head." His brow crimps further. "Yong Da smashed me to the floor, then attacked before I was even halfway up. I acted on reflex." I see him trying to connect this information to Steel Master's head. "My axe kick sent his staff across the room." I twiddle with my fingers. "And...it landed on Steel Master's head."

Such a thing has clearly never happened before because, for a good while, Master Li does not say anything.

"I see." He steeples his fingers. "Let me ask, if he had already smashed you to the floor, how could you go from there to attack mode? So strongly that you surprised an experienced fighter and kicked the staff out of his hands?"

Seikhar. "Like I said, I acted on reflex."

"I hope he recovers."

I want to point out that I have been struggling to recover from his pet student's beatings for years, and those were far worse. Instead, I say, "Yes. I hope so too."

"It's not a good idea to get on the wrong side of Master

Gang. As Head of Fighting, he has more power than you might appreciate. You realize I cannot challenge him within his discipline?"

"He detests me."

"A little humility wouldn't hurt. Confessions have their place in any hierarchy."

He wants me to apologize: I am sorry. It was my fault.

That will not happen.

"Even for a second moon snake, you get into a lot of trouble, Mi La." He looks at me sternly.

"I am not born in second moon," I say quietly.

"What do you mean?"

"My birthing day is the seventeenth day of the first moon." My master looks confounded. "1928," I add, and now he seems doubly confused. "Why did you think I was born in second moon?" I ask.

"1928?"

"Yes, 1928."

"I—" I can almost see the cogs and wheels in his brain whirring, making him stutter out a string of words. "I enquired at the slave market. But they must have just...made it up."

My heart goes cold. "You planned to *buy* me? Like a common slave?"

"No, of course not. I don't deal in human trade."

"Then why did you enquire about me?" The words make me sick, as though I had been inspected like an animal at a livestock market. By my Master, whom I thought had at least some shred of honor in his bones. My legs feel like water.

"It is complicated."

"Not really." I drip with sarcasm, all respect for authority gone. "I was a slave, and you planned to buy me."

"Rescue you," he corrects. "The Nefarious bought you."

"I see. And for that, you needed my birthing date?"

"Actually, yes."

"You only rescue people if they are born on the right day?"

"I do not rescue people. Gorgarath is far too big to tackle alone. It is not my job."

"But you did get me out of the Nefarious' grip," I press. "Why?"

He stares out the window, evading my brazenness.

"*Nide mingtzi shi Xiao Mi*," he says at length. "*Nage Mi, ne?*" He says my nickname, Little Mi, but so many characters are Mi; which one am I?

"*Mimi de mi*," I reply. The one that means secret.

He nods in consent; it was he who gave me this name, *Little Secret*. He turns his head again to the window as he rubs his chin. "*Shenme mimi, ne?*"

I can't answer because I do not know what my secret is. At least not all of it.

I am back at the moon door. Thinking only of what happened in my duel with Yong Da, the pain that flared up in my body as soon as I left Master Li's office is once again subdued by my busy mind. In that moment of focusing on Steel Master's heart, I was *so* strong. It was a fluke victory, but I touched on something. And what about the last time I was here? Something in this cold, dark cellar set off my powers. Seeing people's hearts is obviously part of those powers, but what was the trigger? Why would my hands start to glimmer so far from the northern lights?

I kneel and try the moon door, but it will not budge. So then I do the only thing I can think of: I close my eyes and say, "*Seikhar*."

A flaming sensation races along my arms and I flick my eyes open. My palms are glowing. I swallow a silent gasp and repeat, "*Seikhar*." The light grows slowly stronger. Instinctively, I press my hand to the door.

It opens.

A tunnel is before me. My breath quickens. I take my lantern and enter, progressing by crawling and crouching. At the end is a set of short, steep stone stairs. I climb them, and right above my head is a trap door. I place my palm against it and press upward. Stuck. I put down my lantern and use both hands but to no avail. Frustrated, I climb a step higher, bend my neck, squeeze myself under the wooden board and push with my shoulder. Still no use. Panting, I bend myself even more and manage to ascend another step. Now I engage fully; my legs, my core. I push with everything I have.

With a creaking sound, it gives. The trapdoor flies upward in a cloud of dirt and dust. I cough, cover my mouth with my sleeve and climb out.

I stand with nothing but my rushed breaths for company.

The secret pathway leads outside. No secret chamber, no hidden treasure, only the forest that starts less than a hundred yards from the temple grounds. For a moment, I just stand, feeling all elation run off me. This is a secret entry to Long Si. From out here, you can enter the basement of the first pavilion,

Crouching Tiger, only, there isn't anything *in* there. And Second Archive is not locked. Not even Crouching Tiger is locked; nothing is locked.

I chew the inside of my cheek, vaguely picking out the silhouette of tall conifers around me. The hoot of an owl, the scurry of a mouse. The night is cool and quiet, but it does not give me answers.

I shake my head and go back down the black hole. Carefully, I close the trapdoor, retrieve the lantern and return all the way to Second Archive. But wait, I halt right before it, by the room with the soy sauce urns.

On impulse, I step in, walk up to the closest urn and kneel. After only a moment's hesitation, I lift off the lid. A soft light flares from the open container. My breath is sharp. I blink in surprise as a flaming round shape the size of an apple floats out. When I try to touch it, it floats away but returns to hover above my hand, spreading a light green shimmer into the black space.

A sound from the end of the corridor makes me jump. The flaming shape returns to its home, and I replace the lid as quickly and softly as I can. Then I dash into Second Archive at the speed of a marten, arriving one second before Steel Master.

"What?" he shouts. "Is this all? Have you been asleep, girl?" Even in the faint sheen of lanterns, I can make out the red seam across his forehead. *I hope it hurts.*

"No, Master."

He narrows his eyes. "What is the meaning of this?" His voice takes on a dangerously soft tone. "Are you refusing the tasks I set for you?"

"I, I got a bit—"

"Do you *want* to spend the night down here?"

"No, Master."

With a growl, he grabs his lantern and storms off. I flutter like a leaf at his heels.

CHAPTER 14

THE NEXT MORNING, I STAND BLEARY-EYED IN THE practice yard. I hardly slept a wink. My body ached from my duel with Yong Da, and the flaming pearl kept dancing in my dreams. A trap door, a mysterious hissing, and urns filled not with soy sauce but with...what?

"*Zhuyi*," pay attention, Steel Master snaps. "Something important will be announced at midday today."

Everyone's ears prick up. For a moment, I fear it has something to do with me. Does he know what I have been up to during my detentions? No. He can't.

Then he roars, "Forest track, now!"

Everyone takes off. Aiming for the hills beyond Long Si, onto the goat trails, around and back. A minute ago, I was rubbing sleep from my eyes, and now it feels like death is panting down my neck. Yong Da sprints past, walloping me in the back as he passes. I stumble but do not fall. Everything from the last few days flashes. *Seikhar. Child of the Northern Lights.*

The cold morning air shreds my lungs as I set out after

him. Arms tucked to my sides, I push hard up the first hill and into the forest. Already, I feel like I'm on fire. My heart clashes painfully with my ribs, and acid burns my legs. Second hill. My feet get heavy. *Keep going.*

A slight rolling downhill, then up again. Some boys are falling back. I push past them, up the third hill, onto the goat trail. It's full of stones and roots and hard to see in the shade of the trees, but my *Seikhar* feet know how to tread on Earth Mother.

Soon, though, they feel like lead. My whole body feels like lead. Yong Da is still leading, followed by Apple, who has long legs, and Yong Da's bully-friend, the wicked-looking one. Then me. Gradually, I gain on Wicked as tiredness sets in further. But no, I grit my teeth. *Keep going.* With glacial determination, I force my brain to calculate the exact amount of energy needed to supply my bloodstream with fuel and how much it can expend before the oxygen debt piling up becomes too big to handle. In split-second bursts, it allows muscles, tissue, and bones to correspond and achingly, slowly, plunge through barriers.

I'm neck and neck with Wicked.

Frustration radiates from his gushing breaths as I feel pain eating into my own flesh. *A tiny bit...more...just...a tiny...bit.* I inch past him. Milimeter by milimeter. Yes. Third position. Yes. I spot the curved rooftops. *Almost there.*

Rounding the last patch of trees, my heart dares a weak flip. Long Si is getting near, and I have kept my third position. I sprint into the lower courtyard, wanting to crash on the ground in explosive panting. But I suppress my breath, my euphoria, everything.

Steel Master is watching me and frowns.

It's as if *Seikhar* has given me a boost because, once I've recovered, I move through our continued practice with speed and agility. This brightens my outlook considerably, allowing those missions in my mind to shine a little brighter. The last two days have been good. No one has beaten or humiliated me. Master Li has not been around to give me his look of disappointment. I kicked a staff from Yong Da and whacked Steel Master over the head. I am touched by a brief but delicious feeling of happiness, which seems absurd since, at the rate of things developing, I am also somewhat likely to end up a skeleton in Long Si's underground. Yet, for now, happiness rules. Perhaps my life will come together after all?

Across from me, Wei Wan slurps up his last noodles when the gong sounds, and everyone looks up. Master Li steps forward. He will make the statement we were told about this morning. Behind him stands Steel Master, Master Peng, Head Archivist, Potion Master, and other high-ranking members of Long Si. Behind them, more masters are lined up according to seniority.

"Students, listen up. I trust you have already been informed about today's important announcement. I am sure you are all wondering what it is about." He lets silence work for a moment. "You might or might not have pondered it, but it has, in fact, been very long since we either participated in, or organized, a contest."

Everyone perks up.

"To blow life into an old tradition, we have invited

Temple of the Red Crane and Temple of the Flying Squirrel to join us in a much longed-for tournament."

A chorus of cheering breaks out. Only students who excel will be picked to defend Long Si's honor, and I am as excited as everyone else. A chance to see the very best in real action.

"Each temple will choose twelve students for the tournament, making the total number of contestants thirty-six. The event will open with a lion dance ceremony." This brings a new round of shouts and applause. "Followed by our chosen twelve participants who, together with the competitors from our fellow temples, will perform, first in a group, the Roaring Cheetah sequence, then the Croaking Rooster sequence."

Quiet now; here and there, widened eyes. These are amongst the most difficult sequences, but that was expected. Yong Da leans back with a smug grin, as do his friends.

"The last challenge," Master Li continues, "is the sequence-based free-fighting, where one contestant will be tested against multiple attackers appearing at regular intervals. In honour of our goal to defeat the ancient warlords, it will be performed in the traditional manner."

My subdued gasp blends with the others. This means the fight will not finish until the time limit is reached, no matter what. An old and terrifying display that can result in grisly injuries, even death. Winning this would be most prestigious.

"Our visiting contestants have graciously accepted and have already begun to plan their travels. The tournament will take place in three moons."

More cheering.

"All students will fight together. This is not about beating another school but about excelling in the ancient art of *gong fu*.

You never know who will be by your side in combat. Best make friends with everyone and enemies with no one."

I feel Yong Da's glare lancing me like a piece of meat on a skewer.

"And now, Head of Fighting, Master Gang, will announce our twelve chosen participants."

Master Li takes a step back, and Steel Master advances. He raises his arms and lets his scroll fall open with a snap. The sight of the fat red streak across his forehead ignites a savage glee in me.

"Group four," he begins, referring to the oldest boys and most advanced group. The contestants will mainly be from here. He calls out a number of names, but I am unfamiliar with them. After each one, cheering erupts. "Group Three," he continues. He calls out Apple, which is no surprise. The boy is a pleasant version of Yong Da—not that I would know—I've never talked to him, but he is undoubtedly better-looking. Then comes Yong Da and one of his closest friends, the wicked one. Also, not surprisingly, Yong Da's grin is wide enough to split his ugly face. They all cheer and make thumbs up at each other.

A few seats away, a boy from Group Two is counting on his fingers. "That's eleven," he says to no one.

"And," Steel Master raises his gaze and lowers the parchment by his side. "The last one," he finishes with a menacing note in his voice, "is Lu Mi La."

The refectory goes dead silent. Everyone turns. Their mortified stares hit me like spears. My scalp prickles as I try to decipher what my brain thinks it just heard. Heat floods me, and my mouth feels like dried cement. I can almost hear the others' silent outcries. *Impossible. She can't compete. She is a girl! Not even a good one!*

But no one opposes. It's not what you do to a master. You do not even question. To say just one thing would make him lose face.

"Lastly," Master Li clears his throat and steps forward again. "None of the Twelve Chosen can speak to me. You can talk to your teachers and each other about the competition. Still, since I am ultimately responsible for this tournament, I cannot and will not divulge anything about it. To anyone," he adds. Did his eyes linger on me? They move on quickly, I am not sure. "That will be all," he says into stunned silence. "Now, some final words for the contestants. Everyone else is free to go."

Scraping of chairs and animated voices fill the room. But I do not hear, perceive only a mad rush that blinds me.

All noise floats outside, and the eating hall goes quiet once again.

Master Gang breaks the silence. "As of tomorrow, your initiation period starts. The main element will be a special, daily elite training directed by me and three other teachers. Although we encourage you to practice anything useful, including stealth, agility and mental strength, this new drill will prepare you for the tournament."

He looks at us grimly. "You are freed from chores and regular training but expected to assist in the tournament preparations. Elite practice takes the core slot, so eat your midday meal quickly and spend the remaining time digesting the food. Practice starts at one o'clock sharp. Dismissed."

As in a dream, I head for the door.

"You could go home, you know." Yong Da. Of course. "I'm sure Master Li would make an exception; after all, he's seen what you're capable of."

"Not much," Wicked comes to stand beside him.

"What makes you think I want to go home?" I ask, my cheeks hot.

"Surely you see that little girls don't belong in this competition?" He shoves me into the wall as he passes.

My shoulder is scraped, but I walk out stone-faced. Heart pounding, I push through the crowd outside, descend the stairs and cross the lower courtyard. I walk faster and faster until I run out and up onto the trail into the forest. Further, further, until, panting like a chased animal, I stop. For a while, I can do nothing but bend at the waist, suck in air and absorb my heart's violent beating. Why was I picked? I will be humiliated, kicked, beaten, and thrashed like minced meat.

Clearly, Steel Master is behind it. He must have pushed hard to make Master Li bend the rules. China is old and steeped in tradition. Girls are not allowed to fight, and to pick someone inferior to represent your temple? *Never*. When I get whipped in the arena, it is a face loss for the entire community of Long Si. He's getting me back for that time I stood up for Wei Wan in practice.

And possibly also a little for hitting him in the head with a hickory staff.

I go down to the river. I pick up a stone from the ground and fling it into the water with all my might. Then another one. And another one.

CATARIMA LILLIEHÖÖK

"You're scaring me." Wei Wan stares at my wet clothes and messy hair. "What have you been doing?"

"Throwing rocks in the river."

"Did it help?" I am still toxic from rage. A noxious tiredness descends, making my eyelids thick and heavy. "Are you all right?" he goes on. "Should I get Cook Ma?"

"Why does everyone hate me?"

"I don't hate you."

"Why does everyone else?"

"Not Cook Ma."

"Stop it. You know what I mean."

At length, Wei Wan speaks. "Well," he hesitates. "I guess...because you're a...girl. And..."

"Born in the year of the Snake. Is *no one* else in this entire temple born in the year of the Snake?"

"It's...the combination, I guess."

"I miscalculated. I should have thrown myself in."

"Don't speak like that. It's bad luck."

"Ha!" I scoff. "*I* am bad luck."

"No, you're unlucky. There's a difference." At my hard anger, he says, "Are you okay?"

"Do I *seem* okay?"

I replay the announcement in my head, my name on Steel Master's lips. Master Li saying nothing and I haven't even taken my vows yet! Some old welts on my back start to sting. I rub them, I rub my neck, it hurts. Everything hurts.

Ming Pi comes from supper and looks like he wants to evade me, but I guess he can't run from the person who told him to be brave. No matter how murderous my look.

"So many detentions," he says carefully, as though

128

skirting the most glaring problem would make it disappear.

"Hello, Ming Pi," I say, tired.

"If you collect some bravery at every detention, you must have a big supply by now."

"That's right." Actually, to think that I gain something from Steel Master every time we clash, instead of him leeching me of strength, makes me feel better. "You keep practising, right?"

He says yes, and I go to my room, shivering under my covers. Maybe I am wrong. As Ming Pi just reminded me, so many detentions. Perhaps Steel Master doesn't remember that day I defied him and stood up for Wei Wan. Wishful thinking. Who forgets the tiny girl that causes you to lose face in front of the entire class? I imagine Steel Master's eyes on me, piercing the walls, piercing my blankets.

He will enjoy watching me get smashed to bits.

Elite training for the Chosen, now dubbed the Twelve, begins today. Eleven people attend. Everyone except me. I am paralyzed with fear.

For an entire week, I pretend nothing's happening. I spend unreasonable amounts of time with Habllek. Her silken fur and grounded calm help me immensely. Apart from an insistent chewing on the inside of my cheek, I go through each day mechanically, but already I see the transformation that's beginning to take root. While I do my best to put one foot in front of the other, the rest of the Twelve have changed. They have a gleam in their eyes, an edginess to their moves. They look over their shoulders as though someone is about to steal up and kill them, rob them of this grand opportunity to fame and glory. To win the tournament would bring enormous prestige, especially for someone from a poor background, like most of us here. I watch them, yesterday, today, and tomorrow. And I keep stealing glances at Apple. I've always thought he looks so nice. Is he one of them? Truly?

No one has reprimanded me for my refusal to attend this death camp. Steel Master is probably secretly rejoicing at the speed with which I am falling behind. The bigger my downfall, the greater his pleasure. I went once, but to be in a confined space with the top fighters of Long Si is like being locked into a room with potential mass murderers. All with a new, wildly consuming purpose. What do they do in their spare time? Practice knife throwing on each other?

I never went back. I don't belong there. I want to ignore them, but sometimes their loud shouting calls me, and I walk like a magnet drawn to steel. I squeeze into the crowd of onlookers, filling every free space until Cook Ma comes and sends them back to work, and only I am left. Staring wide-eyed, some morbid fascination with death tying me down, as though my beating heart has moved into my head, dictating my moves, my thoughts, my every breath.

And here I am again, watching.

"Harder, hit harder!" Steel Master bellows.

Yong Da attacks in a blur, spinning his staff like a racing wheel, slamming it at his opponent with an ear-deafening crash.

The other boy roars and charges. They rush, stop, twist, strike high, low, sweep for knee-hits, neck-hits, head-hits and hand-hits. Everyone trains for everything since the discipline won't be announced until the day before the competition.

The other boy lands a full hit on Yong Da's cheek, and there's the sick sound of skin breaking. Blood splatters on their clothes, and Yong Da swears loudly. I recoil, can't even rejoice in Yong Da getting a taste of his own medicine. I know it will infuriate him and make him even more dangerous.

At the room's other end, two boys are free-fighting. Brutally fast, every hit connects with a stomach-churning *thwack*. I can't handle it. I should just leave. But instead, my eyes cling hypnotically to their every move.

Ten days have passed. I walk restlessly. My hands are constantly cold, and my ribcage feels too narrow for all the air I need to suck in. I *can't* face the Twelve. To stay sane, I engage in precisely those things we were freed from. One long, never-ending task of frantic chores, regular *gong fu* and stealth, hiding behind the certainly useless fact that I am at least doing something.

The first few days, Cook Ma looked at me sternly. "I appreciate the help, Mi La. But you really should be practicing."

I think she can feel my fear because she stopped after a few reminders. As though she can't bear to push me. Maybe she's picked up on the treachery too, masters forcing me into a peril with no way out. Or, she has been told by Master Li that she has no right to interfere in my destiny.

What is my destiny?

This morning, I wake with an ache in my chest. I toss around twice, then I get up and slip outside before the gong sounds. I stand in the predawn, considering for a minute. Should I climb my anxiousness away? The ancient walls around Long Si are scarred. Wei Wan found spots where bricks are worn to cavities or where mortared patches stick out like the knuckles of a gnarled old hand. That's where we learned to scale them. The top is wide enough, and if you walk the perimeter, you will find two spots where massive eucalyptus trees stretch their branches into the temple grounds. Strong enough to walk on. If you can handle a few hairy moments, they will take you straight onto the roof of First Archive.

But, no, it's a little dark for climbing.

Instead, I steal around the temple grounds, looking for Cook Ma. I often sneak up on her when she comes with her tray of temple offerings to see how close I can get. She is clever and usually discovers me before I reach her. But she never says anything. I am unsure why she lets me get away with all these things—somehow, I have a feeling she knows. Everything.

Under the eaves of Six Saint's Hall, I stop to peer around; where is she? I can't see her anywhere. Instead, I nearly lose my crouched position as a familiar figure exits Sleeping Bear. Wei Wan. He has been to see *Master Li?*

Master Li, who allowed this to happen. Master Li, the traitor.

It takes until lunchtime before I get him on my own, but Wei Wan quizzes me first, a full-blown attack, most unlike his normal behaviour.

"The elite training?" he demands. "When will you start? You must prepare—no?" he stops my protest, "I mean really prepare."

"How?" I say irritably.

"How? Oh, I don't know. Maybe by *practising*?"

"I'll get slaughtered."

"Not if you start now! They're all so set on winning they might not even notice you. Just act like you belong."

I leave him, too frustrated to press him about Master Li. *Why was I picked?* The rest of the day, I think of asking Cook Ma. Not directly, of course. It's not the Chinese way. As the two of us make our way through the market, I say, "What do you do when you don't have answers?"

She squeezes a tomato. What we grow in our vegetable patch is far from enough. "I meditate."

"And if that doesn't work?"

"Sometimes I ask Buddha. In the Ten Thousand Hall, there is a small wooden Buddha in the upper left corner of the altar. I take him in my hands and ask him questions." She continues through the bustling market.

"Then what?"

"Then I wait."

"Do you get them? The answers?"

She grabs a mango and smells it. "Mostly. If I'm patient."

"Do you ask often?"

"No. Only when it really matters." That faint darkness veils her eyes again, the one that is connected to the falcon. "Buddha sets me straight," she says and puts back the mango, "when I get too lost in myself. When I need a reminder of the path that lies ahead, the sunrise at the horizon."

"The sunrise," I mumble.

"Yes, the sunrise. It's always there, behind the clouds."

She buys *bai cai* and ginger and sesame oil, and half my brain listens to her haggling, making sure she gets a good price.

The other half is back in Sápmi, where I had a tree house. It wasn't really a tree house, more like a pile of branches, but stacked cleverly enough to make a shelter of sorts. Father helped me build it. It was situated on a hill, and I used to get up early and go there. I would close the door, an old worn piece of hide so that it looked like no one was in there.

Silent as a mouse, I sat on the other side of the hide, my one fragile shield against the world at times when I needed it. I could still catch the sunrise if I peered through the branches at just the right angle. It helped me when I was upset, and then no one was allowed in, not even Olli or Maddji.

Now, I hide in my own mind. It's the only safe place.

There *are* safe places here, such as the worship house Cook Ma suggested. This is where the Chinese go to pray, and sometimes I do, too. But this, the whole fishy business with the tournament, I don't know.

"Maybe I'll come back for mangoes," Ma says as we head home. "They will make a nice treat after the tournament."

"Right."

"There will be tons of cooking to do. The day after, we're inviting all our guests for a banquet." I can't bring myself to say anything. "You will help me, won't you? I've already taught you some of the dishes. I must teach you more," she chatters on.

We walk back in silence. I am loaded with rice and vegetables, and after I have carried everything through the busy grounds of Long Si, chores are almost up. I leave the kitchen pavilion. Should I visit the Worship House before the elite group spills out from practice?

"So, mule herder." Yong Da. I bite my lip. Too late.

"What's your strategy? Roll into a ball and protect your brain?" he scoffs. "Oh, wait, you don't have one."

"Get lost," I snap.

"Oooh," bully-friend Wicked teases. "Temper."

"She'll need it," says Ugly Bulldog.

"Anger is stored in the liver," says Yong Da. "It can stagnate the body's *qi*. Though I'm sure it can be kick-started." They break out in evil laughter.

I am sorely tempted to do what he said, roll up into a ball, hide away in some corner and forget about the world. But over by the third worship hall stands a group of boys, and there is Ming Pi. He looks at me, and I look at him. Unease slithers like a snake up my spine. *I* tell *him* to be brave. My made up escape hole just tightened by a mile.

CHAPTER 15

IN THE DUSKY HALF-LIGHT AFTER SUPPER, I SLIP AWAY PAST the Heavenly Emperor's Hall and the Six Saints' Hall and into the Ten Thousand Buddha Hall.

I ensure no one sees me and then proceed to the corner with the Buddha Cook Ma spoke about. Carefully, I pluck the statue from its shelf. I feel a bit bad. Are we supposed to touch him like this? He looks at me in woody silence.

"Why was I picked for the contest?"

Nothing.

"Who will win?"

More nothing.

"Who will come last?" Stupid question; I know the answer. Can I cancel it? "Will anyone die?" Do I really want that answer?

The Buddha is rigid and unresponsive in my hands. Still, his face looks serene, as though he wishes he could answer in some mystical way. Maybe he can find other ways to talk to me. Perhaps I should find different ways to speak to him.

Or to Wei Wan, who is constantly at my throat.

"*Jie*," he snarls as he catches me at the next day's midday meal. "You're not preparing. When are you going to start?"

"Don't you see?" I snap. "I'm up against boys three times my size, boys who could kill in their sleep and know twenty different ways to crush my bones."

"No," he snaps back, gripping his tray hard. "It's *you* who don't see. Whatever the odds, you must still try. You are a fighter of Long Si. Steel Master, Yong Da, this is exactly what they want. You're playing right into their hands."

I hesitate. This is a new thought. Ignoring preparation will ruin the competition. If I get beaten too easily and get too hurt, it will reflect poorly on Long Si. Not only will I lose face, which is undoubtedly the evil duo's plan, but my temple will lose face. Master Li will lose face, and nothing will please me more. *But*...

"Didn't you say you want to be picked for a mission?"

"What's that got to do with it?"

"Yeah," he snorts. "You think on that for a while." He stomps off, leaving me in the throng of people, and pointedly steers to a different table than our usual one.

I can't stop thinking. My mind churns incessantly, and once I lie alone with my demons in my tiny chamber, I have to admit: It's a daring plan but brilliant. If I truly participate and by some miraculous divine intervention, don't get completely smashed to bits, it could, potentially, help me get selected for a mission, no? The fear of getting beaten to a pulp and the hatred of Steel Master for exposing me to this danger has blinded me. Yes, I am still a girl, still smaller than all the other contestants, but...if I could somehow...not focus on that...

I catch Wei Wan alone on kitchen duty the following day.

He is in the side scullery, firmly planted between heaps of sweet potato. He does not look up.

I grab a paring knife and a potato. "You were right."

He lifts his head. "You finally see?"

"You really think it could help me get selected for a mission?"

"Provided you survive."

"That's encouraging."

"Of course you'll survive, *jie*. You're stronger now, you said it yourself." I think of the blood-splattered clothes and raging punches I saw in the elite training. "But you'll need to come up with something special," he adds.

Our conversation stops when Apple comes to pick up potatoes, startling us. "I'm taking a break today," he says.

So, picking chores over elite training. Yeah, I know all about that. I drop my gaze and move aside. I am not overly keen on having any of the Twelve so close. Especially not one who makes my cheeks redden. But another of the regular boys appears, and I am saved, then another one. Potato-peeling has never been so popular. All it takes is one of the Twelve, not me. I obviously don't count.

I see Cook Ma working the big wok at the other end of the kitchen. "Ma," I yell. I stand up and dry my hands on my pants. "Do you need some help over there?"

Without waiting for a reply, I go, and she starts instructing me. This is how you fry the first ingredient, this is when you add the second, this is how you add the spices, this is how you sprinkle soy sauce, and this is how you stir.

"Everything in order, everything at a precise moment, no more, no less, do you understand?"

I confirm soundlessly, trying to shut out Apple in the distance. Even more boys now, talking in excited voices. The tournament, they ask him, are you prepared? How good is the competition? Do you know them? Who will be the judge?

I cook so wildly I disappear in a cloud of steam, and Cook Ma nods approvingly.

"*Bu cuo.*" I can learn, she says, not bad.

The praise warms my heart and shuts me away from Apple and his entourage. I sneak glances at him through the misty smoke. His broad shoulders, strong hands. But now is not the time. I have things to worry about.

I am back in the underground of Long Si. I snuck out in the night and made my way through the dark forest to where the trap door is hidden. Technically, I could enter from inside the pavilion, but that is Steel Master's way; I feel it's bad luck. I did not light my lantern until I was far from the temple. I take no risks. Now, that's wishful thinking. To attempt a nightly jaunt like this is just exactly a risk. It is against the rules, but I have been breaking the rules with Wei Wan for years now. Perhaps it's my way to push an even greater terror out of my mind.

Fifteen days closer.

Moving swiftly, I walk, crawl and sneak through the tunnel, enter the cellar through the moon door and find my way to the room with soy sauce containers. Ahead, Second Archive's honeycomb wall gapes at me like a hundred open mouths.

Inside the room, I drop to my knees, put down my lantern and lift the lid off the nearest container. A glimmering shape floats out, light blue this time. It resembles a gigantic pearl surrounded by a soft, wavering sheen. As my fingertips nudge the wavering light, a stream of life force gushes through me.

Mesmerized, I stare, and then something hits me. Can I move it? Carefully, I move my hands under it. Like last time, it does not rest against my skin but hovers one inch above. I shift my hand slightly left, and the big pearl mirrors my move. Thrilled, I go the other way; again, the pearl follows. As I rise, I nudge it upward and walk deeper into the room. All the way to the far end, realizing that the pearl functions well as a lantern. In the sheen, I see a broom. I am about to pass right by it, but then I stop. A broom? It could not possibly be forgotten here because who would ever bring one in the first place?

I feel a slight tingle in my hand. As though the pearl presses gently into my palm, directing my focus to the ground.

In one spot, the earth is less hardpacked. I put down the pearl, which floats above the dirt floor. Then, I take the broom and make a few rough sweeps until something appears. A knob, a metal ring... I sweep again and make out wood: another trap door.

A thrill rushes up my chest. I toss the broom aside and grip the iron ring. With sweaty hands, I yank until it comes loose. I pull up the door and stare into a black hole with rungs along the side. For a few seconds, the alarm tugs at me. I want to go and get Wei Wan or San Dun.

But my fluttering heart urges me. *Go. Go on.*

I dash back, snatch up my lantern, return, and facing the tunnel wall, I descend into blackness. It's awkward to climb with the lantern; the metal rungs are cold against my palms, and the air of confined space presses against my back. By the time I near the bottom, my body is as stiff as a rattan chair. What if I can't get back up?

Down on the ground, I stare into blackness. The nape of my neck is sweating. I lift the lantern and see a vast underground cavern.

The hissing is so abrupt I jump and gaze wildly. There *is* a beast, and this is where it's hiding! My heart would out-drum a Chinese lion dance, but nothing appears. After a frosty minute, I raise my lantern higher and step deeper into the vast space.

Another hiss. I don't even retrieve my arm. It is stuck in the air like a statue. Still, nothing happens, and I challenge myself, two more steps.

Three more.

Four.

In the end, I circumvent the entire space. After two extra short rounds and a few hissings, I am no wiser. My lantern flickers. The wax is burning low, and I do not want to risk getting stuck in the dark.

Frustrated, I head back up, return the floating pearl to its urn and tell myself that my biggest concern right now is the tournament. Wei Wan's comment plays in my head: *You'll need to come up with something special.* But my mind has snagged on the beast. And the hearts I've seen—oh! Of course! I've been so traumatized since the announcement that I completely forgot about my last duel with Yong Da. I have no idea how I did it, but something connected to Steel Master's heart and gave me that energy boost. What? How? Can I do it again? And this unseen beast, is there a connection?

Yesterday Wei Wan nearly convinced me to join the elite training. I could see Ming Pi hovering in the background and knew he was listening. Today I am still drumming up courage as I am going for the weeding Cook Ma sent me to do. The temple must look its best when our guests arrive. But as I round the armoury, I walk right into a group of sweaty people sitting on the ground. The Twelve or rather, Eleven.

"So." Yong Da is addressing them. "It's important we do well; we must honour Long Si. The extra practice is our key."

I suppress a scowl. Is he some self-proclaimed master now? I pass them and kneel by the strip of young bamboo along the western wall.

"You're all doing well," he goes on. "I keep track."

He speaks a touch too loud, and some warning bell goes off in my head. I glance up and see his gaze migrating from each person in his selected little troupe to me. He narrows his eyes. "Somehow, I didn't see you."

"Hmm?" I blink, pretending I haven't heard.

"Coming to think of it, I'm not sure you've been there even once."

Everyone is looking at me now. The girl. Centre of attention, just like my first day in the lower yard, my first visits to the refectory, or every time I have gotten smashed up in *gong fu*.

"What's your plan, mule herder? Bore us all to death with your peasant fighting?"

"Plan?"

He rises, brows gliding up in a sarcastic arch. "You're not practising; you must be confident, then, to beat us all."

The group's collected gaze prickles my insides. Myriad tiny thorns that stab my skin, triggering my hidden fears. *Loser. Useless. Pathetic.* And most of all: *Dead.*

I rise as well, forcing myself forward. "If you're such an honourable student, Yong Da, surely you have better things to do than harassing fellow acolytes?"

"No, I don't," he says softly. I wish he would yell; it would tell me he is bluffing, making himself seem stronger than he is. Deimatic behaviour. Instead, he comes closer and leans in, only inches from my face and says, "Because you know what, you small piece of dying witch? My only true goal in this tournament is to rid this world of useless girls."

In my peripheral vision, I see Apple. All warmth has drained from his eyes. His expression sends a chill through my heart. Does he approve of Yong Da's behaviour or loathe it?

I can't tell.

CHAPTER 16

THE STIFLING HEAT OF EIGHTH MOON TURNS EVERYTHING into an oppressive, sticky battle. My attempts at finding solace in Habllek's soft form are failing miserably. I am obsessing about my powers that I don't really understand. My skills are somehow connected to the orbs, which represent hearts, but I haven't spotted even one in the last ten trainings. I don't really see or hear people anymore, either. Only the echo of Wei Wan in my head. *You'll need to come up with something special.*

I still run with Master Li. He is not allowed to talk about the competition, but I can feel his concern from a mile away. Why am I not in the elite training? He pushes me hard, flying down the stony hills as though the risk of fatal crashes is non-existent. I am not slowing down. Why should I? I am in the game now with no plan. He put me here.

My blood thunders, and I run faster, lengthen my step and match him stride for stride. It is not safe. If I fall, I might break a bone, but I don't care. I want to break a bone and crush myself on the impossible splendour of the Long Si tournament. Then, at last, he would have to stop. Come to his senses: *I am sorry, Mi La. It was a mistake. It was all a mistake.*

But I am running out of mountain. We are down. It is flat again, secure. And Master Li outpaces me easily.

Sweat trails down my temples as I carry a big basket of lotus roots into the side scullery. Cook Ma is still teaching me to cook. Our long-way guests won't sleep here; Cook Ma has sent boys to enquire in the village, and already they have found housing for almost everyone. It is still considered an honor to host a monk from a monastery, especially such famous ones as Red Crane and Flying Squirrel. The fever of the event is affecting everyone, it's inevitable. This is all too big.

Something scurries across the floor, and I throw my foot out. The cockroach is mushed under my rubber sole, but the long antennae still stick out. *Ew.* I will never get used to those.

"Don't move." Something in Wei Wan's voice makes me stand rock still.

A blur of steel whizzes past my temple.

Twack!

A blade lodges firmly in the wood where the wall fuses to the bench top. On it, a green bamboo snake is skewered.

My tongue glues to the roof of my mouth.

Wei Wan still stands in throwing position, body tense, hand poised.

"How—" I finally stutter. I lick my lips. "Could you *do* that?"

"Some things you are gifted with. From birth."

"*Knife throwing?*"

He shrugs.

All I can say is, "We're not supposed to kill."

"Do you know how deadly that is?"

The snake still moves. Wei Wan grabs a big cleaver, strides across the floor and brings the blade down in one brutal blow. The snake's head falls. Then he yanks the knife loose. "Cook Ma will give it to the villagers. They'll eat it."

He takes the snake and walks out. On the bench top, the clear green head stares at me with open mouth and glistening fangs. My brain is still wildly processing, and for some strange reason I have a feeling I should not tell anyone about this. Wei Wan is my best friend, yet he can do things I can't imagine. And I just now remember I never asked him about his business with Master Li that early morning.

In my little chamber, I use my own candle to light the one I stole at chores today. When clearing out ashes in the Ten Thousand Buddha Hall, right in front of all the deities, I stole a candle meant for worshipping to use for my own selfish reasons. In light of current events, it seems trivial. Perhaps I should steal more things.

From under my thin mattress, I bring out the knife I took from the armoury, then San Dun's parchments, and put the candles close. Again, there is that feeling of song and fire, shooting sparks around my heart.

I steady my hand and scrape carefully at the spilt wax, but

two candles are not much better than one; what I need is sunlight, outside. That won't work. The thought of Head Archivist finding out about my unkind treatment sends a chill up my spine. If he saw what I was doing, San Dun would have nightmares for a moon.

I hold the first paper next to the light and squint. But all I can make out are bits of the last part:

For this to happen, the aid of a twin spirit is required. The strong yang identity demands a yin power. Thus, the one destined to work with the...must be a female. It is only possible if this person is born in the year of the Dragon.

I still don't know what it is that exists, nothing about a purpose or who is destined to do something. Maybe I am all wrong. I should drop it. But the tournament has me in its thrall. Master Li's treachery, like a warm garment being slipped from my skin. *What,* a small voice whispers, *what if this can help?*

"San Dun, wait," I hurry to catch up. Frustrated at getting nowhere with either the hearts, the hissing in the cellar, or *The River God's Chronicles*, I have found another task to pursue; the first scroll I found. "I heard something about a legend," I say as I come close. "The Three Masters of Long Si. What is that? What happened to them? Isn't Master Li supposed to have a brother?"

"Oh, he does." San Dun rests his hands on his round belly, where a tied rope serves as a belt. We have spoken so many times now he is quite relaxed. Even at the daring distance of three feet. "Well, not a blood brother."

"What do you mean?"

"I don't know if you believe in...uh, reincarnation?" San Dun smiles uneasily. "In the Buddhist belief, we do. It is said that the original founders of Long Si were three brothers who fought against enemies who threatened to tear the empire apart. Eventually, they all died, but before that, a prophecy claimed the threat would not disappear. It would just shift into the unseen and surface centuries later. So, the brothers swore to return in a future life when the nation's safety was again at stake."

"You mean the warlords?" At least, that much is clear to me. Reincarnation is not a foreign concept either, but I hadn't thought of it this way. "So...you mean Master Li is supposed to be one of those reincarnated brothers?"

"That's what they say. The prophecy was inscribed on a stone tablet, and some geomancer interpreted signs for the reincarnation, when it would occur, and whom it should be."

"I see," I say, but I don't. "But there were three, so where are the other two? And they must be younger, yes? He is at least fifty by now."

"Just so. He is exactly fifty." San Dun looks pleased, as though I just cracked some big riddle. "But mind you, reincarnated brotherhood is based on soul ties rather than blood. It can be blood relations, but it doesn't have to be. In Master Li's case, the middle brother is a blood brother, the Middle Master of Long Si. He is thirty-eight. The youngest one is supposed to be sixteen."

I crimp my brows at the strange age difference. "But where are they?"

"All I know is that the youngest one is not yet found."

"Then how do you know his age?"

"They are all born in the year of the Dragon."

The cycle of the Chinese zodiac is twelve years, and this is what went wrong the first time. Apparently, this temple on this particular spot needs dragon masters. So, the brothers all decided to be reborn in the year of the Dragon.

"And to spread the births over several cycles to maximize their powers," he adds.

"What about the middle brother? Where is he?"

San Dun shrugs. He doesn't know.

"So, there is only one brother present. That doesn't sound very promising. How will the other two find their way?"

"We believe the powers of destiny will guide them. And there are signs, of course. We might not recognize them yet, but sooner or later, they will stand out."

"You mean *feng shui*?"

"You could say that, in a way, as everything is ultimately steered by earth, metal, fire, wood, or water. Our element often acts as a guide." San Dun nods keenly at my interest. "But—oh, I'm keeping you." He makes a motion toward the practice halls. "How's your *gong fu* going?"

I suppress a grunt.

"We are all thrilled." His hand flutters in excitement. "Both Red Crane and Flying Squirrel coming to visit and everything. I bet you there will be a banquet afterwards." His gaze turns inward as he wanders off toward Archive Number One. "How will we all fit into the refectory?" he muses as he walks.

Entertainment. That is what the tournament is. If I don't think of something soon, my pathetic short life might just end as someone's sick amusement. The idea makes me ill.

Enough that my feet take on a mind of their own. They go to the Pavilion of the Sleeping Bear.

I knock on Master Li's door. "Lu Mi La," he lifts his head as I enter, an irritated look on his face. "You know I am not supposed to talk to any of the Twelve."

"Why was I picked?"

"Did you not hear me?"

"Why?"

"You are going to have to leave. I cannot speak to you of these matters; it is against the rules."

"And risking your students' lives is not?"

"Enough!" he barks.

I overstepped. I am in China, where respect for superiors should be shown, no matter the circumstances. But he stares at me with that hard glint in his eyes, the one from the Silk Road. The one that made me shiver so severely that my skinny knees knocked together. I feared his shifting moods then; I fear them now. Something in him is unstable.

"I know it may not seem like it, but I am trying to help," he says curtly.

"Help?" I taste bile. His distant behaviour, his artificial words and his twisted ideas. "Like when you rescued me from the slave market?" "That was different," he begins, but I don't listen. He conjures up such convincing lies he actually believes them himself.

"Bigger forces are at play. Please, Mi La," his voice loses some of its harshness. "I beg you to understand. It is not simple to follow the oracle bones."

"The oracle bones? What do they have to do with this?"

"Everything. And trust me when I say it is no easy matter." His eyes are veiled, and he looks away, but not before I catch that glimpse again, disappointment. Is it because I don't want to fight in the tournament? Because I'd rather live to see my seventeenth year?

"I don't understand!" I snap.

"Just—" He shuts his eyes and pinches his nose ridge. When he speaks, his voice is low. "Just do as I tell you."

For a moment, his pleading tone shifts something in my chest. It cannot be easy to be the Abbot Superior, the burdens, the responsibility. But why can't he just tell me about the oracle bones and their connection to me? Master Li, my rescuer, my captor. After eight years here, I cannot hate him as much as I want to, but never, never will I forgive him.

"Humility," he says. "You need to learn it."

That is all? He wants me to fight until death, yet he keeps me in the dark speaking of humility? Actually, yes, I decide. I can hate him as much as I want to. "If I were the Master of this place—"

"*Yes*," he cuts me off sharply. "What exactly would you do then, Mi La? Please tell me. I would be interested."

"I would be fair."

"Sometimes things are not what they seem."

I leave without a word.

"You must start." Wei Wan ambushes me as I round the corner of the Blooming Lotus Flower's Palace Hall. "Don't run!" He narrows his eyes and pushes a wooden sword against my throat. I am glad it's not a throwing knife.

"What do you want?"

He presses the tip against my skin.

"Ouch."

"You know what I want. The tournament is a moon and a half away." Before I can say anything, he hisses, "*Elite training.*"

"They'll crush me."

"What do you think they'll do in the tournament?"

His words drop like stones into my gut. A glaring, screaming truth I can no longer ignore. Its high-pitched voice suddenly pushes through to me, delivering but a straightforward choice: Be crushed then or right now. The revelation pierces me like shattered glass. I must have chewed the inside of my cheek again because I taste blood. Wei Wan is right.

Training starts in thirteen minutes. A rush of fear and adrenaline races through me.

I turn on my heel and run.

Panting, I near Practice Hall Number Two, where subdued talking leaks out. But the second I step inside, all sounds die. I instantly know I am in trouble. The Twelve have been here too long. Raged their way through so many sessions their adrenaline-pumped minds are spinning before we have even begun. Hitting, kicking, punching. They want nothing more than to knock you over, bash in your teeth; win. My tongue probes the ragged flesh on the inside of my cheek.

"Look what the cat brought in." Slowly and deliberately, Steel Master crosses his arms. "Welcome to initiation. You're forty-five days late."

I can't back down now. I also can't challenge him in any way. My gaze drops and I say nothing. But even as we begin the warm-up, I can tell that something is wrong. My body is too rigid. Despite having worked hard at regular *gong fu,* it feels like rusty machinery. Gears stuck in the same old ruts, while theirs are well-oiled, instantly responding to their brains' new razor-sharp signals. Humiliation washes over me momentarily, and then I steer my mind back. Focus.

I am paired with a boy I don't know for the first sparring. We're doing empty hand, and so far, I am fine. Then follows technique: blocks, kicks, and punches. By the time we go into free-fighting, I am up against a short, demon-like boy who gives me all he has. I bite my lip and jump back just in time. Nimble. Light.

I evade him once more. Grimly, he charges and then I see it—his heart. Fragmented, hard, crushed. Gravel Heart. *Emotion,* I have time to think. *That's what brings it out.* He spins and lands a reverse backfist strike on my cheek. It's so hard that I fly into the wall. I stumble away and straighten, pretending my face isn't numb from pain. My powers, they must help me now! All I can think of is my magic word. *Seikhar.*

At once, I see shimmering orbs in front of every fighter's chest. I nearly gasp. I *can* bring them out? But why? For what purpose? My magic provides a burst of energy, and I dance away as my opponent charges anew. He tries a foreknuckle strike and a rising knee. I block, spin, and kick, landing a hit. His face tightens, but I focus on his heart until I feel the burst of strength again.

He is a skilled warrior, and my breath is tearing at my

throat, but I manage to hold him off. Until he slams me with a simple roundhouse. I feel dizzy. My head throbs, my ribs hurt, and my cheek has moved from numbness to shooting pain. But, *hai hao,* still okay. He is Group Four. And I am still alive.

After a few more rounds, everyone ends in finishing stance, arms by the sides, fists clenched, and bows. My body is heavy with exhaustion, but my heart tumbles like a free-falling stone. I survived my first elite training.

"Show her the ropes," Steel Master says to a lean boy on his way out.

The boy halts and frowns. "Over there," he nods to a small blackboard with a chart, half hidden by a pillar. "The rankings."

Rankings? Instead of each person's name, on the chart's top row is a string of symbols and animals: star, scorpion, triangle, hatchet, snake, and more. Below are columns.

"The rankings are secret," he warns. "Dead secret. You can't tell anyone." He looks at me shrewdly and points at the rat. "That is you, and you are last."

I look at the ugly hairless creature at the very end of the chart. Below is the number twelve.

Twelve. The number strikes me like a hypnotic spell. *I am one of the Twelve. I will get through this.*

CHAPTER 17

I SURVIVE FIVE MORE DAYS OF PRACTICE BEFORE I CAN GET a minute alone with Wei Wan. I have seen him from a distance, casting worried glances as I drag my bruised and beaten body across the temple grounds. But he's been sucked into the frenzy of preparations and is constantly occupied: Cleaning, repairing, painting.

I scoop up Habllek in my arms and catch him as he descends a ladder on the short side of the Blooming Lotus Flower's Palace Hall.

"Finally," I say as he steps down on the ground, trying to scratch his forehead without getting paint on it. But I get no further, for just as a group of boys passes us, Yong Da and his followers appear.

"Oh, the mule herder and her witch cat, with what? The little mule imp?" Yong Da sneers.

"I can't believe you associate with her," Bulldog says to Wei Wan. "Like why? There are one hundred other people here, perfectly normal."

Wei Wan doesn't say anything, but I get annoyed. Attacking me is one thing. I am used to that, but Wei Wan has done nothing.

"No need to be rude," I snap.

"Oh, no, of course not." The wicked one points at me. "Do you know what she is? A fake." He looks like he is going to spit in my face. "Think we don't know you've bribed your way into this? Taken the spot of a real fighter?"

"Sorry," Wei Wan says gently. "I think you're mistaken."

"Mistaken," Wicked snorts. "You deluded little idiot. How blind can you get? Or are you just plain stupid?"

I put down Habllek. "Don't speak to him like that."

Yong Da takes a step closer. "Or what?"

"Or I'll punch in your foul face."

"*Jie.*" Wei Wan's voice is low.

Yong Da crosses his arms. "I don't think you're going to punch anyone's face. You don't have the guts."

"Oh?" I raise my brows. "That's what you think?"

"*Jie,*" Wei Wan touches my arm. "Let's go. We don't want to bother our fellow acolytes."

His voice is soft, but his fingers dig into my arm so hard I nearly cry out. With a steely grip, he steers me around the corner and all the way in behind the Scurrying Mouse Pavilion, one of the boys' dormitories. He doesn't stop until we are safely away from prying eyes or ears.

"*Jie,*" he bursts out. "I've been so worried. How are you doing? How many fights have you been in? How is your ranking?"

"Ranking?" I hiss angrily. "How did you know about that?"

"It's not so hard."

The lean boy from Group Four said it was a dead secret, and our names are coded. I wouldn't think it was that easy to find out... "Um, not brilliant. Actually, I'm last."

"Good." He looks relieved. "No one bothers with the scraps. Now, *jie*, this is important; how's your special skill going?"

He knows! My Mother's warning pulses in my head. *Be careful, Mila. Careful not to show.* I should tell him I don't know what he's talking about. My mind spins wildly, wondering how he can possibly know.

I study his dark brown eyes and his innocent face. Little dimples appear when he smiles. He smiles a lot. Xiao Wei. I can trust him.

"I have heart magic."

"I knew you had something!" He can't hinder the quick twinkle in his eyes. "Master Li travelled halfway across the globe to get you, see? But *jie*," he throws a look across his shoulder and leans in. "Be careful. Don't excel, don't draw attention to yourself. Understand?"

"I haven't mastered it yet," I say, exasperated. "I don't even know how it works."

"You'll figure it out. Just stay safe. I am your..." I think he means to say friend, but maybe he is embarrassed, so he says, "I want you to be safe."

Does he mean from evil fighters? Others? "Do you mean that I'm a S—"

"No!" He puts a finger to his lips. "Don't say it. Not to anyone."

I am nonplussed. Does he know about *Seikhar*? Who in

157

China would have heard of Children of the Northern Lights? Then I realize he is right. *Seikhar* is dangerous. It's what got me abducted and sold. But surely I can say it here?

"Why?" I ask.

"I can't say."

He looks over his shoulder again, and as some boys walk past, starts to scrape dry paint off his fingers. I wait till they are gone.

"How do you know these things?"

"Practice, *jie*. Practice all you ever learnt. Can you do that for me?"

"No." I narrow my eyes. "Not unless you explain."

"I really can't. We shouldn't even be standing in this off place. Somebody could be watching." He turns and walks back to his ladder, and I am too stunned to follow.

"Wait, what?"

But people are coming, and Wei Wan is already climbing the rungs.

Days pass fast now. The elite training has me in its grip; I have entered their turf and drawn their attention. Still, the geography has shifted. The spaces where I feel safe are starting to bridge the black oceans I have pretended not to notice. Once I understood that I had to call on my powers, pinpricks of light appeared. I am improving, but my adversaries are too. We work out so intensely every day. I have become a part of them whether I want to or not. Today, I was so close to Apple that, for a second, I forgot where I was. I saw the pulse in the skin of his neck. He has a scar on his forehead. He looked at me, too; we looked straight into each other's eyes. Then Steel Master yelled, and all I knew was that I had to defend myself.

These formidable fighters.

Some days, I am in so much pain I have to rest, and Wei Wan hovers around me like a fretting nursemaid. One minute, worrying that I am not getting enough rest, and the next, snapping at me to practice harder.

"You must give it your everything? Do you understand?" he hisses, eyes flashing. *Your magic,* he mouths so no one can hear, then whispers in a sort of subdued scream, "Do you master it yet?"

I ignore him and hurry off, running around like everyone else. Suppress the magic that still eludes me and sneak nervous glances at Apple in between all the cleaning, polishing, and clearing, secretly hoping I will end up right next to him and then not. I learn to cook more new dishes—and explore the hidden underground of Long Si.

Today I will see something. It came during last night's meditation. The tournament is three weeks away, and exhaustion has kept me from Second Archive, but something is there and I have to *call* it. Ukko, how could I have missed it?

The secret passage, the tiny moon door, corridors and the soy-that-is-not-soy-sauce-room. Here I am, and as I pass the ceramic containers, I hear a faint grinding. It's an urn, the one next to last in the second row, but I ignore it, go to the trap door and climb inside. As soon as I am down, I raise my lantern and speak loudly. "*Seikhar.*"

Two more attempts, and my hands glimmer.

A golden light flares.

Slamming my eyes shut I jump back, arm raised. Then I look—and nearly choke on my own breath.

The magnificent creature in front of me has sharp teeth, claws, and golden scales across its massive, undulating body. It locks my gaze with crystal eyes, and immediately, I feel its power. A drumming beat that ripples through my legs, arms, hands, the tips of my fingers, my earlobes.

I exist outside of time. In this vast dark underground, I am separated from the world and yet merging with it. My palms sweat with an echo of something remembered. I don't know what, but my brain emerges victoriously, and everything comes together in one long gush of whirling thoughts. *The River God's Chronicles*. The secret that made this the most auspicious and powerful spot in all of China was the symbol embroidered on the emperor's robes. *Feng shui jixiang*. Of course. In China, dragons are bringers of luck and good fortune. With the aid of such a magical creature, how could the *feng shui* be anything but most auspicious? This is the core of Long Si, its mystical, vast source of strength, the base of energy that has helped to craft the best *gong fu* fighters for centuries. But my scrambling mind rears. Dragons don't exist.

The creature arches its huge neck, stretching toward me as though it is sniffing me. Fear and excitement blast like quicksilver through my body.

I am Hidden Eyes, spirit dragon of Long Si. The voice is in my head. Otherworldly, rich, carrying the strength of a thousand mountains.

Lightheaded and wobbly, I stand until I manage to crack my stupor. *I am Lu Mi La, Seikhar.* I think back to him. *Child of the Northern Lights.*

I am hungry.

I blink. What?

The creature tilts its enormous head, the glowing spikes along its forehead and neck gliding like a billowing wave. It does not look like it is about to devour me, but...its light flickers and fatigue floods me as though there is nothing in my stomach. As though the last *baozi* I ate was an eternity ago. Soon, I feel drained, so drained. The dragon's light... I squint. Did it just grow dimmer?

I have waited for ten thousand years.

For what, I want to ask, but the words garble in my mind. I want to drag myself out of here, into the kitchen...steal food, like Yong Da...

Upstairs.

Some part of me gets it. Perhaps it is like the *vajans* instinctively knowing that colostrum, the nutrient-rich first milk they produce, is crucial for the calf's life. She urges it to get up and drink, nudges it with her muzzle and legs, and puts herself in position. She makes sure they get it.

I break away from the dragon's thrall. He is drawing on my energy. He has no other choice. Turning, I grab my lantern and force myself on, up the rungs, but my legs are so heavy, up, up...heavy... In the chamber above, I go to the urn that made a noise.

As I lift the lid, a soft yellow light floods my face, and before I know it, the pearl has floated up and into my hand. Legs dragging, I return to the trap door. For short periods, I can steer the yellow light with my will alone, which I do when I climb down. Sometimes, I have to stop and herd it back with my hand before it floats away.

In the underground chamber, Hidden Eyes' light has dimmed to an eerie outline. He is lying down, his *qi* so low I can hardly pick it up.

I mean to bring the pearl close, but before I can take another step, it disengages and sails off on its own. Carefully, it coasts down to his talons, where his enormous head is resting. He raises his head two inches and slowly clasps the big pearl in his talons. Ten feet away, I kneel, watching breathlessly until he has fed and gradually regains his glowing light. He releases his grip, and the pearl floats back to my open palms.

Then again, he rests his head on the floor and shuts his eyes. *Now I sleep.*

My energy is back to normal, and I reluctantly rise and leave, walking first backwards, then forward, but turning at least five times to look at his sleeping, glowing figure. *A spirit dragon.* I nudge the floating pearl, trying to keep it in the crook of my arm while I climb up and return it to its urn. I feel weightless, as though all the cells in my body have simultaneously decided to become air and something sparkly. Delirious with my find, I choose to skip the long secret tunnel and just go through the cellar door, straight into Pavilion of the Crouching Tiger. I have to get Wei Wan! Which dormitory again? Wise Panda?

I take a left outside the urn room, hurry along the corridor and climb the stairs at the end. At the top, I open the door an inch, peek in and listen. Then I slip through, past the refectory, quiet and softly, as Wei Wan and I have practiced. Stalk the cat. Away from any creaking floorboard, I progress onto the open seating area.

And there stands a figure.

I nearly drop my lantern.

Steel Master is surrounded by deadly stillness. All I can hear is my beating heart, which thumps so loudly that it echoes in my head. My Master's look could drill through a mountain.

"Reindeer Girl," he says at last.

"Master Gang."

"What"—his voice is so muted I can't tell if the reason is to intimidate me or not wake up Cook Ma and Ah Mei on second floor—"are you doing?"

His eyes hold me vice-like, brimming with hatred. Beyond stern master; cold, calculating evil. "Where have you been? We both know you are breaking the rules, herder girl. Know trouble awaits, so you might as well speak."

"I..." It's hard to breathe.

"If you can't explain yourself, you sneaky little minx, I'll just have to...help you." A faint *pop* is heard as he slowly and deliberately cracks his knuckles. That is the only sound. "Do you understand that every time you break the rules, you are insulting all the masters of Long Si?"

The stillness drowns me like white noise.

"There're many interesting methods of legal punishment. Even some that break bones."

He can't do that. He *wouldn't*. I curse myself for my stupidity. Of course, he can, of course he would.

"So now," his hands curl into fists. "Tell me, what is it you are hiding?"

He grips my arm. My heart rate triples. I fear my skull will shatter. *No, no, no.* Guilt seems to slide physically over my tight cheeks, jamming my teeth together like mortar.

The door opens.

163

In walks Master Li.

My breath leaves me in a rush, and my knees go weak.

"What now?" he says. I try to radiate silent desperation, but he ignores me.

"Nothing to do with you," Steel Master says sharply. He lets go of my arm.

"Whatever it is, let it go, Master Gang," Li says. "She's just a witless girl, not worth your time."

"Witless girl!" Steel Master retorts. "She's reached level three, and she's competing in the tournament, is she not?"

Yes, that you forced me into. I silently fume, *Both of you.* My hands are shaking.

"I caught her breaking the rules. You have no power over me here, Li."

Master Li clasps his hands and throws me just a quick glance. But it reaches me. He wants me to say something; I feel it all the way in my bones. My mind races. What? Is there something he taught me? The word humbleness comes to mind. Confessions.

"I...just went for a walk. I feel so stupid and useless sometimes." I look at the ground. "Everyone here's so good, and it was wrong, but I just tried to..." I snivel into my sleeve.

"Tried to what?" Steel Master snaps.

I rub a spot over my left eye. The roof of my mouth has merged with my tongue, and I am waiting for the blow to fall. This is the end.

"Bribe me," says Li.

I dare not look at him. I could give myself away.

Li claps his hands. "It was I who sent her into the woods. I thought a walk alone in the dark would teach her a lesson. I just came to see if she was back."

"*Bribe* you?"

"Yes, to earn leniency. She believes we are pushing too hard. It's what foolish young people do."

"How?" Steel Master draws his brows into one low line. "She is as poor as they come."

"Well," Li shifts his gaze as though broaching a delicate matter, "what is the oldest trick in the book?"

I clench my fingers to keep from gasping. Is he saying I tried to bed him?

"What?" Steel Master goes wild around the eyes. "You are three times her age!" he shouts.

Master Li lifts a hand. "Let's not wake everyone up." He speaks in a low voice. "It was stupid and immature, but that's all it was. No need to drag her through the mud. She is already embarrassed by my rejection. Surely you can see how a girl must get confused around so many boys?" He clasps his hands. "Particularly at this age," he mumbles, leaning in slightly.

I don't have to fake embarrassment. My face is pulsing with heat. I wipe my cheek with the heel of my hand, drying an imaginary tear. "Am I permitted to leave?"

Steel Master flaps an irritated hand. "Go."

CHAPTER 18

THE MORNING IS EARLY, AND MY HEAD IS FULL OF HIDDEN Eyes. And Steel Master and Master Li, pretending I tried to...the thought nearly drowns me in embarrassment. He saved me, though. Regardless, a scolding awaits. But Hidden Eyes, was it real? It must have been; I fed him. He got strength from the floating pearl.

At morning meal, I never get the chance to tell Wei Wan, it is noisy and the dining hall has too many ears. Anyway, his sharp gaze tells me he has his agenda: Are you practising? Are you working on your special skill? I am too wound up to care, but he watches me like a hawk, cutting me to pieces. *Fourteen days*, he mouths.

I push the words away, spoon up the last of my eight-treasure soup, gulp it down, and rise. I walk away fast, leave my tray at the drop-off table, and rush outside. San Dun. There, on his way to First Archive.

"San Dun!" I prevent myself from grasping at his brown jacket. "Do you know anything about dragon lore?"

"Oh," he lights up. "I forgot to tell you, I found some more of *The River God's Chronicles*. You got me intrigued. I have been reading all that I could find. Well, when Head Archivist is not around." He whisks his head side to side, but no one is nearby. "So, yes," he finishes proudly. "I do know some. What is it you wish to know?"

Lots. "What—" I breathe. "What do—what did they eat when such creatures were still around, if they ever were? Especially the ones that are...not solid. According to legend, they came in all shapes and forms, right?"

"Do you perhaps mean a spirit dragon?"

I press my fingernails into my palms. "Perhaps."

"According to the chronicles, they fed off flaming pearls. A sort of floating round mass, I guess you could call it. Actually, if you look at old paintings, they are often depicted holding a flaming pearl under their chin or as two dragons fighting over one."

"And this pearl...?"

"It is associated with wisdom, power, immortality, and spiritual energy. So that, I assume, is where they got their nourishment from. I know it sounds odd."

"I understand," I say too quickly.

"You do?"

But I am already leaving, nearly bumping into Ming Pi, who reflexively flings up a book in his defence.

"Sorry, Mi La." He steps aside. "I didn't mean to... I was just returning..."

I halt. "What're you reading?"

"Just some Sun Tzu."

"The famous theorist? Military stuff?"

He shrugs. Why not? My thoughts go to Yong Da and his perfect quote from Sun Tzu about how important it is to know your enemies. It is clear who Ming Pi's enemy is. It is clear who my enemy is. We happen to have the same.

"Perhaps you can teach me someday," I say and continue. I think he says something about being brave that I don't quite hear and I don't get very far. On the stairs of the Heavenly Emperor's Palace Hall stands Master Li. I am considering my options, but it is too late. He's seen me. At his wave, it's evident that I am meant to follow.

As we enter his study, I shake my hands to remove the jitters and wait for the scolding to begin.

"How are you doing, Lu Mi La?" he says, sitting by his desk.

I don't know how I dare to say the following words, but I do. "You can be either a cruel master, or an unbiased teacher, or a savior, or a captor. But nowhere in world history has anyone managed to be all of those at the same time."

I expect a slap in the face.

"Cruel might not be fair."

"I know you think you rescued me and all that rubbish." I stiffen as the word rubbish flies from my mouth. I had not meant to use it so flippantly.

"I got you out of trouble just last night."

I turn red at the idea of how he did it and rub my arm a little too hard. "In a way that I will pay for. If word gets out that I tried to—"

"It won't."

"How can you be so sure?" Though I already know, to have a student acting so imprudent as to try and charm a master

168

is too big a face loss for Long Si. Steel Master won't tell anyone. I make a gesture that I understand. "But you invented a cheap story." My accusatory tone vibrates in the silence.

"I invented a story. It worked, didn't it?"

I am hard-pressed to argue. He did risk clashing with Steel Master to save me.

"Hopefully, we've convinced him you're nothing but a silly girl. Now, away with you." He waves me out before I can reply.

As I walk the corridor, I see Wei Wan through the window, waiting for me. No, I can't handle it, not now. I turn, slink through the house and out the back door. Unfortunately, this is another game we have played. Trick the stalker.

Outside sits Wei Wan.

He is angry, I can tell from his tight shoulders. But the bells for second chanting ring, and I rush off, pretending that I don't see him chasing me, quickly dropping onto one of the cushions. At one point, I thought Apple would come and sit next to me, but he didn't. Somehow, that annoys me. Annoyance feels better than guilt.

Afterwards, we go straight to morning *gong fu*. But I am unfocused. Too much going on. I am hit so many times I catch Wei Wan wincing as he looks away, even though we're never supposed to do that. We must be present at all times, see all things, the wanted and the unwanted.

I drag myself out and try to appease Wei Wan by telling him about Hidden Eyes. But he fails to see what the fuss is all about.

"Don't you understand," I snap. "A spirit dragon, a creature of myth and magic! And in fact—" I lean close. "I suspect this is Long Si's secret weapon. Just think, a dragon."

"What are you going to do with a stupid creature if you're *dead?*"

It is the first time he has shouted at me. The first time I see his fear. "How's your fighting going?" He whips his head around to see that no one is listening. "Your magic," he hisses. "Is it working? Because it sure as stone didn't look like it."

I stare at Wei Wan. There is a tear in his fighting jacket. He is so angry his eyes bulge, and he reminds me of a bullfrog. A small, friendly bullfrog that has temporarily lost it.

"You must work on your powers. Are you even trying? Hard enough?"

A shimmering orb appears in front of his chest. It shivers in true light blue but with streaks of red, gripped and tormented by something. Fear.

"You're a terrible friend!" he blurts. He turns away and then turns back. "Terrible!" The round, light blue shape whirls with him. Sky Heart.

Speak, I mentally urge myself. *Say something.* What can I say? Yes, I am working on my magic and making progress. Strangely enough, I am still near the bottom of the ranking. No, actually, I am last. Dead last.

He storms off, and my face slackens. *Oh, Wei Wan.* I feel as though all my bones have turned to liquid. Almost nauseated, I go and sit on the stairs of the Heavenly Emperor's Palace Hall, taking Habllek in my lap. But her interest is piqued by some unseen lure, and she scoots off. My stomach heaves, and lunch does not tempt me.

I climb the stairs to my room with heavy steps, but as I reach the second floor, I spot something on my door. It's...a doll? Unease fills me. I approach slowly as though it might burst into flames or explode in my face. Without moving my eyes, I come to a stop. A doll is hanging from a string tied around her neck. No, it's not a doll; it's a dead girl. Me.

I rip the doll from the string and squeeze it hard, but I can't feel it through the tingling numbness. My heart jumps unsteadily in my chest. How many days left?

One more week has passed. Filled with creepy nightmares where strangled dolls hang from a hundred trees and multiple Yong Das attack from every direction. He has an eye patch and horrible battle scars. And even when a fight is over, he comes after me, slow but unstoppable, with a dream-silent laugh that sends an icy shiver up my neck.

It feels like choppy waters are pulling me toward a waterfall, and time narrows into a tunnel. I had hoped my heart magic would bring me further than just surviving. But I am still ranked last, and I still get thrashed, just at a higher level.

I am helping Ah Mei in the laundry, and someone steps through the door. It is Apple. My mouth goes dry.

"Hi," he says.

I try to think of a clever reply. "Hi."

"Ah, Mei?"

"She's not here." I sound tight. I wish I didn't. "I mean, I'm helping her."

He makes a faint gesture at his chest. "I've only had this top since yesterday, but I spilt in the kitchen." He gives a half smile. "Cook Ma. Big pots."

I nod. "Big pots." He waits. "I'll get you a new one," I

hurry.

He looks relieved and tugs his jacket over his head. In here? I see his lean waist, and a tingle rushes through my stomach. The skin is smooth and tight, defining the muscles on his belly in a pattern of perfect squares. Apple holds out his top, but I am fixated on his body until he makes a slight noise. I'm staring.

"Right." I snatch the top. The tips of his fingers brush against mine, sending a rush through my arm. I dig around in the nearest basket, find a new top and hand it over. He puts it on and heads for the door. I still hold the old one as I look after him, the thin silk a crumpled ball in my hand.

As he reaches the door, he turns. "And...good luck, I guess."

"Yeah," I breathe. "Good luck."

The door clicks shut, and I stand alone in the empty space. I don't know why, but I lift his top and touch it to my cheek. It's soft. It smells of Ah Mei's scrubbing soap. And something else, something...male. My pulse won't slow. He wished me luck. He didn't look at me like I am a meal for the adepts in the arena. I know I am not one of them. I probably am a meal, but he treated me like an equal. It changes everything. I force myself back to sorting pants, shirts, socks, but I can't quite focus.

As soon as I leave the laundry, Wei Wan ambushes me.

"Have you figured it out?" My failing magic twists like a blade in my gut. All it has done is make me slightly stronger and faster. Not nearly enough. He grabs my arm. "Look at me," he says angrily. "Have you figured it out?"

"I'm *trying*," I snap.

"How hard?"

I throw out my arms. "What do you want me to do?" I yell. "Show you all my bruises? Describe exactly how close I am to having my teeth knocked out or an arm broken every day. I'm working on it, I am!"

"You need to think. Don't you see? Connect your brain to your heart. Listen to your intuition. What does it tell you? How is it guiding you?" Behind his anger, I see sadness hinting of new fear and worry. "Please, Mi La *jie*," he begs. "You must do this, you must defend yourself."

My heart breaks. "Your hair is getting long." I frown. All the boys are shaved every two weeks.

"*Jie jie*."

He never cries in the open, but his eyes are red-rimmed and dark smudges have appeared beneath them. I wonder what would happen to him if I were gone. I haven't really saved him from much, but I guess the emptiness of a lost friendship can tip the steadiest vessel. I wonder why he is here. Has he lost his family? Is he a stray? Has he fought for survival, and is he as far away from home as I am? I have never thought to ask.

Why have I never asked?

CHAPTER 19

HIDDEN EYES TOWERS ABOVE ME. I HAVE BEEN DOWN to feed him twice, and now he says he has recovered. From what? I ask, but he flings his head irritably and tells me not to waste his time.

Or yours. He scrutinizes me with arched brow ridges. *You called Seikharinne, Girl-Child of the Northern Lights, with your magic word.*

I don't bother asking how he knows because, in that instant, everything becomes clear, like pieces of a puzzle fitting all at once. *And you called me? That is why my hands lit up in here. You triggered my magic, and I used it to call you!*

This is correct. Can you think of why?

The competition. It strikes me at this moment, and instead of recoiling at the thought, like I would have only yesterday, excitement knocks away my leaden feeling. *You're going to help me! Help me survive. No, wait.* I gasp at my own insight; *help me win?*

Hmpf, he snorts. *There's a greedy girl.*

Okay, maybe not. *But will you help me?*

Perhaps I will, perhaps I won't. It depends on if you deserve it.

How can I deserve it?

By learning the most important quality: Courage. When you are courageous, you have earned the right to borrow.

Borrow what?

There are precisely four days left until our guests arrive. The grand red entrance doors have been wiped countless times, the big brass knockers shine, and endless intricate patterns in the worship halls have been repainted. The road leading up to the temple has been cleared. There is nothing but forest framing it, and you cannot see any neighbours from here, but soon they will all come. Not only our guests but every person from all the nearby villages. We must look perfect.

Ma is testing me on the new dishes. I have skipped morning *gong fu*, taking my lunch in the side scullery where I am hiding away as I work. I can't face them, Wei Wan, Master Li, San Dun, Yong Da, everyone. I am skipping the elite training as well. I have pushed through for twelve days straight and am bereft of all strength. I need to be alone. Focus. How many lotus roots for one hundred persons? How much of the pumpkins will be left after I cut off the leathery skin?

I slice with silent efficiency. Accompanied by loud fizzing and crackling as I throw the first batch of lotus roots into the big wok. Then, star anise, sliced pumpkin, aubergine and green beans. Flames engulf the old blackened metal, and as I stir, the contents hiss and sputter, releasing hefty clouds of steam.

I don't hear him; I feel him.

Through the haze of rising vapour, Wei Wan stares like a wraith that has come to haunt me. A deep, hollow, empty stare.

I swallow. "What?"

He just looks.

"*What?*" I repeat.

"You scared yet?" he whispers.

"What kind of a stupid question is that?" I snap.

"'Cause if you were, perhaps you'd train instead of playing kitchen aid."

If I believe that in my dreams lurk a thousand one-eyed Yong Das, then inside this boy lurks a monster ten thousand times worse. The monster of my unresolved fear.

"I can't!" With a scream, I lose hold of my bucking desperation, anger flaring so hotly that I swipe up a fistful from the tasting plate and chuck it at him. There is no sound as cooked pumpkin collides with his chest. Only a soft thud as it drops to the floor like slushy orange snow.

He turns and walks out. My body shakes. I drop to the floor and stir the soaking rice. The smashed pumpkin glares at me. I stir with my hand, around and around, until the water splashes and rice swirls like white waves in the bucket.

Courage, I hear Hidden Eyes boom in my head. The most essential quality. And here I am, staring at a mushy pumpkin and scratching my knuckles raw from stirring rice. That is not courage. Courage, Mila, can only come from inside.

I drop everything and run.

Gasping, I slide into my spot amongst the Twelve just in

time, the hair of my sloppy bun in disarray. I left everything in the kitchen. Cook Ma will scold me, but I don't care. Four days. Four more practices. Wei Wan's words tumble in my head. *You need to come up with something special. You need to think.* Hidden Eyes: *When you are courageous, you have earned the right to borrow.*

My first sparring partner is Apple. He gives me a faint smile before we start, and under any other circumstances, I might have melted into a puddle. Not now. *Courage.* We bounce around each other for a while, and I call on my powers. His orb is green, swinging like plants in the wind. Grass Heart. No wonder he is so fast and flexible.

He does a front kick followed by a parallel punch. I dodge and shoot up my clenched fists between his arms. With a swift scissor, I have forced them out and away. Fast, I jump back. Grass Heart. Grass Heart. My mind churns out a rhythm matching my bouncing steps. Lighter, faster, more flexible. The more I focus on his heart, the more it seems I can take on his abilities. Can I? My heart does an extra spin. I try again, focusing so hard I see only his heart, hardly noticing what he is doing. Again, I manage to evade him, landing a sidekick as I whirl out of the way. I catch a look of surprise on his face.

His next kick hits me square in the side, and I sway. *His heart, focus.* We dabble back and forth, but in the end, I am tired, and he's bigger. However, I didn't get badly hit. Was he being kind?

As Apple passes me on the way out, he mumbles something. Good job? Really? I can't be sure. Jittery, I collect myself, pass the extra masters that help set the rankings and pass Steel Master. Did he notice my shift?

Three more days until our guests arrive. Then: Tournament. Fight until death. The words want to throttle my throat, but I won't let them. Something changed yesterday. *Courage.* That is my mantra as I now face a skilful fighter from Group Four. I take calm, steady steps to measure out my kicks and punches, focusing on the floating orb in front of me. It shimmers in faint, earthy golden hues and gives off little but peace and calm. Buddha Heart. The more I focus on it, the more grounded I feel. All my moves seem to follow a pattern. I block, I punch, I dodge. He is good, but so am I. Confidence spreads in my gut. Steel Master is watching. I see it from the corner of my eyes. It throws me. And Buddha Heart is stronger. Three kicks, eagle beak strike, palm heel strike, and I am on the floor. Frustrated, I bounce up and wonder why they are still all stronger than me. I see two of the other masters conferring with Steel Master.

I am about to leave as we finish, but I see Apple over by the ranking board. He gives me a meaningful look, then turns and walks out. What?

I walk up to the board. Under the rat sits the number eleven. I nearly shout with joy.

Outside, I run to find Wei Wan.

"I did it," I pant as I grab him and drag him in behind Pavilion of the Silent Grasshopper. He is on his way to afternoon *gong fu,* and he looks sullen. "I'm sorry," I hurry and say, "for throwing pumpkin at you. Really, I am, but I moved up one notch in the rankings. I wasn't last today."

"Do you master your heart magic?"

"Hey, I just improved, didn't I?"

"And you think that's enough?" At my surprised look, he says, "Master it, or they will kill you."

Today is my second to last chance at the elite training. I have a roaring Sea Heart in front of me, and a rolling wave flashes by in my mind. It spits out foam at the crest just as it's breaking, throwing itself off in one long, beautiful arch.

And understanding comes so fast.

I can hardly breathe. It's not mine; it's their strength I must use! *When you are courageous, you have earned the right to borrow.*

I concentrate on my own heart, visualizing my energy as that spluttering foam, making it stretch and stretch until it forms a white tendril only I can see. Then I fling it out. Reaching my opponent's heart as we jump and kick is hard. But I send the white string a bit further every time I duck. Finally, I succeed in latching it onto his heart orb. Instantly, I feel a burst of power. I attack: punch, punch, knife-hand, and roundhouse. I am shocked at my own strength. He doesn't go down, but neither do I. I notice Steel Master watching me again. I end in eleventh place. I kept my ranking.

The next day is my last day of elite training. I move through it with only one thought in my head: Borrow. Again and again, I practice shaping my heart energy into a slim tendril that I shoot out to whichever orb is shimmering in front of me. All I need to be able to borrow my opponent's strength is a moment of connection. And when I get it, my brain clicks, and my muscles charge. It is hard work but energizing. As I pass the ranking board, exhausted and bruised, the ugly rat glares stubbornly from the end of the chart. Beneath is the number ten.

I straighten my back and raise my chin as our guests arrive. As one of the Twelve, I am lined up on top of the stairs at the lower courtyard. We are all wearing clean clothes and stand straight-backed in a file, six on each side of Master Li, Steel Master, Master Peng and Head Archivist. Behind, the rest of the Long Si masters are placed in order of seniority. Cook Ma. All the students.

Master Li waves at the oncoming masters, and everyone smiles and laughs as they greet each other, but I detect their glances. No doubt our guests have heard rumours.

One boy elbows his friend. "*Jiu shi ta.*"

That's her. My stomach clenches, partly because an overwhelming male presence tightens it on any day and partly because something new stirs inside, an inner demon I didn't know I had but now see clearly. A demon born of intimidation, shaped by growing boys and the passing of time. I ball my hands and dare their gazes. *Yes, it's me. The odd one, the girl who makes everyone uncomfortable.* I think of my heart magic and feel a thread of relaxation.

As soon as the parading is over and Steel Master has presented Yong Da to anyone who possibly wants to meet him and a few more, I am saved by Cook Ma. She calls me to the kitchen like I have asked her to do. I refuse to be the object on exhibit. And while the other thirty-five contestants and their masters mingle, I concentrate on chopping and peeling.

For the following three days, our guests are invited to use one of our training halls and have midday meal with us. Training is by choice; the idea is to rest up for the competition and make new friends.

I notice that all the bigger boys instantly gravitate toward each other, perhaps one or two smaller ones, but what they all seem to have in common is a vast, bloated self-confidence. Rowdily, they gather at mealtime as if to demonstrate that they're not afraid of each other, not to mention the rest of us, who are obviously beneath notice.

Except me. I get a fair share of glares, regardless.

"A girl," says a boy at the next table over. "What could she possibly do?"

"I see it as one contestant less," says the one beside him.

Wei Wan squeezes his *baozi* so hard yeasty dough swells like miniature walls between his fingers. "That's not fair."

"She's been in detention so many times," says Ming Pi, and I cringe. The two boys look confused. "Do you know what she does to get there?" Ming Pi nails them with what can only be his sharpest gaze so far. He has a certain brazenness I have to admire. "Brave things," he hisses.

A skinny boy named Chen Wen says, "Some of her kicks are lethal."

I am unsure if these comments make things better or worse for me, but my meager crowd of defendants has spoken, and I am strangely touched.

Even San Dun looks affronted. "She's really good with tales and chronicles, too," he adds.

That didn't come out right.

"Wonderful," smirks the first boy.

"Yeah, watch out," warns the second. "She could narrate us to death."

It's the day before the tournament, and the fighting style has been announced: Empty hand. I cling to my last shred of comfort, Wei Wan. Last night, he came to find me in a moment of truce. I was so frantic Cook Ma had put me to work. I scrubbed pots, stacked them, scrubbed them and stacked them again.

"Hey." Wei Wan.

I jolted to a stop. "Hey."

He twiddled with his fingers. "I saw the light."

"Right."

"Just checking who's here."

"Right."

"And, uhm, about tomorrow," he said to the nearest pot stack. "I just wanted to say...good luck. And all."

My throat closed up. "Yeah."

"I never meant to. All I wanted was to—"

"I know."

"Don't, don't..." the last words came out so quietly I could barely hear. "Leave me," he whispered.

"Never."

"You wouldn't, right?"

"I wouldn't."

Before I knew it, he was in my raw dishwashing arms, and we hugged, a fast, clumsy attempt. I had the urge to hug him harder, to give in to the storm about to break out inside me, but I let him go. He walked toward the exit, and my heart clapped hard.

As it does now, an hour before the ceremony is about to start when dark clouds cover the heavens. Perhaps not even the gods want to watch this ugly spectacle. A strange wind blows up, making the two eucalyptus trees outside the walls bend in the gusts. Despite that, people are streaming in, gathering in the lower courtyard. Ready to climb statues and stairs to get the best view, ready to set eyes on a feast of gore and blood and one piece of broken oddity. My palms feel sticky. I need to warm up. No, I should try to relax. Where is Wei Wan?

I need him now. I need his calm presence. The mere thought of performing advanced series like Roaring Cheetah and Croaking Rooster in front of all these people makes me jittery. And then: free-fighting. Terrifying scenarios flash in my head. I feel heavy. All of me; my hands, my arms, my legs.

I wish heaven's gates would open in the worst downpour ever. I want a white bird on the eastern rooftop, white the colour of death, and lightning that strikes in series of four, the number pronounced like death. I want someone to mysteriously appear and present a big clock to Long Si because *song zhong*, to give a clock, sounds like a farewell to someone on their deathbed. I want omens so ominous that everyone flees in panic. It is me, Lu Mi La, the strange girl who does not even belong here. Yes, let them think I cursed them all! W*here* is Wei Wan? I scan the crowds but can't find him. He should be somewhere I can easily spot him. I feel sick.

The contestants are being told to get ready. For the last two hours, our visiting fighters and masters have been resting in Practice Hall Number One. But now they are spilling out, and I scramble to join the procession that is forming, about to head down toward the lower courtyard. But I can't shake Wei Wan; where is he?

A crazy impulse hits me. I turn and run. Back across the upper courtyard, first straight, then right, all the way to Pavilion of the Wise Panda. I tear up the door, rush in, and pound up the stairs into dormitory number three.

I search the room, not even caring that I am breaking rules and intruding, knowing only that I am panicking at its empty austerity.

There are rows of narrow beds and lantern hooks in the walls. But still, I pick out something. Stalk the cat. The game we played has sharpened my senses. There. The last bed, all the way in the corner. There is someone in it. I stride over, clomping.

"What are you doing?" I demand.

Wei Wan moves his head. His eyes are glazed, his voice thick. "I'm, I'm sick," he wheezes. "I've been..."

I storm out. Run down the stairs and back across the upper courtyard, throw myself at the very end of the procession that is still advancing. I scramble to get in line.

"Where's your little friend?" Yong Da, who else?

I ignore him.

"Doesn't have the stomach to see you get smashed, huh?" He stresses the word stomach.

"Leave me alone." I take one last look at the face I loathe

more than anything.

I want to destroy that smirk forever, crush his nose and bash his teeth down his throat. My hands fist by my sides. I clamp my jaws. But for once, it's not really him I am angry at. It is not Wei Wan either, probably delirious from the guilt I just heaped on him by storming out. It is the fact that I need him so badly to survive this tournament and that he is my only anchor in this painful reality. I make it through my days here for him, and he for me. Without each other, we are lost.

Yong Da offers a derisive smile. "What?"

"I hate you."

"I know." He will use it to his advantage. Never lose your calm; isn't that what we're told all day long? Control. I have already lost mine.

As promised, the tournament is opened with a lion dance for fortune and good luck. The contestants are herded toward the top end of the lower courtyard, the spectators are directed toward the back and sides, and the performers, supposedly the best in southern Guangxi, dressed in elaborate costumes, begin to mimic a lion's movement. The red and golden shape is operated by two people and accompanied by a team of musicians beating drums, gongs and clashing cymbals. The dancers are accomplished; they roll, wrestle, leap and jump under their costumes despite the heavy attire. The onlookers press closer all around the perimeter of the yard, cheering and clapping. The pressure from jostling bodies increases, and the noise gets louder and louder in my ears.

I have to fight to stay on my feet, and soon I don't see anything. Dread rises like murky water. The volume of the beating music increases. The lion comes close, pushing through the throng as though it knows I am there, sniffing me, seeing me. It could be Steel Master in disguise with a last fiery attempt to unseat me. People jostle, and the lion whirls to scatter the crowd before rising on its hind legs. For a screaming moment, it towers above me. Then it bounces down on all fours, gusting the hair from my face. It snaps its wide costume jaws and shakes its head in a blur of red and golden tassels. A host of tiny bells showers me in its jingling crescendo.

Then all stops; the lion, the accompanying musicians, the drums, the cymbals. A storm of clapping and shouting takes over and fills the space of silence the Chinese find so uncomfortable, until the mighty temple gong sounds.

My bowels turn to water.

CHAPTER 20

S PECTATORS ARE PUSHED BACK, AND THE CONTESTANTS are called to take their places in the middle of the arena. We stand evenly spaced in straight lines, the boys all bigger than me.

As I shift into opening stance, I feel the crowd watching me. They have never seen a girl fight. I imagine I am alone, with only birds and swaying trees for companions. Wei Wan in the crowds, sending me strength. But the gusty winds push and tear at the leafy trees, and no birds can be heard. Voices, however, I hear clearly. I focus on the opening steps and moves. But the crowd is too close, drawing my ears to sounds around me.

"Why is a girl fighting?" says a disdainful voice.

"She can't be any good."

"They're going to crush her."

My cheeks burn, but somewhere from the corner of my eye, I pick up something that feels familiar. Cook Ma. I risk a fleeting glance. She gives me the thumbs up. I quickly tighten the messy bun on my head and let my gaze traipse across the men, women, and children around me. Somewhere in the throng, I see San Dun. Ming Pi.

Together with two fighting masters from the visiting temples, Steel Master stands on top of the stairs to the upper courtyard, ready to preside over the competition.

Master Li appears, and the crowd falls silent. As Abbot Superior, he greets all the visitors and bids the travellers officially welcome. "It has been long since we organized something like this, but now," he almost smiles, "the moment is here."

Shouts and applause follow, and Master Li talks about fair fighting and may the best contestant win. More cheering, louder, until excitement bounces like a cat around the yard, and the lion musicians follow with a wild burst of drums and clanging cymbals.

The three referees step forward, and Steel Master clarifies that the contest will begin with two fixed sequences, followed by free-fighting.

The master on the left lifts his arm and drops it. "Roaring Cheetah. *Kaishi!*"

I click into action. My body moves like a marionette, step by step, punch by punch, breath by breath. The crowds have gone quiet—I think—I can no longer hear. My ears are roaring like a sonorous ocean. I let years of practice take over. My motions are a little tight and not completely mature, but not bad. My muscles bend and flex in rhythm. I push so hard to make my moves look powerful that my lungs burn. *Halfway, keep going.* Focus, relax, breathe, from action to action, like one long chain of synchronized kicks and strikes.

As we all simultaneously come together in finishing stance, I try to silence my gushing breath.

The three masters confer while we stand to attention. I pray they will discuss at length, allowing my heart and lungs to catch up. I want to bend forward for easier breathing, but I keep my stance. We are not allowed to move. Besides, it would show weakness.

Already an arm is raised by the master on the right. "Sequence two, Croaking Rooster. *Kaishi!*"

I start a little too hard and sway but quickly recover. I focus on fluidity and speed. Front kick, side kick, high touch, low sweep. Bear punch, knife hand, spear hand, tiger claw. My breaths are getting steady. Sweat trickles down my temples; I can feel each drop, like warm wet pearls travelling down the sides of my face. I shut everything out and do my duty to Long Si. Some strange solitude finds me, embracing me with the strength of Ukko. I am not sure, exactly, what sense is picking up on it, coordinating my limbs, my heartbeats, my muscles and joints, my gaze, my focus, the adrenaline rushing through my body. But as though a thin silver stream is coursing through me, intertwining every part of me and solidifying them into one, I know.

I am a gong fu fighter.

When we finish, I am in a daze. I performed all the correct moves, I managed to keep up. I slip a silent sigh of relief that I have not shamed anyone. Yet.

Again, the masters confer, but no winner will be announced until everything is over. We are given a longer break and a drink of water before the final event. Also this discipline is based on a sequence of idealized combat application, but the performer is alone and a trickling but steady flow of real opponents is sent in to attack. It means you are surrounded by enemies which, in this thousand-year-old tradition, are as real as any vicious warlords.

We are told to line up as we are called. I pray I am first. All I want is to get this over with. By the time my name is called, I am numb. From cold, from the drizzle that has begun to fall, and from fear. My name is last.

Thirty-five contestants will fight before me.

As the tournament begins, I watch from the upper courtyard. The first performer is a tall, strong boy who systematically wards off the attackers released into the open space. The next one is slightly shorter but stocky. He fights aggressively and strikes so hard that some of the contestants buckle under his blows. I watch and listen in dread as each student takes his place. Out of all the lessons and years of learning, nothing has prepared me for this. Nothing has taught me how to stop tension from creeping into my body like multiplying insects, or how to hinder the vicious monsters that mushroom in my head. The tightening of my arms, my back, my neck. *Courage.*

At last, my name is called, and I step out into the arena and take my opening stance. The first opponent rushes in, he is not from Long Si, and he has a graceful fighting style. I do not dare to use my heart magic yet. It requires a lot of concentration, and it could deplete me.

The first blocks of the sequence we are supposed to follow are relatively simple, and I manage to ward him off. The next is Apple. I manage him too. But the following is Wicked, Yong Da's stout friend. He has an evil glare in his eyes, and I need to watch out. I succeed in a front-kick, side-kick, elbow strike, which takes care of him. For the moment.

I whirl toward my next opponent. But they come faster now, boys I have never seen and whose fighting styles are unknown to me. The stone surface is getting slick from the drizzle, and from the corner of my eye, I detect a large familiar shape. Yong Da.

The spectators shout and pump their fists, but I feel as if I have walked into a tunnel and left everyone behind. Fatigue is gripping me, and the world seems hollow. My adversaries are getting closer. A foot connects with my hip in flesh-numbing pain. I take a strike to my cheek that leaves my ears ringing. For the first time this day, I am getting scared, really scared.

Yong Da draws near. To him, this is not a tournament. He wants me dead. I can feel his *shaqi*, his murderous energy, reaching out for me, thick and dark like bitumen tar.

As I turn, I catch a glance of Steel Master. He stands with arms crossed, a sneer on his face. He and Yong Da are cut from the same cloth, not even bothering to keep up the pretence. They want me gone.

That is my cue: heart magic. I need it now.

I have barely called my powers before shimmering orbs appear in front of each fighter's chest.

I chart their true colours, duck and make a fast retreat. It earns me precious seconds. Here comes one with dense brown at its core. Wood Heart. Not too fast, not too strong. I evade him. The next one is transparent and brings a feeling of lightness. Wind Heart, fast then, very fast. I am too tired to fight such speed; instead, I visualize the thin white stream flowing from my heart to his. Swiftly, I nip at his power and a burst of lightness fills me. I whirl out of his way.

Behind, I see a shape of pure silver; that one is not out to take my life. He fights for technique and perfection. Again, I send out my white tendril, latch onto his floating orb and borrow some of his qualities. As we clash into close combat, I do a palm-heel strike and a roundhouse, performing beautifully.

Blood pumps through my veins, and life sucks me back out of my imaginary tunnel. But I know I won't ever be able to strike them all down; I will have to make it until the time limit.

Yong Da is before me, the orb at his chest black as pitch. Ink Heart.

His fast triple sequence knocks me so badly I fly across the arena and crash into the spectators. They scatter like frightened chickens. I struggle to see, but all is hazy. Someone is calling.

"Get up, Mi La. Get up!" San Dun. Behind him, Ming Pi, also shouting. Others? I don't know. Shouting, shouting, shouting.

I must do as they say. If I am down for longer than ten seconds, it is over. I stagger up on one foot, then a second foot, and face the fighters in a half-circle around me. *Quick. Identify.* To the left, Yong Da's orb shimmers like black oil. I move right. They close in on me again, and I go straight for a Steel Heart. I throw my white force like a grip hook onto his grey ball of energy and retrieve. A gush of strength fills me, and I take aim and shoot a kick at his waist.

A Sand Heart. I draw a chunk of light-brown power and round on Yong Da, landing a heavy blow on his cheek. At his look of surprise and anger, I dodge fast. There, the Wind Heart again, I clasp his vibration of lightness and dance out of Yong

Da's way. His black orb seems to nearly explode with hatred. It's pumping and pulsating, power for the taking, but evil, too evil. I dare not touch it.

Hot and red-faced, my opponents attack with renewed vigour. In a desperate attempt, I spread my own force, sending out multiple white streams, but it is too difficult to hit several targets at once. I hit no one.

Instead, I am knocked to the ground.

Screaming voices rouse me. I raise my eyes as though dragging myself from some great depth, and looking without focus, I slowly drag myself to sitting. It is impossible to converge the chaos in my head. My body is a kaleidoscope of shattering pains and aches. But the spectators, they...they have rallied in my defence? Or are they just screaming?

I force myself up, stumbling twice, and walk unsteadily back to the middle of the arena.

As one, they swamp me. Blows rain down, draining what paltry bit of energy I have. How much longer? I entwine myself with the Silver Heart. He is tall and could be handsome, but I see only his glimmering orb of power. I reach with my tendril and clutch at it, gaining another hit from a stout Stone Heart, Wicked, Yong Da's closest henchman. I tense my muscles and round-house kick three opponents in one go. They go down. But this has gone on for too long, and there are too many. Blood pours from my nose and my cracked lip, my hand is scraped and shooting pains in my left side make me deliriously think I have been kicked by a horse.

Wind Heart, where is he? If I can grab some of his lightness, I might be able to stay upright. There, behind Yong Da. Sluggishly, I manage to duck under Yong Da's blow, but he catches me in the shoulder, and I catapult to the side. I sway and grasp for Wind Heart. Latching with every last bit of force, my white tendril hits home. If we are too tightly engaged, another fighter cannot come in, and I cling to his energy tightly, tightly.

Like two courting cranes, we fight and dodge in a mirror sequence that takes my breath away. On an energy plane, we are so connected that we could be two wings of the same bird. He cannot beat me, and he cannot shake me off; the faster he moves, the faster I move.

And no one can get near us.

The gong sounds.

We all stop where we are, bow, and leave the arena.

The audience is wild, but I feel like I have been sucked into a vacuum. The tang of blood fills my mouth. I am slick from sweat, bruised, and broken.

I collapse to the ground. Vaguely, I hear sounds; vaguely, I know that I am moved and that time passes. How much, I do not know.

Sleep.

CHAPTER 21

L ONG BEFORE THE GONG SOUNDS IN THE GLOOM OF post-tournament predawn, I try to move my sorry excuse for a body, but as it has during the entire night, chaos rages within. A wound on my hand has scabbed over. My cheek is bruised and dried blood cakes my face. My left eye is black and swollen shut. My ribs feel as though they have been cracked, and my muscles groan in painful protest. Weakly, I burrow into the stale, musty blanket on my bed and go back to sleep. Except for one trip to the privy, I do not stir until midday.

There is a knock on the door. It is Cook Ma, but not now. Another day, another year. I am too exhausted. Vaguely, I hear her say that she will leave food outside the door. Whatever.

Eventually, hunger wins, and I force myself up through an avalanche of agony, nudging the door open. Outside is a tray with a covered bowl of broth and a ceramic spoon. A bowl of white rice and one *baozi*. Chopsticks neatly placed in between never stuck into the rice, which resembles incense for mourning the dead. I take tiny sips until I have gotten some sort of control of my jaw, my shaking arm, and my hand. The rice I eat faster. Then, the *baozi*.

I sleep all day. Don't go down for the banquet, even though it is loud enough to be taken for a visit by Diermmes, the hammer-wielding thunder god who controls storms and lightning.

After all has died down, there is another knock on the door. "Mi La," says Cook Ma. "I want to see you. Please let me in."

She stares in shock as I open the door.

"Yeah," I say, and it hurts to move my cheeks. "Not too pretty, huh?"

I take two steps back, and she hesitantly follows. There is an awkward silence, as though she feels guilty, the Chinese way, taking on an embarrassment that isn't even hers to bear.

"Can I see your body? Please, Mi La, I need to know if we must send for Potion Master."

I bring my loose jacket down over my shoulders and turn around. I hear her stifle a gasp. Tentatively, she reaches out. Her hand butterflies across my back and stops at a point on my right shoulder blade.

"I am so sorry," she says softly. "I wish this had never happened. And I am sorry for Wei Wan as well. Don't be too hard on him. He wanted to be there for you, but he got sick. Violently stomach sick."

I slide my garment up and turn to face her. My face so grave it feels like mortar. "Why was I picked?"

Unease flits across her face.

"I know Steel Master was behind it. He loves to hurt and debase me, nothing new."

"I don't think anyone meant for you to—"

"I could have died. How could Master Li endorse it?"

Cook Ma twists uncomfortably. "It's not that simple."

"It's straightforward. He is the Abbot Superior, is he not?" My tone makes her shrink, but I am too upset to feel bad.

"Yes and no."

"What's that supposed to mean? He could have stopped it before it even happened."

Another embarrassed smile. She is so disturbed that her heart energy manifests, a warm yellow orb fluttering with red; apprehension and distress.

"Cook Ma, please. Help me make sense of all this. How could this be? Why didn't Master Li stop it?"

The silence is deafening. Then she licks her lips once. "It was Master Li who ordered it."

This is my chance. For years, I have wanted to hate Master Li. Instead of bringing me back home, he dragged me across a continent. A *child*. I know he thinks he rescued me; he did take me from the Nefarious, but to me, it felt like a betrayal. And now he's done it again.

I am sure of it now: When I die, I will never be taken by Guan Yin in her lotus flower and brought to the Pure Lands Beyond because today I will set my fire free. And probably burn in the Netherworld for it.

Five hours have passed since Cook Ma left me in silent shock. I snapped out of it long ago and let the familiar cold rage take its place. Palming the knife I took from the armory, I step into the corridor. Cold, damp air hits my face, and I relish it. I look carefully as I make my way downstairs and outside. Stealth I have practised to near perfection, and dark glee is oiling my stiff and sore muscles. No one will hear me.

In the late night, I sneak softly like Habllek, my animal sister. I pick out a small shape in the dark. Is she watching over me? At the Sleeping Bear Pavilion, I carefully push open the door and enter. Master Li's bedroom is up the stairs and to the left.

The door is ajar. Master Li is inside, up despite midnight's fast approach. He sits by a desk, his back turned, and a candle and writing tools are in his hands.

Soundlessly, I slip in.

But his calm voice stops me. "It has been exactly eight years, one moon, and three days." So, he was expecting me then. It doesn't change a thing. "Since we met," he adds.

"Such precise records of trivial things?"

"Not trivial."

"No, I guess not. After all, removing a child from her family is a rather big thing."

"I didn't take you."

"Oh, that's right, I came running to you with open arms. Or no, actually, I had planned to fight my way out, but I felt sorry for you; I mean, what could you possibly have to match a skinny, hungry, frightened little girl?"

"Your anger is quick today."

"There is nothing quick about eight years."

"Lu Mi La," he slowly rises. "There are things you do not understand."

"No, you don't understand!" I yell, feeling my broken

body throb. "You don't understand what it's like to have a family and to lose that family, because you don't *have* a family." Meanness fuels me. I want his pain.

"I do have family."

"Right," I scoff. "What, parents that no one has ever heard of? No sisters, a brother last seen when? Yeah, he must really miss you!"

His slap hits my cheek like a hammer blow.

I strike with my knife, but like a snake, he grips my wrist. I swing my other hand for tiger claw, and before he grips it, I have already kicked at his groin. He evades, and I whirl from his grip, kick high, whirl again, low sweep. Ukko is with me. Adrenaline floods my system, and for a few heated moments, I cannot even feel my pains and aches. Perhaps the room's *feng shui* is conducive to fighting.

There—perfect lock, and he freezes. I thrust my knife. And stop. An inch from his throat.

He locks my gaze. Then says in a low voice, "Is this what you really want?"

His hands are up in surrender, and I spot that strange scar on his underarm. My breath is quick and short. *Do it. Do it now.*

But.

I let my knife hand drop.

Master Li straightens his jacket. "So, you are ready."

Although his reaction confuses me, I do not let it show. I am shaken by how close I got. The candle on his desk is still flickering, feeding off the *shaqi* my heart produced, my murderous intent. I wanted to kill him. Part of me still does.

"Why did you make me compete?"

"This is not the time."

"Of course not," I say sarcastically and leave, but I keep the knife. He does not ask for it.

As I step outside, a light drizzle is falling.

Habllek is waiting for me.

The rush from trying to kill Master Li last night ebbed out quickly. My aches and pains have returned with double impact. I feel terrible for what I did. Yet I can't regret it. I survived the most brutal fight of my life and got within killing range of my Master. How fast my spark is returning. I first felt that strange mix when Wei Wan and I began our secret practice—of terror and thrill. Am I not here to fight warlords?

I hear a faint scraping by the door in the dark of predawn. My head hurts over my right eye, and my body feels like it's weighted by one of the stone turtles in the yard. Slowly, I lift my head and see a small crinkled note pushed in through the wide gap between the door and floor.

I watch it for a while. What now? A death threat from Yong Da? No dolls this time. With effort, I rise and fetch it. Fingers fumbling, I sit on my bed and light the candle on my nightstand. After smoothing out the grubby note, I hold it close to the flame. *Zao ri kang fu.*

I notice the uneven characters, how the lower horizontal line of the *zao* is slightly too long and makes the character out of proportion. How the complicated *kang,* with no less than eleven pen strokes, looks a mess. Pretty handwriting was never Wei Wan's forte, but that is irrelevant. The meaning has already seeped into my heart. Never has a wish to get well caused my heart to swell so, and for a long while, my body does not hurt. Tears crowd behind my eyelids.

Today, I will go out properly, not just to the privy. Hopefully, I will get more than snippets of gossip leaking from the men's room. When I passed yesterday, somebody talked about Wei Wan's hair and why it was not shaved. Scabies, they speculated. Hives said another.

As the day brightens, I hobble out and sit on the stone steps of the Heavenly Emperor's Palace Hall. The first person I see is San Dun.

"Mi La," he calls. "There you are! I have been worried about you. Oh," he comes running over, grimacing as he nears. "Look at you."

My hand instinctively touches my bruised cheek. Drifts to my black eye.

The quick Chinese smile. "Some of the others got beaten up pretty badly too." He leans in. "And Yong Da didn't win." We both smile conspiratorially, even though it hurts my face. I do not ask him who won, and I do not tell him I tried to kill Master Li.

Near Practice Hall Number Two, a figure stops. I know that outline: Apple. He leaves his companions and walks toward me. I push myself to my feet.

"Hey," says Apple.

"Hey."

"How're you?"

He is asking how I am. I nearly have to hold my jaw to prevent it from dropping. "Umh, fine. Yeah, fine. I mean, I'm okay."

"Really?" He scrutinizes my face. "Does it hurt?"

I stop my hand from darting up to my cheek a second time, and rather than recoiling from his gaze, I match his look with my own. "No. I mean, yeah. Some."

His friends call him back, but the leaden feeling in my body is all gone.

"Mi La," I turn to see Ming Pi. "That was so brave!" he gasps. "To meet all those fighters in close-up combat. And you held out."

"Yeah," I manage to raise the corners of my lips a bit. "Perhaps it was all that detention."

"Your style was amazing." He stares, excited. "It was almost like you knew how to fight them, as though you could figure out their strengths and, and, I don't know, use it against them. Did you also read Sun Tzu?"

I tell him no, no military strategy, and he runs off to morning practice. I go to look for Wei Wan, but like Ming Pi, he's already in the hall.

Instead, Master Peng comes my way. He gets almost teary-eyed and says I performed exceptionally, even though I came last. "The odds were...not in your favor," he gives me a distressed look.

After he is gone, I sit with Habllek on the stone steps and wait for Wei Wan. Nothing is as soothing as stroking her soft fur and listening to her purring.

As he sees me, he runs over. "You did it, *jie*!" He beams with his whole face. "I knew you would. I knew it." He looks so proud of me and I find myself blinking a little too fast. But then he lowers his voice. "I'm sorry I wasn't there, *jie*. I failed you."

"Of course not. It's not your fault you were sick. Nausea

is awful. Why is your hair so long? I heard someone say you have scabies and can't be shaved. Is it true?"

He ignores my question. "I don't think Yong Da will be so mean to you anymore."

"Why do you say that?"

"Before the tournament, he was urging me to be there and cheer you on."

Strange.

"He even gave me a *baozi* because it would go on for many hours, he said, and I would get hungry."

"Oh, Wei Wan," I close my eyes and sigh. "After all our secret practice, shouldn't you know better than to eat anything Yong Da gives you?"

"But?" he stops, unable to put words on this absurdity. "What do you mean?" he stammers. "You think..."

"I don't think, I know. He poisoned you."

He absorbs this, speaking only after several moments, and then sullenly, "Well, his days are over."

Wei Wan claims that people talk about me and that it's not slander. "They think you were brave," he says. "And you held out a lot longer than anyone expected. All those boys were bigger and stronger than you. They're not blind, *jie*, they saw, they were impressed."

I don't know if it's bad luck to say anything good about me or anything, but as if on a given signal, Yong Da and his minions appear.

Two of them step in front of Wei Wan, and Yong Da slams me into the wall. My aching body screams in protest, but I am not a skinny child anymore.

"Get off me," I push him, furious.

CATARINA LILLIEHÖÖK

He towers above me. "I know what you did."

"I know what *you* did. Poisoned an innocent boy." I ensure I don't look at Wei Wan; I don't want to drag him into this.

"You're a witch."

"That's getting old, Yong Da."

"You bewitched everyone. It helped you in the tournament."

"Helped? In case you didn't notice, I came last."

"You should be dead," he spits and kicks at Habllek, who scoots away. "And that stupid cat, is that your link to witchcraft?"

"Stay away from her," I hiss.

"Or what?" He gives me one last shove and walks away.

I straighten my jacket, and we continue on our way, history class awaits. Why doesn't anyone stop this bully? It's like they're all just…watching.

"I got to go," says Wei Wan. "I promised to help Ma."

CHAPTER 22

ONSIDERING I DON'T LOOK AT MASTER LI AND HE doesn't look at me, my first history class is awkward. It has been two days since I ambushed him in his workroom, but he makes nothing of it. At the moment, we are studying more recent affairs, like the Long March, which began in October 1934 and marked the emergence of political leader Mao Zedong as the undisputed leader of the Chinese Communists.

"It saved the Communist Party from the Nationalists," he drones. I look forward to lunch break. I will find Habllek. "Why was the Long March important?" I see him look out into the room from the corner of my eye.

"The Communist army survived," says Ming Pi.

"And that is important. Why, exactly, Lu Mi La?"

I was waiting for that; he clearly saw me losing concentration. "They help our cause." I amend, "We help their cause."

He doesn't contradict me. That must mean I am right. I

know that warlords and communists hate each other. My Master and I do not exactly see eye to eye either. When class is over, I can't get out fast enough, but it's strange because I find myself in the throng of everyone heading for lunch. It's been a long time since there was a complete hole around me, but seldom have I moved with the crowd as one. Now, there is no gap between me and them. Only between Master Li and me. And suddenly, it strikes me, perhaps also between him and his brother?

I sneak into the kitchen where Cook Ma is running full pelt between pots and pans. I grab the big black wok filled with stir-fried vegetables and tip it into a bowl, telling her I wonder about Master Li's brother.

She stops stirring her pot. "Why do you ask?"

"I said something about him and clearly hit a sore spot." I leave out the knife bit.

"He used to be here." Was that a tremble in her voice? "He went on a mission years ago and never returned." Her face tightens, as though I just asked something forbidden, and I quickly hobble back out to join Wei Wan for lunch.

It is the fourth night since the tournament. I glance over my shoulder to make sure no one is around. Then I put down my lantern and reach for the trap door in the forest. Every move I make still sends a rush of aches and pains through my body, and I walk down the stairs carefully, negotiating the tunnel where roots and stones poke from walls and floor. Eventually, I am back in the soy sauce room. Or rather, the pearl of flame room.

I hesitate; best bring a pearl. Then I open the hatch and climb into blackness. I must take it slowly, but as soon as I reach the bottom, I turn and raise my lantern.

You came back.

For a rushing instant, all I do is gawk. My gaze takes in the shimmering outline of jaws, spikes, and horns. His crystal eyes glitter, and a soft light flares around him when he arches his huge neck. Yong Da flashes by in my mind, scared witless, about to be skewered in the maws of a golden dragon.

I do not eat arrogant boys. I eat pearls of flame. He produces a hard glint under his scaly brows, which has me sending off my pearl in a blink.

I didn't die, I say. And after a while, I add, *though, you didn't really help me, did you?*

I most certainly didn't. And nor did you die. He settles with the pearl in his claws.

So, I called you for another reason.

That is right. What do you think it means?

That you are Long Si's secret weapon? That I am ready for something?

To stop feeding me. I am fully recovered and only need occasional sustenance.

What am I ready for?

I don't know. I like the green pearls better.

He neither denies nor confirms that he might be Long Si's secret weapon. I get nothing out of him.

207

It is midday meal, but Wei Wan is nowhere to be seen, so I gobble down some food and go out to play with Habllek. I find her near the boys' second dormitory. My heart swells, and I tease her with the stick I have made, a string with a small rag ball tied to it.

Suddenly, she scurries off. I follow, still limping, all the way behind the Pavilion of the Wise Panda, where voices spill through a screen window.

"Why don't they let *me* go?"

"Keep your voice down." The angry reprimand comes from Steel Master, aimed at Yong Da.

"I'm far superior."

"It's not up to you."

Before I think to hide, Steel Master spots me through the screen. "Let's go," he says.

Yong Da leans in to see who is there. He scowls and turns to follow his master.

I scoop up Habllek and walk back, seeing Wei Wan. "Hey, wait, you." I catch up with him, and Habllek jumps from my arms. "What're you doing? What're you so busy with all the time?"

"I'm not busy."

"You are. I hardly see you. I haven't seen you since before the tournament."

"You're imagining things. When will you come back to practice?"

"Tomorrow." I narrow my eyes. Is he holding back something?

He throws out his arms. "Stop glowering, *jie.* I haven't done anything. I have to go."

"Now? Where?" I snap.

"I promised I'd help Ah Mei in the laundry, then San Dun. Not illegal, is it?"

"You're ridiculously busy."

"No, *jie*, I'm not. It's you who's ridiculously *un*-busy. So now I ask you again: Are you ready for fighting practice tomorrow?"

"I am."

"Good. Because for the future of Long Si, none of us can afford to appear broken."

"Of course not." I battle with wanting to be irritated and knowing that he is right. I want to praise him; I also want to cuff his obnoxious little head.

I go and look for Habllek again, allowing my body its fourth day of rest. It is slowly healing, and my focus is good during evening meditation. I sleep better than I have in a long time, and the next day, during midday break, I get the idea to try my magic. I silently say *Seikhar and* focus on seeing *all* the hearts.

It takes three attempts, and I don't really succeed. Still, my breath catches because, even though the orbs have not revealed themselves, I can pick up their underlying sentiment. I can only keep the sensation for a few seconds, but clearly, there is a shift. Less ill will, a *lot* less.

"What ugly sorcery this time?" Yong Da snarls.

I restrain my jolt. Did he see? No, I can read his expression; he wishes to catch me doing something I shouldn't.

"Witch-snake," he hisses. "I have my eye on you."

I glare at his back as he walks away. That's just the feeling I get from Steel Master. But in the shadows of the Blooming Lotus Flower's Palace Hall stands Master Li. Now, why is *he* watching me? Is everyone watching me?

For my first chore, I find myself with Cook Ma and Apple weeding in the veggie patch.

Ma kneels on the ground. "See these little green shoots here in between?" she points. "Those I planted, do not pull them out."

All I can think of is how close I am to Apple.

"Is all clear?"

I blink. I haven't heard a word.

"What're you waiting for?" She points at the gloves on the ground. "Get started."

We both drop to our knees and almost knock heads. I laugh, embarrassed, tugging at the leather around my wrist.

"How did you do in the tournament?" I ask, immediately regretting it. Why did I bring up an event where I came last?

"Okay." He lifts a shoulder. "I don't really care."

I observe him. Was it a mistake to ask?

"I'm sorry they put you through it," he says. "You did really well. Everyone in my dorm bet against—"

He stops himself, and I feel a slide in my gut. Do they bet against me? So, blatantly wishing for my crushing defeat?

Stiffly, I move down the row. "And you, Apple, did you also bet against me?" My voice comes out strangled. "Were you all betting that I was going to die?"

"No, Mi La, listen," he comes after me, plucking the weeds quickly. "It wasn't like that. I didn't bet at all, and no one bet that you were going to die. At least not in my dormitory," he adds.

So, they did, then. They bet that I was going to die. I will have to keep that in mind. I pull hard at the weeds and feel Apple drifting behind.

For the rest of the chores, I am distracted. I don't know if it is because I am actually having an almost proper conversation with Apple or because they bet on my life. Well, I clench my jaw. Whatever they bet, they lost. The thought gives me satisfaction, and when I am done, I leave the veggie patch feeling not so bad.

By the rookery, I spot Cook Ma.

She holds the falcon in both hands. Just as I near, she throws it up in the air.

"Oh, I missed him," I say, disappointed. "Are you sending him somewhere?"

She looks after the departing bird. "No, just exercising."

My brow creases. I could have sworn I saw something tied to its leg.

Eventually, she turns to me, shielding her face from the afternoon sun with her hand. "Master Li wants to see you this evening after supper."

"What for?"

"I don't know," she says, but I get a distinct feeling that she does.

CHAPTER 23

"**I** KNOW YOU'VE BEEN TRYING TO FIGURE THINGS OUT," says Master Li. "What have you learned about the legend of the Three Masters? About The River God?"

I can just barely stop my jaw from dropping. "How did you know?"

"Feeding Hidden Eyes was a giveaway."

"You *know?*"

"I do. For the first time in centuries, he has been fed, and for those of us sensitive to energies, everything at Long Si has shifted."

"Oh," I can't help feeling a wave of disappointment. I thought something had changed because of how I performed in the tournament.

"That too," says Li, as though he just read my mind. "You. Yong Da is losing followers, which is why he is so angry."

"Does he know about Hidden Eyes?"

"No. Neither him nor Master Gang."

"This is the secret weapon you taught us about. Why haven't you used it? And he was starving, why haven't you fed him?"

"We could not call him. That is why we needed you. If you managed to steal the dusty, wax-blotched *River God's Chronicles* from right under the Head Archivist's nose and I suspect you did, since you had a knife so handy the day you planned to kill me, then you probably know." He ignores my shock.

"I..." I feel deflated. "The light was too dim; even scraping off the wax with the knife, I couldn't see."

"Then let me fill you in. The lesser deity mentioned, connected to the River God, is Hidden Eyes. As you know, dragons are associated with water. He is here to help us finish what could not be done the last time when feudal lords threatened to tear the empire apart a thousand years ago. But he needs a twin spirit to help him, and this person must be *yin*, female, to balance his strong male powers, the *yang*. She must also be born in the year of the Dragon; otherwise, they are incompatible."

An odd sensation grows in my chest, but I focus on his tale. The first part I was sort of getting; the creature, the legend, spoke of what could be Hidden Eyes, but the rest...is new.

"Can you guess who the twin spirit is, Mi La?"

My heart flutters. *No.*

"Yes, you. This is why I went all the way to the slave market. To find you, as the omens told me all those years ago. This is why you must be here, at Long Si. You and Hidden Eyes belong together."

I feel like my stomach just dropped from the bottom of

the world. I realize that after all this time, I am still struggling to stay in sync with this place that keeps serving me rude awakenings. Twin spirit to a dragon deity?

All I can manage is, "Connected to me?"

"That is right."

"I am not born in the year of the Dragon."

"You are. Have I not taught you well enough? You need the exact date to know which zodiac you are born in. Our lunar system overlaps the moon calendar. You can be born in the beginning of a year but still belong to the sign of the year before."

My mind blanks.

"In your case, Wu Chen Year commenced the first day of first moon 1928. I am sorry, I got your dates all wrong."

"So, you mean...all that taunting I suffered, it was for nothing?"

"There is nothing wrong with being born in the year of the Snake, but no, you are not."

"I am not a snake, a dragon is my twin spirit, and I am supposed to...help him?"

"You are, and you will. It is your destiny."

My destiny. He mentioned that so many years ago at that market in Kashgar but then never explained it. He tells me he couldn't have said it before; he needed to see if I could call the dragon. I probably look as if I am going to faint because he asks if I am all right, and I say that I am a reindeer herder, but he reminds me that was long ago.

I glance at the scar on his arm and feel a strange attachment. Three long marks that make me think of a river. I don't know how it comes to me, but in this instant, I understand that this tug and pull between us will always be there. I have been trying to live both my old and new lives simultaneously. The one he had planned for me has not been a straight road, and my old life is long since gone. I am not a reindeer herder anymore, yet it was the first thing I said.

Despite everything, it is still in there, that diminished part of me whose only outer proof is my Sámi bracelet, sitting on the chair in my room.

And now they bubble up, those memories I have suppressed for years; what did my mother do after my abduction? The panic that must have consumed her, how she must have been torn between pursuing my captors and rushing off to get Father. What might she have said to him, yelled? Screamed? I have imagined his breathlessness, his widening eyes. His mind trying to make sense of her insane words. *She is here, she must be. I saw her only minutes ago.* A mass of cold desperation, tearing through your chest like a vicious beast. And later: Guilt. Self-blame. Because who in their right mind cannot protect their own child? Who in their right mind can allow anyone to stomp in and shatter the most privileged of unions, your family?

Who can lose their daughter?

Here, I would always end my reflections. As a skinny, scared and detested orphan at Long Si, this was as much as I could handle. A shell of my former self that I have now slowly wriggled out of for eight long years.

Then came a dragon and set off my powers.

I am not sure I can take much more. "A dragon's helper?"

"Yes," Master Li says. "You are the Spirit Dragon's Keeper. Do you believe me?"

I want to.

"I understand this must be difficult, but I promise you, it is the truth. And I know it is hard for you to see anything positive in me coming to the slave market, but if you, for just a moment, would give me the benefit of the doubt, you will see that it was at a great cost for Long Si. And for me."

My brain grudgingly calculates. Going all the way to Gorgarath and back, it must have taken more than...a year and a half. The expenses and the physical and mental efforts of being on the road for so long. The danger of freeing me from a fate I don't even dare to contemplate, of constantly looking out for me, saving me from thieves and bandits. Feeding me, finding shelter, paying for it, dragging me along, hearing my complaints...

My heart softens. A bit. I am still mad. "The tournament." I stare. The forbidden challenge from student to master. Things between us changed at our last encounter. I held a knife to his throat, and he let me go, not even taking my weapon. But still. "To throw me in the arena like a slave in the fighting pits. You knew I was nowhere near their strength."

"Lu Mi La," he opens his hands. "Surely you must know I did not put you in that contest for something as simple as physical strength? Anyone can master that, even Yong Da."

I miss a breath.

In some twisted way, that is the kindest thing he has ever said to me. No teacher must ever say anything degrading about a student, and I understand that it is to stay between us, but finally, for the first time in nearly a decade, he has put me above my bully. He recognizes me. A wave of warmth floods my chest.

"Little Secret is your name. Now we know what your secret is: heart magic." He does not see me gulp, and I do not ask how he knows. "We knew you possessed some skill," he continues. "The oracle bones said as much, but we weren't sure which one. We had to test you to see what it was."

A test? "You mean there was actually a reason for this stupid contest?"

"I know it was not easy for you to go through, I understand that. But please, believe me when I say it was the only way. We had to know."

I blink. An apology? Not really, but most likely as close as I will ever get. "Why did you have to know about my heart magic?"

"It is crucial for our resistance. Only heart magic will defeat our enemy. But it is wielded only by a few."

I stay composed even though this feels close to praise, and I am half out of my wits for it. I must have earned it. Perhaps it is my Reindeer Heart.

"But just as much," he continues. "I wanted to gauge if you could handle a big challenge. This contest was the only way to see if you are ready."

"Ready for what?"

"Ready to save Long Si."

The next few days slow to an ant's crawl. I was told not to say anything to anyone, so I have only whispered it to Habllek. My animal sister keeps any secret. But I am sure something leaks out of my system because Apple has glanced in my direction several times, and just today, he offered to spar with me. It's the second time.

I casually leave practice, managing to make it through supper. Though, I am desperately curious to see where Apple is.

In the busy refectory, Wei Wan thumps down his food tray opposite me. "Who're you looking for?"

"What? No one."

"Waiting for? Hoping for?" His eyes sparkle, and now he looks like that little frog again, just as he did before the tournament when he yelled at me to work on my powers. This time, though, he seems happy.

"Your brain will trip on itself one day."

"I wonder who will trip you."

I ignore him, thinking of my brother Olli. Small brats need to be kept in place.

"I'm thirteen, you know," he says, nearly making me drop my spoon.

"You a mind reader now?"

"I do understand things."

"Like what?"

"Now is not the time to trip."

What's that supposed to mean? But he is already busy talking to Ming Pi. I furrow my brow.

CHAPTER 24

I HAVE ENDURED TWO DAYS OF EXCRUCIATING WAITING FOR either Master Li or Apple. I keep searching for Apple's broad shoulders and tall stature. If I spot them, I dodge away. He looked at me once, but I looked away. I instantly regretted it.

Today Cook Ma let me have a go with the hunting falcon. I carried him outside on my arm, and she let me take his hood off. I felt his force as he pushed his talons into my leathered wrist for take-off. That moment of contact made me gasp in wonder. Usually, Cook Ma tells me that an apprentice must work closely with an experienced falconer for two years to be allowed to do anything. She made an exception today. As it came flying back, I stood tall, holding up my arm to show my position, then lowered it for landing. She helped me put it back in its cage, and now I am staying behind to clean up.

At eight o'clock, right after supper, I am finally called to Master Li.

"Sit." He points to a chair and proceeds to tell me about

his brother. "I sent him on a mission nine years ago. He traveled to the Qinling Mountains, for centuries home to one of the biggest warlord cartels in China. His orders were to build local resistance, find information, and map their operations. A mission," he says as he presses his lips into a thin line, "from which he never returned."

The pain in his eyes is so palpable I hardly dare ask. But then I do. "Did he make it there? Have you heard from him?"

"We know he reached his destination and started along his path. In the first few years, we used messenger birds, but with his growing entrenchment, the messages got less frequent, sometimes carrying only vague or coded reports. We suspected he might have been watched and worried the birds would get intercepted." A crease forms on his brow. "In the last few years, we haven't heard...anything."

"You believe him to be alive?"

"Our theory is that the local warlord has taken him prisoner."

"And?"

"You will travel to the Qinling Mountains and infiltrate his fort."

My heart stops. *Mission.*

"You are ready. This is what you have been trained for."

I can hardly think. Waves of heat pirouette across my face. "But," I stutter, "alone? With a pack of warlords?"

"And you wouldn't know how to get yourself out of trouble, Lu Mi La? What have you been doing here for the past eight years?"

He is right. Fear and excitement blaze through my chest. This is what I have been waiting for. Planning for.

"You will identify the *Da Laoban*, their highest leader, and, if necessary, take him out. Then, locate and free my brother."

Assassination? A thousand what-ifs form in my head. Why me? I want to ask. Instead, I say, "Who will be coming with me?"

"Wei Wan."

"Wei Wan? He's just a child!"

"Exactly, you will be going as children." I shoot him a sharp glare, and he amends, "Well, you will be his *jie jie.*"

I raise my brows. His big sister?

"As you know, the term is widely used in China, someone like a sister is enough, not necessarily related. I believe he already calls you *jie?*" Does nothing elude my sharp-eyed Master? "Your command of the *Putonghua,*" he continues, "is perfect. You are dark enough in eyes and hair to pass for some of our ethnic minorities. Ma has told me you already do at the market." He drums his fingers on his desk. "You will say that your mother is from Xinjiang and your father from Inner Mongolia; no one will think any further of it. You and Wei Wan grew up together, and now you are traveling to find a lost uncle. Last time anyone heard of him was in this area."

I am still not convinced Wei Wan will be the best companion. How will he be able to protect me if I need help? He is a thirteen-year-old boy. A skinny one at that.

But Master Li says, "Wei Wan will play the part perfectly. He already looks upon you as an older sister."

I cannot disregard the quick flush on my cheeks. The notion still touches me.

"You probably are the closest to a family he will ever

have. He was left at the temple doors when he was just an infant."

He is an orphan? Instantly, I am filled with guilt. Here, I have been moaning and complaining. I, who grew up in the best of loving circumstances for the first eight years of my life, had a wonderful father, mother, two siblings, and a home, while he's never had anyone. I understand now his reactions at the tournament, how horribly, deeply and vastly his fear of losing me must reach. And I, the only family he ever had, refused to prepare myself for an event that might have claimed my life. Might have left him all alone.

I battle to make my lips move. "That's why you let his hair grow."

"Yes. Neither of you can, in any way, be even remotely connected to a temple, to Long Si."

"How will we get there?"

"First, you will go on a bamboo raft up the Yulong River until you reach Li River. You will purchase a ticket on a sampan and travel up the Li to Guilin. From then on, you must continue by horse, donkey, and foot. It will be at least two moons until you reach Shaanxi province."

"And then?"

Once we get closer, Master Li tells me, we must ask locals for directions. The warlords have spies in the entire region. If we just show up on their doorstep, they will be suspicious. But the locals, I ask, will they really help us?

"Ah." Master Li smiles. "Some of them will." He hands me a scroll. "Here is a map and the names of villages, places and locals to look out for, our spies. They will point you in the right direction. Read this, memorize it, and burn it."

My fingers close around the scroll. "And once we reach their lair? Why should they take us in?"

"You will get a fake tattoo on the inside of your right wrist. I have arranged for the ink master to come tonight. He will prick your skin very lightly. It will wear off with time: the tattoo of the Nefarious, the witch triads, the small mark that all their abducted victims get. It means you are their property."

"But," I start.

"All crooks are opportunists. As much as they collaborate with the Syndicate, they wouldn't miss a chance to double-cross them."

It takes me a moment to see the brilliance. The warlord and his Sworn Brothers will think I am doing the witch triad's bidding, which means I have some sort of supernatural ability that can help *them*. They will allow me to enter with the aim of outsmarting the witch triads, take me and use me for their own purpose.

"There will be guards who will catch you," Li says. "You must appear as though you are hiding the tattoo, and they happen to see it by mistake."

"What if they turn me away before they see it?"

"Well," Master Li purses his lips. "I assume you might have to use a bit of womanly charm."

My hands go clammy at the embarrassing memory of being saved from Steel Master. "You expect me to..."

"A little flirting might be necessary. Or it might not. I can't tell you."

"I haven't been trained in that."

"I'm sure you can think of something."

I snort. "We will be armed?"

"Of course. Unfortunately, you cannot bring any of our quality weapons, that would be a clear giveaway. You will each be given two worn swords of inferior grade, purely as a decoy, to take unwanted attention off hidden weapons."

I think of the older boys picked for herblore that Wei Wan told me about. "Poison?"

He nods.

"I haven't been trained in herblore either."

"Not you."

My reply is a few seconds late. "Wei Wan?" I gape. "I thought only older boys got selected for that."

"We made an exception. We have been training him intensively for the past five moons." He scoffs at my expression, "No, you can't get mad at him. We made him swear to keep it a secret."

"He has been trained for this?"

"He has. He will carry the bag of a healer's apprentice."

"Since when have you known? That I was...the one who might have heart magic?"

"Since your first moon bleeding."

My face grows so hot with embarrassment my gaze slides all over the place. I want to sink through the earth.

Thankfully, he says, "You can talk more about that with Cook Ma. She will set you up with money and equipment."

"When do we leave?"

"Tomorrow, an hour before dawn, before anyone awakes. Only me, three other masters, and Cook Ma know about this."

"I understand." I turn to leave.

"And Lu Mi La."

I turn in the doorway.

"Don't fail me."

CHAPTER 25

A S I LEAVE THE PAVILION OF THE SLEEPING BEAR, MY heart rushes. *Mission*. Me and Wei Wan. We did it; we got picked! Out of all the one hundred students, it was us. Excitement builds so rapidly that a bubble of laughter swells and nearly explodes in my chest. I sway with giddiness at the thought of the look on Yong Da's face; just imagine when he finds out. I stop short.

It feels like losing my balance. That fluttering sensation that things are not as they should be. Something is wrong. Terribly wrong.

On the ground is a mess of fur and dark patches. Warning signals wail in my entire system. *No*. The outside lanterns are too far away, and I can't see, but as I approach, my stomach wrenches. I want to stop and turn around, but something compels me, some twisted inner darkness that shouts and screams at me to run and stay simultaneously. There is blood, so much blood. White fur smeared in blood. Glazed eyes and no life. Habllek.

I sink to my knees. Stabbed by cold blades, I break into hysterical sobbing. Someone is nearby. Wei Wan. He must have known Master Li was going to tell me of the mission and waited out here. He kneels beside me and puts an awkward hand on my shoulder. I can't talk to him, I can't say thank you, I can't think. I touch the smeared fur as though trying to heal her, breathe life back into my beloved friend—sister. Wei Wan just sits silently by my side. I do not know how long has passed, but my eyes are sore from gushing tears, and I have moved up the scale from bottomless sorrow to vicious hatred.

"I'm going to kill him."

"Not now."

"I have a knife. What dormitory is he in? Which bed?"

"No, stop."

I rise and stomp away, but Wei Wan grabs my arm.

It is his touch that sends me over. The slight pull of his fingers holding me back triggers an uncontrollable urge to hit, to *hurt*.

I yank my shoulder free, and he yanks it back.

I whirl before I can stop myself, and my fist connects with his cheek. A sickening sound, and I nearly fling him into the nearest wall. "Stay out of it!"

"No," he bounces after me, hand on cheek. "You can't!" he hisses, hardly able to move his jaw. "Tomorrow, we leave for our mission."

"I don't care about a stupid mission!"

"Quiet! You'll wake the others."

I stride off, but he jumps me from behind. The impact is so hard I crash to the ground in a bone-jarring thud. I struggle to fight him off, but he is all over me, pushing me down, digging sharp fingers into my arms. "Stop it," he begs. "Stop it."

I have never felt his strength like this before or met him in actual combat. A skinny kid, only thirteen, but as tall as me now. My back screams from pain, and fury overtakes me. I try to get up, but he pushes me down and strikes me, trying to slap some sense into me and force me to calm down. I fight him wildly. I cry, bite, snarl, twist, and soon his strikes rain down on me. But I do not feel them anymore. I do not feel the hard stone that grinds into my spine. I do not feel anything except the strangling grip on my heart. The one that stops my blood and makes it impossible to breathe.

I stop fighting. I stopped long ago.

Crouched over me, Wei Wan is crying.

We bury Habllek in the hills behind the temple. We take a small shovel from the tool shed and a lantern to see in the forest, and I go to my room and get my Sámi bracelet of pewter and reindeer hide. After we reach the hills, we find a good spot away from the trail. Wei Wan digs a deep hole, and I scour the grounds for a suitable gravestone.

My heart feels skewered by a thousand nails. She was my first friend here, but now she is gone. I inscribe her name with charcoal on the stone and place it at the top of the grave. Then, I loop my bracelet around a straight, hard branch and stick it in the ground beside it. *Goodbye, sister*. The Sámi bracelet was the last evidence of my heritage. Together, they form the bridge between my new and old lives, but now the bridge has collapsed. And me, have I truly moved from that initial feeling, that weightless state where I felt stared at yet unseen? This feeling that I could not name? Not at eight. Or nine. Or sixteen.

I clamp my jaws together. Yes.

Yes, I have.

Cook Ma has managed to get us ready with knapsacks, leather harnesses for our cheap, worn swords, the healer's bag with potions for Wei Wan, money, food, and a small cage with two pigeons for messaging.

"And," she says as I bend to inspect my knapsack. "Several thin towels for your moon bleedings."

How could I think she would forget? The three of us slip quietly out of Long Si and walk east, first up into the forest, then down to the riverbank, but further away than I have been before, to where the water is wide and swollen.

"Once you find him," she whispers, nodding at the cage, "we'll be waiting for your message." In the early dawn, I see a glimmer in her eyes, and finally, I fully understand that veiled darkness. It must originate from the lost brother, the Middle Master of Long Si. He is the one who owns her heart. He is the one we must find and free.

She stops whispering and changes the topic. "Remember, ancient fortresses were originally designed to protect in times of war. You will be spied upon. There are always ways."

She gives us both a quick embrace, and we climb up on the raft. Hands on the bamboo, she follows us into the water and gives the raft a strong push. As we glide into the dusky morning of the tenth moon, I look back at her standing waist-high in water, her hand raised in a silent goodbye. I raise my hand back, touching the small bandage that still covers my fresh tattoo.

Eventually, I turn my head, and we begin using our poles to push ourselves forward, passing through endless rice fields and the pointy karst mountains that characterize the region. An early morning fisherman is out with his cormorants, the big black birds trained to catch fish and keep them in their throats. Beyond his wide-brimmed hat, in the light of a lantern pegged to a pole, I see them hop from the water and up onto his raft. Silvery streaks glide out of their mouths as they bend their necks forward.

We push on until midday. The lush green landscape is hypnotic, and the blooming jasmine drapes us with a heavy, perfumed scent. I feel the connection to the water, and when kingfishers fly by like streaks of blue, they etch long, thin trails of beauty in my heart.

This should be wild and adventurous, but all I can think of is Habllek. I see her broken body, the white fur smeared with red, and my heart wants to split. Gush out a sorrow so great it brings me all the way back to Sápmi, this almost forgotten place that is still not. In my mind, I find myself among lost reindeer calves and their mourning *vajans*, not understanding, searching, calling and running. *Where are you, my child? Come back.* Habllek was my sister. My grief is too deep.

I recall my hushed conversation with Cook Ma in those dark hours before we left. It was not long after the Ink Master had finished the tattoo on the inside of my wrist that I asked about my powers, only marginally less embarrassed than I was with Master Li.

"Cook Ma," I began. "My heart magic." She smiled in

recognition, a proud smile. "Master Li said you've both known about it, or at least suspected it, since my first moon bleeding." I could not stop blushing when I said the word. "How did you do it? How did you work it out?"

"By watching Yong Da." The reply hit me with a mixture of genuine alarm and disgust, but Ma continued, "You may have noticed that he's become angrier and more frustrated with you at certain times."

I could only snort as I continued packing.

"Do you recall when the first time was?"

"When I had my first moon bleeding."

"Many gifts start to manifest more strongly, or take root in the body when a girl moves into womanhood."

This I knew, the Triple Goddess, Ah Mei taught me. The moon bleeding represents the conclusion of a cycle in the Goddess's life: the maiden, the mother, and the crone, which symbolize a separate stage in the female life cycle and a phase of the moon.

I gaped in horror. "He could tell I had my moon bleeding?"

"Not exactly, but Yong Da, like me, is very sensitive to energies. He noticed a shift at some level. Consciously or subconsciously, he could sense that you were coming into your powers. And that is what he fears."

I was stunned. That pig-headed brute, sensitive to energies? It hit me then: *That's* why I had the feeling of the Hexfinder that time when he was staring at me in scripture class so many years ago. He was checking out my energies and probably gauging them as well.

"And the second time?" I asked.

"You tell me."

"The tournament?"

"Exactly. You aligned better with your powers; the challenge forced you to command them." She placed a hand on my shoulder. "I really *am* sorry you had to go through that." But we both knew all of that was past us now. Still, she squeezed my shoulder, and I briefly put my hand on top of hers. "It made him furious. Even though he couldn't grasp any of this with his analytical mind, he could sense your shift. His worst fears were coming true." She glanced at me in the flickering light of a candle. "In a few moons' time, you'll be back here. I know you won't forgive him for Habllek, but remember, you can beat him with your inner strength."

Yes, I will remember. Now, here on the Yulong River, Cook Ma's words churn in tandem with my pole pushing in and out of the water. Yong Da is the foulest person I know, and he has proved himself more dangerous than I ever imagined. Clever, too. He killed my animal sister out of jealousy for not being sent on this mission. How did he know I was going on a mission?

It is dusk when we moor our raft and climb onto dry land to settle for the night. I give the pigeons water and seeds while Wei Wan plucks out *baozi* and tofu that Cook Ma has packed for us. I am ravenous. And excited. I have frequently been out of Long Si, but never this far, not since the Silk Road. Too long ago. I bite into my bread.

"And this," Wei Wan says and hauls out a bundle from

his knapsack. And then another one.

"Is what?" I ask between mouthfuls.

He unrolls the first one to reveal six shining throwing knives; Skyhawk, the top brand. My *baozi* sticks to the roof of my mouth.

"Where did you get those from?" I manage.

"Master Li."

"Whatever for? We don't know how to use them."

"You don't."

My mind processes this. "No. Don't tell me they trained you in this as well. I am the only one left out, again?"

"Honestly, *jie*. You have been struggling since you got to Long Si. Don't you think you had enough on your plate?"

"No one gets trained in knives until group four," I protest.

"I was an exception."

"How long?"

"Two years."

"Two years?"

"Master Bao taught me privately. Nobody was to know."

"Both knife throwing and herblore, no wonder you've been busy. And no wonder you gave me all those vague excuses every time I pressed you."

"I also practised on my own."

"That's why you were able to hit that bamboo snake in the kitchen. And that's why I ran into you at the armory," I say triumphantly.

"You never told me what *you* were doing there," he counters.

I grin. "Stealing a knife."

It hits me, then. Wei Wan has always been small and

skinny and never excelled at anything. Never had a role to play. Until now. This makes him feel important and valuable. "I'm very grateful that you are here to protect me," I add.

A hint of relief crosses his features. He pulls out another bundle. Six throwing stars. "We'll split them."

"But I don't know how to use them," I protest.

"I will teach you."

"In two moons?"

"Some skill is better than no skill," he says wisely.

CHAPTER 26

"OUR OWN JOURNEY WEST," WEI WAN SAYS. WE are taking a break, munching dried fruit in the shade of a huge sequoia tree. He means the famous Song Dynasty legends about the Monkey King. The *Journey to the West* tells of a pilgrimage where the young monk Xuanzang goes in search of sacred texts. The Monkey King, who, for the most part, created chaos wherever he went, was made protector of the young monk. Together with two fellow disciples, they set out on their long journey.

"Right. Only it's north."

"Direction is irrelevant. It's an allegory."

"True," I say. "They had a mission; we have a mission."

"*But,*" Wei Wan's hands move in every direction, and his voice slows for dramatic effect. "Will the travelers reach their destination safely? Will they find what they are looking for?"

I catch on his animated style, "And do they have enough courage to conquer beasts and demons?"

Making his eyes big, Wei Wan leans in and whispers,

"Both those lurking around them and those within their own hearts?"

I burst out laughing. "I think you're the only demon around here."

"Really," he straightens up. "Fair enough. I thought you were going to dub me the Monkey King."

"Good idea, if I hadn't already done it to Yong Da. He's the Monkey King."

"Ew."

"I know. Luckily, I deem you better suited to protect me than to protect a sixteenth-century monk. You're not the obnoxious Monkey King, but the sworn defender of Mi La Reindeer, the amazing but primitive Ice Witch."

Wei Wan scoffs. "Don't adopt the nasty nicknames Yong Da calls you. Could be bad luck."

"Well, we know what happens to the Monkey King; the Buddha seals him under a mountain, and he's trapped for five hundred years."

"I wish."

"We should practice," I say.

"I'm resting."

"I thought you said you were on a pilgrimage."

"I am."

"And what, you think Xuanzang and the Monkey King sat around stuffing their faces with Beijing duck?"

"It's dried apricot."

"They were busy looking for demons."

He chews frantically. "Stale, too."

"Humor me this once, will you?"

"What's the rush?"

"Your pilgrimage. It set my mind on the warlords. We can't come unprepared."

"I guess." Wei Wan tosses the kernel over his shoulder. "First, any respectable envoy should know the characteristics of a good throwing knife. Dull edges and rounded corners but sharp points. It should be thick enough that the tip doesn't bend on impact. And no fancy grips or handles."

"Okay. What else?"

"For an accurate throw, you should stand up, and your body must be relaxed." He rises. "Place your right foot forward, left foot slightly behind. Like this."

I stand up and mimic his movements.

It's so different from using a sword I feel awkward already. The actual throwing is even worse.

After two days of marching, we finally spot Li River and the ferry harbour.

"Hurry up." I quicken my pace. "We don't want to miss the last sampan."

But as we wind through the crowds, following signs to find the right boat, our hopes sink. By the sign for Guilin, a horde of people is squashing themselves into something that, with only utmost imagination, might pass for a line.

The man at the front holds up his hand and shouts, "*Manle, manle.*"

"Oh, no," Wei Wan slows, but I grip his arm and push through the throng.

I address the man with the polite title *Shifu* and say, "We

really must get on this boat. My little brother here is very sick."
I squeeze Wei Wan's arm, and he immediately slumps his shoulders and lolls his head.

"*Manle.*"

"Yes, I understand it's full," I twist to keep eye contact through the mass of pressing arms and bodies. "Perhaps you could make an exception?"

"*Manle!*"

"Yes, *Shifu*, I understand, but you see, it's very important. He must see a specialist in Guilin."

I can see his mind go: A specialist? And you ragged lot can afford that? I squeeze like an eel through the last bit of people-barrier, step close and smile. A timid smile, a sad smile, but still, a *girl* smile.

The man's grunt disappears in the hustle and bustle of shouting travelers, and I press closer again. Very close. "He's all I have, our parents," I stop as though the memory is too painful. "*Bu haoyisi,*" this universal excuse erases the embarrassment for my emotional display. I try the timid smile again. Then, slightly bolder. Still sad, I bat my eyelashes.

"*Hao ba,*" he snaps, okay. He lifts the rope and waves us in, pigeons and all. "*Manle! Manle!*" He shouts to the crowd behind us, telling them to return tomorrow.

Next, we are aboard the sampan and gliding away in the water. Wei Wan smirks under his slumping posture. It's best to look sick for a few more minutes. "Stars above, *jie*. Did Master Li tell you to do that?"

"What?" I suppress the faint rush of adrenaline.

"I don't know. To use your womanly charms or something?"

"Don't be ridiculous."

"Ha, so he did, then. Good." With a grin, he squeezes in between a goat and a wrinkled old lady. "This will make things easier."

"Don't count on it, brat," I scowl as I search for an empty spot, but secretly, I am thrilled. It *worked*.

It is dark when we arrive in Guilin, and we skirt the city, finding a northbound road to keep us in the right direction. When everything has quieted and the solid night surrounds us, we find a small forest. We place our bedrolls on the ground and try to get some sleep. This we keep doing for several days. Street stalls with cheap food can be found almost anywhere, and they are usually good too, but the nights are rough.

After a week, I decide we have earned rest in a proper bed. We settle for a rustic inn with affordable prices. Wafts of fried *pak choy* and soy sauce hit our nostrils as we cross the noisy downstairs, where patrons loudly slurp and gobble down noodles and rice. No one takes any notice of us despite our sword harnesses and a cage with cooing pigeons. The room is basic, with two hard beds and a small mirror mottled from dampness and age.

Wei Wan goes back out again, but I stop in front of the mirror, staring mutely at my own reflection. I cannot recognize the person who stares back. I have not seen myself since the Silk Road, and the skinny child is long gone. My face and the rest of my body have filled out. I take a few steps back, pull my clothes tight and stare at my own curves. The hair that's come loose from my usual sloppy bun is long and thick. The brown eyes seem richer than I remember, as though years of hardship have deepened them. And the tattoo on my wrist still feels foreign.

The door opens and slams shut again. "So, are you going to tell me?"

I see Wei Wan in the mirror behind me. He stands with a wrap of three tofu skewers in each hand. My mouth waters.

I take the one he offers and start nibbling. "Tell you what?"

"About your magic."

I stop chewing. "Not unless you tell me how you knew."

"Master Li." He sits down on his bed and tears off a piece of tofu with his teeth.

"He told you?" I am about to embark on a tirade, but he holds up a placating hand.

"He had to. The mission. I had to know what I was getting myself into. And help you get your act together. Only I knew you were likely to get picked." He manages a grimace between mouthfuls, "None of us were too happy when you refused the elite training."

"So that's why I spotted you coming out of his office that morning, ha!" I triumph at his surprise. "You never knew I saw you."

"Only once?"

"What? You met several times? Ukko take you." I cuff him on the head, but he dodges with a grin, and I go back to devouring my food.

I tell him I can sometimes see people's hearts, and gauge their personalities. "Hidden Eyes said I must learn courage. Only then have I earned the right to borrow strength, and only then would my magic enable me to grow. Did I tell you it was me who called him? Well, I mean, *he* called *me*, activated my powers because he could tell I'm S—"

"No!" Wei Wan says sharply. "Don't say it. We don't talk about it."

"But why? Surely, it's safe here?" I gesture around the empty room, lowering my voice. "I want to know how you knew, Wei Wan." I lower my skewer and give him a hard glance. "That bit *no one* knows."

"We don't talk about it." He looks so alarmed I go quiet. As does he, a strange sort of quiet I can't read. But something tells me not to push.

I finish my last bit of tofu and lick my fingers. To break the silence, I say, "I'm glad you don't mind magic."

"Why would I?"

"I dunno," I shrug. "Yong Da hates magic. He's always accusing me of practicing it, even though he can't possibly have any idea..." With a frown, my words trail off.

"He's just afraid," says Wei Wan and finishes his skewer.

CHAPTER 27

WEI WAN PATIENTLY TRIES TO TRAIN ME IN MY NEW weapons. A knife does not travel through the air point first, like an arrow. Instead, it circles around its centre of gravity, which requires rotation and lateral movement.

"You must be consistent," he says as my fifth knife bounces off the target with a dull thud. For practice, we have picked a wall of an old, dilapidated house on the outskirts of some village. He hands me another knife. "Again."

I raise my arm over my head, elbow slightly bent, take aim and swing from the shoulder forward and downward. I follow through with my arm, letting go with my hand pointed.

Another sad thud.

"You snapped your wrist."

I growl.

"I told you, you don't need to do anything. These are professional throwing knives, their center of gravity sits exactly halfway between the end of the handle and the blade's tip."

"Both ends will trace out equal circles as it flies through

the air," I snap. "Yes, thank you, you told me."

He walks over to the wall and picks up all six knives. It takes until long into the evening before I am to hear my sad thud change to a *thwack*. But eventually, it does. And even though, from then on, it still only happens occasionally, I am overcome with relief.

After knife throwing, we burrow into our bedrolls and go to sleep. The following few days and nights are much the same; we are cold, stiff and miserable. Wei Wan begs for an inn, but I think of Old Bai, the trash collector, and tell him *xi shui chang liu*. We must live frugally so the money will last. And so, we push a bit further until we decide our need for a bed is desperate enough.

This evening we did, and I am now practicing meditation. Even just to sit on a bed is a luxury. However, I might be more prone to do so than Wei Wan.

"Are we done?"

"What does it look like, you clodhead?" I open one eye.

He gives me an insolent grin. "Well, your body posture kind of looked like you were done. And we've been going for ages." Throughout the journey, we practiced meditation, but Wei Wan moans, "I'm hungry."

"We already had supper."

"It was boring."

I have to admit, it was. This inn is very poor, and the food is no better. I have half a mind to go down and check that they don't throw our pigeons into some slow-cooking stew.

"Go get a cup of tea. Maybe they'll throw in a *wotou*," the steamed cornbread.

"Why don't you come? You're more persuasive; work

your womanly charms."

"In your dreams. Now go. And don't come back for a while," I order as he walks out the door. "I'm not done."

"Old nun," he says as he leaves.

It is the worst he can come up with, and I laugh. He just doesn't have a bad bone in him. I am tempted to follow, except I need my meditation to stay sharp. We are halfway through our trip, and once we reach our target, I must be at my best. A touch of worry breathes down my neck. *No.* I push it away. We will find our "uncle," and we will rescue him.

Through the countryside, we travel undisturbed in a steady rhythm for another week until a drunken guest at one of the taverns where we have stopped for a meal decides to take Wei Wan's bone carving. The round, flat piece with some obscure pattern is only a cheap trinket I bought for him at a market, I don't know why he's so attached to it. Wei Wan does not get riled easily, but this time he does. The drunken man holds the carving out of reach until Wei Wan is furious and left with two options: Jump for it or let it go. He does neither. At least he has the good sense not to start a *gong fu* fight right here.

Instead, he stomps on the thief's foot, just where small, fragile bones connect to the toes. The man roars angrily and drops the bone carving, which Wei Wan quickly snatches, and I step between them.

"That kid a friend of yours?" the man barks in my face.

Though I would much prefer to knock him out with a spear hand, all I do is bat my eyelashes. "Please forgive me. My little brother can be such a nuisance." I nod across his shoulder. "And are those your friends?" Two menacing figures have risen from the throng of curious gazes around us.

He produces a blurry smile and quickly waves them off. "My brothers can be a bit of a nuisance, too,". He grins, his gaze sliding up and down my body. "We should have a talk." He leans closer, breath thick and sharp. "Without brothers."

"You're right." I smile, though I'd rather vomit. "Let's sit over there, *shuai ge*," I say, pointing to the farthest table.

He laughs, embarrassed but pleased. "*Handsome guy*, heh."

"Oh, but you are."

He slumps on the rough bench across from me. "So, what's your name?"

"Let's have a beer." I wave at the serving girl and tell her two *pijiu*, which soon arrive. She places them in front of us, and I grab one, but just then, from the bushes behind me, comes the call of a bamboo partridge. Wei Wan.

"Did you hear?" I say. "Such an unusual bird?" I point at the bushes, and when he looks that way, I quickly swap our glasses. Pray Ukko I am guessing right: Wei Wan has dipped into his healer's bag and placed a drug in the glass that happened to land in front of me.

"The most unusual bird around here is you," my company slurs, gaze sliding back to me. "I'd like to get to know you." He offers a sleazy smile, and I offer one too. He puts his hand on my leg under the table, and I make a silly girl laugh, push it away and raise my glass.

"To you, *shuai ge*."

He takes a big draft, and his eyes slither unpleasantly across mine.

Not nearly drunk enough. I raise my glass again. "*Gan bei*."

"Right." He takes another two long drafts.

"I'm so thirsty, aren't you?" Up comes my glass once more, pretending to drink. "*Gan bei, shuai ge*," I bat my lashes, hoping desperately that the words *cheers* and *handsome* in one sentence will work their own magic. They do.

In a few gulping drafts, he empties the glass, bangs it down and produces an even sleazier smile. "Now, what was your nam—?" With a heavy thud, his head plonks onto the table.

I glance around. When no one is looking, I rise and slide smoothly into the bushes. Thank Ukko for rural taverns. Wei Wan stands with our harnesses and knapsacks ready. The pigeons sit quietly in the cage by his feet.

"I have to pay."

"I already did. Let's go." He tosses me my pack and takes off, pigeons flapping wildly at the cage's swinging motion.

I slip into my harness, wriggle into my pack and trot after him. "Heavens, you knocked him out fast; what was that?"

"Valerian root."

"It's not that strong."

"Five times the normal dosage it is."

"How did you do it?"

"*Jie*, what a stupid question."

He is right. After all our secret practice, that was a stupid question. I remind him I still haven't forgiven him for the time he slipped bitter melon juice into my food. We walk in the dark until we are too tired to continue, and Wei Wan is too exhausted to hear me tell him I got him out of trouble and that it wasn't the first time. *No, you're right*, he counters, *nor was it the last*.

"But look at it this way, *jie*, with all this practice, you're getting really good at your womanly charms."

"Would be good if you practiced something too."

"I do." He holds out his hand. A white stone with amber streaks lies in his open palm.

"You stole from him?"

"I figured I should prepare. You never know what skills might come in handy."

"You stole!" I repeat accusingly.

"He stole first." And I say he gave the bone carving back, and Wei Wan says he didn't. "I earned it back. There's a difference. And anyway, it's only a stone."

I frown in the dark. "I'll look at it tomorrow."

"Describe your homeland," Wei Wan says as we are taking a break along a dusty road. We have been walking for hours, and in the end, we decide to pause and regroup by a river that meanders peacefully through the landscape.

"You're asking me this now? After all these years?"

"Yeah. At Long Si, we're always so busy. There's not much time to really just...ponder things. Like small things."

"It seems so far away," I say.

Yet, I can still feel the dry press of cold on the *lávvu* walls. Smell the warm bodies from the herd, hear the Elders *joiking*, the traditional Sámi singing, filling the air like insistent prayers. But eventually, all sounds would subside, and the breaths around me would turn even. Only I would still be awake, part of me whispering what I could not understand. Twin spirit with a dragon? I did not know then what threads my soul was pulling.

I only knew that I had to step outside. Walk alone under the thick stars of the Polar night.

"It's white," I say.

"White?" says Wei Wan. "The color of death?"

"Well, I mean in winter. But that's how I think of it. Cold, sharp, beautiful and nothing to do with death. It's my favorite color, especially on animals." I think of Habllek and pain stabs my heart. "Our animal brothers and sisters never have an agenda. To me, they represent pure spirit."

Wei Wan chews on a straw and lays back on the sloping river bank. "If I die, I'm going to come back as something else and find you. So we can always be together."

"Why would you die?"

"Well, our battle will move from the practice yard to real life one day. It already has, right now. Things happen."

"You're not going to die."

"I know. But if I do, I'll come for you. Maybe I'll be a bird, a white bird, then I can fly and find you easily."

"You don't need to find me, I'll be at Long Si."

"But if you're not."

"You're being silly."

"I know."

"Long Si is for life, so stop your doleful predictions." Long Si is my place, even though they still haven't asked me to take my vows. Whenever I ask, Master Li waves me off.

"Just saying."

We both fall silent. Wei Wan fingers the stone he nicked at the tavern. I have looked at it more carefully, and it is not just a stone; it's *hetian* jade from Xinjiang. I saw it at the market in Kashgar. It is not very big, but still worth money.

"It fits in the middle of my palm," he says.

"Thief."

"In our trade, all skills are worthy."

I roll my eyes, but he says you'll see. Another two weeks have passed of journeying and practicing. We do as much *gong fu* as possible in the early mornings when our energy is still high. Sometimes, I am too tired when evening comes and can't focus on my knife throwing. But we keep at it a little every day.

Sometimes, he brings them out when we take a break, like now, and we practice away for an hour. But not this time. His talk of death has quieted us both. Nobody is going to die, I tell myself. But the idea of worming myself right into the tiger's lair sets a chill in my bones. Surrounded by heavily armed men, probably outnumbered one to a hundred.

"We should move." I rise and brush off my clothes. "I want to get some proper knife throwing in this evening."

CHAPTER 28

WE REACH THE SMALL TOWN OF JINGXIE FENG, NEAR the border of Shaanxi province, early in the evening. It is an old, poor area. The motor-driven vehicles I only spotted once or twice on the Silk Road do not exist here either. Nor do we see any traces of the Long March, where political leader Mao Ze Dong led his troops over a distance of six thousand miles. They came here right through Shaanxi, though that was several years ago. I am glad for the lack of any traces because the threat of a communist troop in every bush would have pushed our targets even deeper into their secret dens.

By now, we have traveled straight up through the country on boats, ox carts, donkeys and foot for nearly two moons. Winter is drawing near, and I detect a coolness in the evenings. The only thing motivating me to keep the pole with the pigeon cage bouncing off my shoulder is the faint rush of warmth it brings my body.

Soon, we will cross into the Han River Valley, the longest tributary of the famous Yangtze River. And then north again.

Always north.

I breathe a sigh of relief when lights penetrate the falling dusk. Naked electric bulbs glare from inside townhouses. Lit-up street stalls, simple shops and the murmur of voices once again surround us. The smell of roasted pigeon wafts into our nostrils as we pass vendors touting everything from thousand-year-old eggs to snake soup, deep-fried scorpion, grasshopper, and squid.

Wei Wan and I are starving. We decide on scallion pancakes and bean paste made with soy and rice vinegar. I extract some coins from my drawstring pouch and pay. Heat leaks through the pancake's thin wrapping, warming my hands and the smell makes my mouth water. We make our way through villagers gathered around the small town square, take off our knapsacks and settle down on a stone stair.

"What about the food?" He munches his pancake.

"What about it?"

"When we get to the fort, what do we do? First of all, we're vegetarians," he gobbles down some more. "Second, as Buddhist monks and nuns..."

"Yeah, I know." We're not allowed garlic, preferably not even onion, as it stimulates the senses and disturbs a peaceful mind, though, for the scallion pancakes, we made an exception. "Well, we..." I finish my delicacy far too quickly. "Hope that we don't get served any."

"I want to try garlic." Wei Wan rubs his brow. "How much longer?"

I don't know, and quite frankly, there are many things I don't know. Why did we get picked for this mission? Yong Da has probably read every book by Sun Tzu and practiced spying to perfection. And so many other strong fighters, like everyone in Group Four. Or Ya Li Shan Da, or Apple. For a fleeting second, I fantasize that it is Apple beside me. The thought is gone as fast as it comes, but still, I wonder, why did Master Li send an inferior girl and a thirteen-year-old boy on a principal mission? Is it because we can play the sister-brother thing? Making the setup believable? Perhaps.

The money Cook Ma gave us would last well enough if we were frugal, like Old Bai, she said, and it has, though I don't know how much will be left for our return. Still, tonight, again, we decide on the luxury of an inn, though it is full, and I have to use all my charm to get us a room. It is very basic, just like at Long Si. I must stop comparing everything to Long Si. It may cause me to slip, say something that will give us away once we find the warlords. If we find them.

"Master Li was right," I begin after I have wriggled out of my knapsack and harness. The pigeons had to go in the stable. I would rather keep them close in such poor quarters, but getting just the two of us into a room was as far as the flirting took me. "It really does work."

"Of course, it works." Wei Wan throws himself on one of the simple beds. "Girl delights, the oldest trick in the book."

"Girl delights," I say with a scowl. "That's not what I'm doing. Just...smiling a little."

"Of course."

I scowl some more.

"Hey, you hear me complain?" He raises mollifying palms. "You've helped us plenty. I knew you'd be good; I've seen you practice on Apple."

"What! You cheeky little—"

He jumps up, but I slam a pillow with such force it hits him square in the head, and the threadbare cover tears. Scrawny, moth-eaten feathers fly all over the room. He looks so ridiculous I burst into hysterical laughter.

"We'll see," he says, snorting through a flurry of white, "if the grumpy owner thinks it's funny." He brushes down from his arms. "I doubt your womanly charms will get you out of this one."

The closer we get to our target, the more thoroughly we perform our routines. We spar and refine kicks and punches, standard sequences and more advanced ones. And, of course, our new weapons. The stars are smaller, thinner and have lesser mass than the knives, which makes them more accurate. Still, mastering an unfamiliar tool in such a short time presents a great challenge.

Wei Wan disagrees. "You know the star is easier to learn," he presses. "It's got better spin than the knife."

I have worked on letting the star slip out of my hand by itself rather than flinging it, and now I stand ready, holding the stack horizontally in my left hand. As he nods, I let the edge of my right thumb catch the star's center hole to slide it off the stack and grasp it, eyes still on the target. Only a light tensing of the fingers and wrist at the moment of release, and I send the top one on its way. And the next and the next and the next.

Thud, thud, thud. *Thwack, thwack, thwack.*

I stare in disbelief.

"Not bad," says Wei Wan.

"What do you mean not bad? That was awesome!"

"It's surrounded by pointed tips. That increases its chance to pierce a target."

"A hit is a hit," I snap.

"The piercing capability is low compared to a knife, though."

"Still very damaging. Especially if you hit a major artery, or eyes, or throat."

"When I had practiced as long as you, I was hitting moving targets in multiple directions."

"Of course you were." I go to pick up my stars.

That's when I hear a chuckling and turn. "I was only teasing. You're doing really well." Wei Wan snorts with laughter at my outburst. "It took me twice as long to get to that level."

"Oh, you clod!" I lunge at him.

More than a week has passed since we reached the southern tip of Shaanxi province. I am starting to recognize the names of villages from the map Master Li gave me. So far, we have asked the way twice and *think* we got the correct directions from the right people.

Now we are in Ying Pei, a sleepy place closer to the mountains, and we try not to attract attention by walking at a slow but steady pace, looking as if we know where we are going.

I sneak surreptitious glances. "Search for a shack with a wire fence around it."

Wei Wan nods right, and I let my gaze slide. Outside a ramshackle hut, on a rickety chair, a lady who looks to be a hundred years old is busy smoking a pipe. We slowly draw near, but the lady pays us no heed.

I stop by the fence and clear my throat.

"*Zhao shei ah?*" She hardly looks up as she inquires whom we're looking for.

I explain that me and my little brother are searching for our lost uncle. The last time we heard of him, he was in this area. But we have no idea where to look.

"*Bu zhidao,*" she slurs lazily. Don't know.

"But it's our uncle," I stress. "Can you really not help?"

She sucks on her pipe and waves a bony arm at the deep forest behind us. "Perhaps he went to the lair. Some beast there apparently. Luring people in..." Her dreamy expression tells me we've already lost her.

"A beast?" Wei Wan blurts. "That's not what we're—"

I put an arm around his shoulder and tell him, don't worry, little brother. "*Xiao didi, bie danxin.* I'm sure we'll find Uncle." I thank the old lady and steer him back onto the gravel road.

"We must ask someone else," he protests under his breath.

"No," I hiss. "Lair is the code word for the warlord's fortress. She is one of us; she just pointed us in the right direction."

We continue until night falls. Then we head into the forest and make camp. It has been a long time since we passed a street stall or a food market, but we have eaten our fill of the Shaanxi spiced food. We've had to use lots of soy sauce and vinegar to dilute the heat. Right now, even just the wrinkled apples we have are good. All I want is to get there. It has been a long trip, and gloom is beginning to set on me.

Two more days pass, and three times we ask locals for help, and one of them speaks of the beast in a lair. Again, pointed in the right direction, we trudge along forgotten roads, forging deeper into the Qinling base. The fresh mulberries we bought are already gone, but we nibble on our stash of dried bayberries, jujubes, and walnuts. In a last tribute to Old Bai, I had gotten the ones with shells; they were cheaper. We use stones to crush them, and twice I hit my thumb and swear out loud. The temperature is dropping, bringing a harsh dusty wind from the north. We have not climbed any proper mountains, just various degrees of incline, but I am exhausted. Dirt is collecting under my fingernails, and hunger has begun to gnaw at my stomach. I glance at the tattoo on my wrist. My ticket into the fort. Yet I cannot shake the feeling that I am marked.

We place the bedrolls close to each other and tuck in for yet another chilly night. I am so tired I sleep deeply, dreaming that something pokes my forehead. Something steely. And sharp. I blink awake.

And gasp at the sword tip between my eyes.

CHAPTER 29

WITH A YELP, I LEAP FROM MY BEDROLL. WEI WAN is at my heels, the pigeons flapping wildly in their cage, frightened by the early commotion.

"What are you doing here?" asks a stern voice.

It belongs to a meaty, broad-shouldered man with a knotty beard and long hair. His old-style rough leathers are reinforced with spiked arm guards, just like in the history books at Long Si. Beside him stands a second man, and in the woods behind them, I see horses tethered to a tree.

"We're looking for our uncle," says Wei Wan in a trembling voice. The man flicks the sword to his throat, and he shrinks.

"Please." I shift my weight. "Don't hurt my little brother. It's true, we're searching."

"For your uncle?" The second man looks just as nasty.

"Brother? You don't even look the same," the first one snorts.

"She's my sister!" Wei Wan yells in an outburst so

convincing I am not even sure it's an act.

"We are like siblings," I hurry. "My mother comes from Xinjiang, and my father from Inner Mongolia, but none of that matters. *Xiao didi* and I grew up together, and now we have come to search."

"*Shushu,*" Wei Wan sobs quietly. *Uncle.*

"This is where he was last heard from. They say there is a beast in some lair where people get lured in and disappear. Do you know where that is? Do you know where we can find him?"

The men exchange a look.

"No idea," says the first one.

"But we've heard a rumor," I insist.

"And we don't care," the second one snaps. "Off with you."

"Xingjiang, Inner Mongolia," number one snorts. "You're probably both from some pigsty around the corner."

Wei Wan slips another quiet sob and fingers something that flashes white. The stone he nicked.

"What's that?" says number one, the meaty man.

"*Hetian* jade," Wei Wan whispers. "From Xinjiang."

"How come you have it?"

Wei Wan only sniffles.

"My grandmother gave it to him," I say. "Our families knew each other before we were born. Please," I hint at tears. "We must find Uncle."

"I *said*—" the second man starts.

But the meaty one interrupts, "Give it here."

Wei Wan reluctantly hands over the white stone, sobbing even more as the big man inspects it and slips it into his pocket. "*Hetian* jade, all right. I'll keep this one."

Good, he gained something. "We really must find him." I hide my face in the crook of my arm, hitching up the sleeve just a fraction. I pretend to be sniveling, but I catch the guard's glance at my tattoo and then at his companion, who glances back.

I suppress a sob.

"Well...we might know something," says number two.

Number one gestures. "Pick up your stuff."

We scramble to get our gear together, then gravitate to each other like two petrified mice. My heart lurches in fright as rough hands put a blindfold over my eyes, and for a moment, I am eight years old again. *Breathe. Calm. Not the slave market.*

But is a warlord fort any better?

After several hours on horseback, I am so weary I can hardly sit up. My seat is sore, and my legs ache. When we finally dismount and are relieved of our blinders, I gawk at a monumental stone fortress surrounded by forest and mountains. The big square building is fringed by three crenelated walls of different heights. The outer, widest one, which is the lowest, is a good ten feet high with massive gates. It is an ancient structure, repaired with big patches of mortar and ill-fitting stone. Beauty was never a factor. This is solid strength.

As we pass through enormous gates, lead fills my body. I dare not even look at Wei Wan. Armed guards glare and step aside, and we cross the expansive outer yard, every step feeling like one further away from safety.

There are no sentries at the second gate, and we proceed

toward the main entrance. I surreptitiously observe, and my eyes fall upon a faint circle drawn on the stone wall. Right beside a big wrought iron cauldron, a fire holder, it's not even three feet tall, and with the wall's poor state, I can just barely discern it.

I am back at Long Si for a moment, which is strange. Then I realize it is not a drawing; it's a small moon door. It reminds me of Second Archive.

We enter through the next set of gates, and I feel I am going back in time. The wood is grooved and worm-holed, studded with worn metal rivets and held by heavy hinges of cast iron. The score of guards that spill out from the fort all exude the same vibration of bygone eras; that brutal roughness, dirty, bearded, leather-clad.

"What'd you bring this lot for?" a man growls but quiets as our captors give him some signal I cannot see.

Mutters are exchanged, and they move on to inspecting.

"Do you always go armed when you're looking for relatives?"

"Roads can be dangerous," I mumble.

Somebody pulls the sword from my back and scoffs. "Cheap trash."

Another one adds, "When'd you last sharpen this, girl? Couldn't kill a mouse with it."

They break out in harsh laughter. As Wei Wan's bag is opened, they rifle through it, but when he tells them that he is a healer's apprentice, they quickly tire. They tear the black cloth off our small cage, and inside, the two pigeons screech in a whirl of feathers.

"So we can send word back home when we find Uncle,"

I offer.

Wei Wan and I keep our gazes lowered, and I pray to Ukko they won't search our clothing. Beneath my linen binding, a dirk presses against my breastbone. The insides of my thighs are sweaty from the straps with the three morning stars and six Skyhawk knives.

A guard appears and breaks up the scoffing. "Enough," he sneers. "*Laoban* is ready."

The boss.

In China, important people make you wait, a sign of dominance. This was unusually fast, but I guess we are already as dominated as they come.

"This way," says the guard and leads us inside.

We are marched along corridors, through open rooms and across two courtyards. As we reach a set of tall doors, the guard who leads us stops and knocks.

The doors swing open, manned by two guards inside, swords at their hips. I shiver. This is the big boss, the one we must fool, maybe kill, and save our "uncle." My palms begin to sweat.

We enter a hall with an open fire crackling at one end, a large table and an old-style Chinese sofa complemented by several ceramic stools that you can heat by putting coal inside. The walls are hung with large paintings, traditional motifs of the Yellow Mountains, calligraphy, and Chinese tigers. It could have been an illustration from our schoolbooks. Small trees in pots covered with white stones line one entire wall. It is sparse yet classically stylish, displaying ample wealth in this poor province.

Two men at the table look up from a map, and by the

window, a third man turns to inspect us. He does not wear a military uniform bedecked with medals like the modern warlords of the 1920s, which, as far as warlords go, would be the closest to the present time. Instead, he looks like something out of the Qing Dynasty. Long leather coat with shoulder caps and breastplate, a fur-lined mantle and dirks in golden sheaths. I blink. This one sticks to tradition.

The greeting I receive is one long, cold stare. "My men tell me you are looking for a lost uncle?"

"Yes."

"Armed?"

For a second, I freeze, before I realize he means our cheap swords. "Danger can appear where you least expect it."

"Pigeons?"

"To send a message when we find him."

"And you're from?"

I tell the story we have rehearsed in as much detail as I can without it seeming forced. He softens a little, and I battle to keep my nerves under control. "Can you help—"

One of the men at the table rises. "Laoban, let me take care of this. I'll have my men interrogate them properly."

Laoban keeps his distance, but I can see his gaze searching my right arm. I am careful to keep my tattoo hidden. "That won't be necessary."

"Should you really waste your time on such trivial matters?" The man by the table gives me a stern look. "I've executed all present orders. I have time." This must be his second. A savage. For a moment, I think of Yong Da.

"That, Urg, will be all." Laoban nods. "Warg." Another nod.

The second man rises as well. Urg's mantle flutters over his studded leather outfit as he sweeps past, Warg at his heels. They glare like hyenas.

I notice Laoban has a tattoo of his own, the character for water, on the inside of his forearm. As soon as the doors click shut, I try anew. "Uncle, we must find him."

He looks out the window. "Yeah, you said."

"Can you help?"

He weighs the answer. "*Keneng ba*," perhaps. "At any rate, you are my guests for the night, and I will provide you with the meager comforts I can offer."

The famous false modesty, which we can only accept and show appreciation for. Right now, I am mostly grateful that he kept us from his second; thank Ukko, this one ranks higher. However, it feels like a thin reassurance.

"*Xie xie nin, duo xie.*" We thank profusely, smile, bow our heads and press our palms together. Despite everything, I feel a sense of relief. We are in, and we still have our weapons and Wei Wan's healer bag.

He waves away our praise. "You will sleep on the second floor, on the east side, not far from my office."

I almost snort. *How very helpful, thank you.*

"There will be a man posted outside your door. For your protection."

"Of course." I was waiting for that. I have a feeling moving around might not be so easy.

He waves a guard over. "Show our guests to the bathing cellar and then to their room."

I dare a smile. "Thank you. I'm so glad you will try to help us find *Shushu,*" Uncle. "*Xiao didi*"—little brother—"did you hear that? The kind man is going to help us."

Wei Wan nods appreciatively.

A short while later, we are in the cellar, where an excavated chamber holds a roaring fire and several wooden bathtubs. A man and a woman with rolled-up sleeves begin to fill two tubs with warm water, then place a screen between them so Wei Wan and I are separated. A hot bath. Too good to be true. Shivers race up my arms in the cold, dank cellar.

I quickly undress, careful not to reveal my weapons. We have already anticipated this scenario and practised undoing hidden weapons and slipping them off together with our clothes.

But just as I get naked, I freeze—my fake tattoo! It is only very lightly etched into my skin, and even though it is safe with water, I am not sure it can take a serious scrubbing. Already, the lady has armed herself with a brush that looks fit to clean a horse's hooves. Demanding, she points at the tub.

"Ah, *bu hao yisi*," the fake embarrassment to excuse myself. To decline her service will make her lose face, as though she is not good enough. "My skin is very sensitive. *Yisheng* says I should never scrub it."

"*Yisheng?*" A frisson of relaxation touches her face.

"*Dui, yisheng.*" That's correct, the doctor.

"*Na, hao ba. Suibian nin.*" She tells me to do as I please, leaves her tools on a chair and walks away. Because if the doctor says it, you must listen. The ubiquitous respect for authority is seldom questioned.

I climb into my bath, shut my eyes and sink into pleasant heat until a yelp snaps me from my heavenly comfort. On the other side of the screen, Wei Wan is being harshly scrubbed by the man with the rolled-up sleeves, making me grin.

Robes have been provided, and once we are done, we put them on, grab our clothes and step outside. The guards are waiting. They take us from the cellars up to the second floor. We walk silently, passing storage rooms, halls and chambers with locked doors. At regular intervals, torches cast their dim sheen across barren walls.

Up here, it is quiet. All I hear is our own footsteps that echo ominously in the long corridors. But then I pick up something else. Two men come around the corner.

One of them pushes me against the cold stone wall so fast I flinch, dropping the bundle of clothes and hidden weapons. My heart races, but no *clink* is heard. Wei Wan is already seized. Urg and Warg.

Warg jerks his chin, and our guards disappear. He covers Wei Wan's mouth and drags him off.

Urg's scarred face is two inches from mine, his stink of sweat suffocating. "You're hurting me," I huff.

"Who are you?"

"My name is Lu Mi La."

"What do you want?"

"I'm looking for my uncle."

"Wrong answer."

"What are *you* doing?" I snarl. "We're guests of Laoban. I will tell him."

"Oh yeah. And how do you know it wasn't him that sent us?"

I suppress my fear. "Let me go."

He pushes me even harder against the wall, grips my right wrist and squints at my tattoo. "It's true then," he mutters.

"Let *go* of me." I curl away from him and yank back my arm.

"You better have some skill to show us, girl. Or your days are numbered."

"Where's my brother?"

"I wouldn't worry about him just yet. Especially since he isn't your brother." He gives me an icy look and walks away.

Before the shudder down my spine has even waned, the original guards materialize and resume their escort.

We proceed as if nothing has happened.

CHAPTER 30

O UTSIDE OUR DOORS, ANOTHER GUARD IS WAITING. He opens it and lets me in. Wei Wan is standing in the middle of the room.

"Ukko, save me," I gasp.

We rush close and unite in a tight embrace.

Face pale, he steps back, voice low. "Do you think they know?"

"They know we're not who we say we are."

"Do you think it was Laoban? Did he order them to rough us up?"

I sit on one of the beds. "I'm not sure, but they're ready to devour me."

"What are we going to do?"

"Nothing changes. Have supper. Try and find out about Master Li's brother. He must be here somewhere."

"Can you use your magic?"

"In close combat, I can; for anything else, I'm not sure."

Clean clothes have been laid out, neutral garments that fit

well enough. I guess they don't have too many women working here, apart from possible pleasure girls. Now that we've had a close-up taste of the inhabitants, the idea of being inside probably the best-organized warlord cartel in China makes my chest hurt.

We debate in hushed voices whether to bring weapons or not. Finally, we settle for just two each. I have not been properly trained in throwing, but according to Wei Wan, Master Li wanted me to have them, nonetheless. Any weapon, he had claimed, is better than none.

I settle for two of the slim Skyhawks on the inside of my thigh. They're meant to be worn on the outside, but I dare not, lest my linen clothing reveal any shape.

A knock on the door is followed by a voice that tells us to be ready in ten minutes. Silently, we wait. I am so hungry I could eat a horse, yet my stomach clenches. How will I convince the warlord, Laoban, to reveal anything? Make him slip information about an important prisoner? He seemed courteous enough, but that was just for face. And he wants me because he thinks I am property of the witch triads. What if he asks about my paranormal skill that I'm supposed to have? I will have to tell him something, or should I pretend I don't know what he is talking about? No. Yes?

A bang on the door. I jump.

We rise and look at each other. "Whatever happens," I whisper. "Stay calm. Do not anger them."

"And look for useful things," Wei Wan whispers back.

Our guards lead us away, for protection. I silently snort at this silly idea and wonder if I could outsmart them in a fight. I nudge my thighs together. *Knives in place.*

Laoban welcomes us to a table where servants bring a host of traditional delicacies. He insists we must try common dishes and those unique to the region. There is; *biang biang*—the spicy, long-style, thick noodles, *rou jia mo*—the open bun stuffed with pork, hot and sour dumplings, tofu, and steamed spinach with garlic. And several pots of green tea.

I dip a vegetable dumpling in soy sauce and vinegar, which melts on my tongue.

"*Lai, lai.*" Here, here, our host points at various plates. "You must try this one. And this one."

In China, the only way to honor your host is to eat as much as possible. Not until you are unpleasantly full will he be satisfied. I am about to take a *baozi* before I realize they have meat filling. It's usually very little, but I haven't had meat for eight years. My stomach will not take it.

I excuse myself. "*Bu hao yisi*"—I'm sorry—"but I won't be eating the *baozi*."

Laoban doesn't listen. "*Lai ba, lai ba.*" Here, have some more.

"So sorry, but no, thank you."

He insists, and unease crawls up my spine. If I do not eat, he will lose face. In China, it is not common to eat only vegetables unless you are Buddhist, somehow tied to a temple, or very poor. I cannot risk him making the connection to Long Si, but to readily reveal that my family is so impoverished that we cannot afford meat means a face loss for *me*. In China, I have to play their game.

Can I use the doctor trick twice? I doubt the bath lady has informed anyone of my skin condition, it would be safest for her not to. After all, she could have in some way displeased me, the honored guest of Laoban.

"I have a—uh, my stomach gets very easily upset. The doctor said I should not have meat."

"Ah, the doctor?"

I nod.

Our host accepts this, and I feel a massive relief until I see that Wei Wan has not at all caught onto what I was doing. Greedily, he reaches for a *baozi* and devours it. I wince. Could he not tell there was meat in it?

We exchange some pleasantries. Laoban asks how our baths were and if everything is to our satisfaction. We reply in the positive and eat with good appetites to give our host honor, but I am anxious. How long before Wei Wan's stomach reacts?

He devours another *baozi*.

Ukko, take you. I feel the muscles in my face tightening, but I can't say anything. We are not alone for even one moment. Servants dash in and out, guards at the door. I am burning to find out about Master Li's brother, but I brace myself. Appearing stressed during a meal will not do. We must take our time and enjoy the hospitality.

Wei Wan is getting a glazed look in his eyes. *Oh, no.* Soon, he starts to look uncomfortable. He came to Long Si as a baby, he has never had meat in his whole life.

He rises abruptly. "*Bu shufu.*" Not feeling well.

I rush up, every inch the worried sister. "*Xiao didi,* What's wrong? Are you sick?"

"Bathroom," he mumbles and rushes out.

The guards snap to attention. I make an attempt to accompany him, but outside, two other guards wait, and he waves me away.

As soon as the doors close, I wring my hands in distress. "Oh, *xiao didi*, what can be wrong? I hope it's nothing serious."

"I'm sure he will be fine," says my host.

I bite my lip, as if struggling with emotion. "He's all I have. Mother and Father are dead, and Uncle—" I stop. "Do you really think you can help us find him?"

"Let us eat some more."

I overstepped. I flash a quick smile and praise the food again. And the tea, fantastic, I have not had such a good tea ever.

"Try the garlic sautéed spinach."

We don't eat onion, but to refuse both meat and garlic is too unusual.

He looks at me expectantly.

"I am so very full."

He persists, and in the end, I give in, hoping I will not get any reaction. He seems more relaxed now that it is just the two of us. No servants at the moment, but still two guards at the door. Is the man never alone? I make myself smile until I am tired of it. Do I dare bring up Uncle again?

"I'm sure we have a lot in common." He puts his hand closer to mine on the table. "*Ni hen mei*," You are very beautiful.

I glance at the guards. They stand stone-faced by the exit. Should I be grateful or annoyed that they are there?

"As a token of my appreciation, I will call you Lu Mei Mei," Lu the beautiful. "You understand the depth of my appreciation, yes? Just listen to this name; you must tell everyone I named you so." He gives me a meaningful look and repeats it. But something gets stuck in his throat, and he spits out the name in a sharp cough, "Lu *Mei Mei*."

That was a strange intonation.

I ignore him. The bare thought of using my womanly charms sets panic in my chest. I do not want to encourage him. But he locks his gaze with me, and some strong emotion flashes in his eyes. A warning. Then his sickening smile is back. He is trying to frighten me. I press my legs together and feel my Skyhawks. "You're flattering me."

"I only express my sincere meaning."

He glances at my wrist. Still, I hide the tattoo. That should keep his interest.

The doors are opened, and Wei Wan is let in.

"*Bu hao yisi*," he apologizes and returns to the table. But his skin is white, and he dips his head. This is my cue to get out. We are not going to get any further tonight.

"*Kelian de xiao didi*." Expressing sympathy for my poor little brother, I fold the napkin and rise. "I think I best put him to bed."

"Of course," says Laoban, but I detect disappointment. *Good*. Let him hope.

He stands and motions for the guards. "Take them to their room."

We again thank him and apologize for Wei Wan again, and the inside guards hand us over to the two guards waiting outside. We climb one set of stairs, then twist and turn corridors and rows of doors. Which one is Laoban's office? I must enter and search for information. How will I access it?

I memorize as we go, every nook and cranny. Anywhere that could serve as a hiding place. One guard points out the privy, and soon, we are ushered into our lodging. It is sparsely decorated with only two beds, small plain tables, one flickering candle, and two spare ones. A side table holds a pitcher of water, a towel, and a washbasin.

As soon as we are alone, I whisper, "How are we going to figure out which one is his office?"

"Third corridor, second door on the right."

I gape. "How do you know?"

"I asked." He grins. "None of the guards were too interested in watching me getting sick. Or smelling it."

"You!" I blurt. "You ate that meat on purpose!"

"Got to make it look real, right?" He grins some more. "I asked for some privacy, so they backed off enough that I could sneak sideways as soon as I came out from the privy. I ran to the kitchen, caught a servant girl and asked her where Laoban's office was."

"And she told you?"

"No. But I reminded her I'm an honored guest of Laoban. Told her he'd said that if I needed anything at all, just ask the servants." He mock-sharpens his gaze as though he's speaking to the girl. "Is there a problem?"

"Oh, you clod, you're brilliant." A rush flits through me. "Now, all we need is the key."

Wei Wan opens his healer's bag and pulls out something that glimmers.

I gasp. "A picklock?"

"A healer's tool, useful for pricking blisters." He shows me the sharp end. "And draining pus from a boil." At the other end, a thin hoop shrinks as he adjusts it. "And...other things." He grins. "They did teach me a tad more than herblore."

I am exhilarated. In whispering tones, we plot our night.

Finally, I blow out the candle and slide between the sheets. They are soft like silk, and the blanket is not stale and musty. I am far from Long Si. I am at a warlord fortress in the Qinling Mountains.

It must be well past midnight when I finally hear a faint scraping and see Wei Wan's eyes glimmer in the dark. I look at him and nod.

He slips out of bed and steps outside.

The guard snaps, "Where do you think you're going?"

"*Xishoujian*," he mumbles, the privy.

"Off then. Quick."

In his seamless canvas shoes, Wei Wan's steps are too soft to hear. I wait a few minutes, and then I step out.

"What now?" snaps the guard. "You too?"

"What?" I look confused, making sure my eyes are bleary and my hair is a mess. "Has my little brother gone out?"

"You can't both go. You'll have to wait until he is back."

"Oh, *bu hao yisi*," I say as I twist uncomfortably, "but I have to go. I'm afraid it's an emergency."

He looks at me like I am trying the oldest trick in the book. "Those are the rules."

"Boys and girls have different needs."

He snorts.

"The moon is waxing and waning," I say. "Influencing tides, on the planet and...in our bodies..."

His expression morphs into that of a bovine creature.

"*Yin*," I whisper, the feminine energy, dropping my gaze as though terribly embarrassed. I sketch a move towards my groin. "It's, eh, quite urgent."

He jolts, likely horrified by the prospect of a girl moon

bleeding right in front of him. "Go," he waves me off, and I hurry with short, girlish steps, almost sure I hear a faint "Take your time," as I round the first corner.

In the light of flickering torches, I find our designated intersection. I slide in behind a protruding column which conceals a spiraling staircase. Then I wait. Focus all my senses, and yes, after a while, soft, measured steps near. *Stalk the cat.*

Wei Wan reaches my spot. He turns his head as he walks past. A nearly imperceptible nod. It is done; the lock is breached. But just as I am about to step out, I hear a noise at the end of the corridor. I dare a quick peek and see Wei Wan slow his pace and walk in a sleepy, unsteady manner.

Two guards pull their swords. "What's the meaning of this?" one of them demands.

"*Xishoujian.*" Wei Wan mumbles about the restroom, rubbing his eyes. "*Wo yao...shui jiao,*" he wants to go to sleep.

The guards wave him off and continue.

I leave my hiding and tiptoe to the boss's office. Quietly, I push the handle and slide in.

Inside, I let my eyes adjust to the dark, then feel my way over to the desk and find a lantern. I pick up the nearby matches and light it. *I'm in.* Now, records of prisoners?

I quickly go through shelves and drawers, calculating how long the guard will believe I need for my womanly needs. The shelves are filled with scrolls and documents, but nothing even close to prisoner reports.

A cold thought finds me: What if they don't keep any books? But, no, I tell myself, warlords do organized crime. They are part of a large network. They have targets, people on lists, debts to claim and debts to be repaid. They must keep track of it all.

I begin to lose hope when I come across something. Registers, names, but it turns out to be deceased warlords, Sworn Brothers, and their outstanding blood revenge, most dated decades back.

Frustrated, I place my lantern on the desk, but my eye catches something. A small piece of rolled-up parchment, partly open. Something alerts me; I don't know what. But I lean in and straighten it with shivering hands.

My jaw drops.

CHAPTER 31

THE REST OF THE NIGHT, I TOSS AND TURN. BACK IN MY room, I can't get the parchment out of my mind. Again and again, I see it before me.

Zhaodaole. Tade mingtzi shi Lu Mi La. We found her. Her name is Lu Mi La.

Laoban knew my name? How is it possible? The punishment for cheating a warlord is severe. I imagine horrible torture, beatings, rape. The more I think, the more feverish my tossing and turning. The bed is uncomfortably hot, and I feel sticky all over. And if he knows who I am, then why does he pretend he doesn't?

Hours pass before I finally drift off. The following day, the knock on the door jerks me out of a deep sleep. I am exhausted.

"Just a minute," I shout, dragging myself out of bed and over to the wash basin on the side table. "Let me get ready."

Wei Wan is already up, watching me hopefully. "Later" is all I say.

We are breaking fast with Laoban. If I disliked sharing a meal with him last night, I loathe it now. I can't believe the note in his office had my name on it.

The servants bring soy milk, rice porridge, and a whole plate of *baozi*. They're vegetarian today, he points out. "Since the doctor says you can't have meat."

I give an embarrassed smile. "*Gei nin tian mafan.*"

"Not at all," he says. "No hassle". "Here, try the sweet bean paste. We Manchus love bean paste."

"Manchu?" I say. "You're a long way from home."

"It has been centuries since we were only found in the north. And for that matter, I don't think I'm the only one who's a long way from home."

My bowels clench. How much more does he know than my name? But then he smiles, and I wonder if he is hoping for my womanly charms. I force myself to smile back and ask about Uncle. Can they help us?

"I am sure we can," he says and rises. He turns to Wei Wan, "*Xiao pengyou,*" little friend, "are you interested in seeing the cavalry of carved wooden horses on the second floor? *Ayi* will take you." He nods at the lady who, most of the time, stands quietly by the side door. One more face in his infinite army of servants.

I quickly say, "Oh, *xiao didi,* that sounds wonderful."

Wei Wan nods. The lady is already by his side, leading him out.

Laoban walks over to the *kang*, the traditional Chinese

wooden sofa. It has a large, wide bamboo bottom with a small table on top.

"Tea," he orders with a wave of the hand. Then he takes off his shoes and climbs up. He settles cross-legged on the cushion by the low table and motions for me to sit opposite. "It is good your little brother left. We can talk about your uncle."

"What do you mean?" Hiding my excitement, I adjust the cushion under my seat. "Has something happened to Uncle?" Servants bring steaming tea in covered bowls. I make big eyes. "Do you know something?"

He takes a sip of tea. "Ah, oolong. To sharpen thinking and improve alertness."

The most expensive tea. Of course. I try it. "It's exquisite. A chance to enjoy oolong; how fortunate I am." I must steer him back on track. "It's Uncle's favorite as well."

"You know something very unusual happened this morning."

"Oh?" I softly put down my cup.

"When I came to my office, it was unlocked. That has never happened before." He looks me straight in the eyes.

"How strange. What can have happened?"

"What do you think happened?"

"Hmm," I purse my lips and furrow my brow, trying desperately to mask my fluttering heart. "Well, someone else must have a key, obviously. *Or*," I say and sit up straighter, as though I just thought of something, "someone has, at some point, borrowed your key and made a copy of it."

"If they had a key, then why didn't they lock it as they left to ensure I never realized?"

"Perhaps they aren't very smart?"

"Or perhaps that's not at all what happened." Across the table, he moves a bit closer.

I veil my dread with another inflated smile and lean in, too. "So, what *do* you think happened?"

"Maybe I just forgot to lock it?"

I get so shocked that for a moment, all I do is stare. "Oh, of course! That must be it."

He nods at the two guards by the door. "Xin and Wang here think I'm getting old."

"Old? But you're no more than..."

I realize it was a joke. We both laugh out loud, and I relax like a squeezed-out sponge.

Then he shifts to dead serious. "I never forget to lock."

I grip my teacup. *He knows*.

I fake surprise. "I really have no idea what could have happened. Do you have a lot of valuables in there?"

But he obviously believes he has given me enough warning and drops the subject. "Lu Mei Mei, are you interested in plants?" Again, he makes the strange intonation of *mei mei,* but I ignore it.

And I am interested in Earth Mother. "Always."

"Let me show you, then." He gets off the wooden sofa and heads over to the row of small trees. "These are a miniature version of China fir, native to the central parts of our country. They need a lot of water." I think of his tattoo, the character for water.

"They're beautiful," I say as I stop beside him. "A symbol of longevity." I bend down to touch the plants, and on impulse, I snatch two of the small white stones at their base.

Laoban is already at the other end of the hall, where more

plants are lined up. And next, we leave the room.

The two guards fall in step like mute gorillas, but Laoban snaps impatiently, *"Juli."* He wants distance, and they melt back into the shadows.

As we tour the fort, he points out different types of flowers and trees inside and out in the yards. I snatch a few more white stones every time he isn't looking. My impulse has set me thinking. Perhaps Wei Wan and I can use them for some sort of signaling? I don't know; possibly show that one of us has been in a certain place? I pretend to be heavily into the fortress's flora, but wherever we go, I pay attention.

The ground floor has a kitchen, several storage rooms, a canteen, meeting rooms, grand halls, an armory, and a guard post by the main entrance. If only I could turn into a tiny mouse, crouch in a dark corner, and listen. Sooner or later, someone must mention something about Uncle.

Cook Ma's words surface. *Ancient fortresses were designed to protect in war times. You will be spied upon. There are always ways.*

"Bamboo shoots." Laoban is showing a whole row of pots. "They require massive amounts of water. *So* much water," he says.

Water again, I vaguely think. What did Cook Ma mean, there are always ways? Secret passages? Spy holes?

"I love bamboo." I carefully touch the bright green leaves, then give a small smile. Patience. He is still assessing me, trying to figure out my paranormal skill. He has not asked, and I have not volunteered. Which one of us will make the first move? "Thank you for showing me your plants. It has been a pleasure. Only..."

"What?"

"I was thinking, it's rather horrible for a girl to be followed so closely by these *men*. I am sure they are trustworthy," I say hurriedly, "but...it's been so nice to walk around freely. Do you think, I mean...would it be possible that they could just keep a bit of distance from me and Wei Wan like they are right now, I mean?"

It is a risk, and considering my break-in last night, I am sure I have asked in vain. He thinks for so long I fear I have angered him. Finally, he seems to reach a decision.

"I suppose that can be arranged." He makes a sharp nod. "Guests should not feel watched."

Only with restraint do I manage not to thank him profusely. A plan is forming in my mind.

Wei Wan looks at me in disbelief. "He will stop the guards?"

"Were you escorted back here to our room?"

"No."

"See?"

"But why? You said he knows it's us who broke into his room. He should be watching us even more closely."

I keep my voice down. "Perhaps it's just an act."

"Exactly," Wei Wan nods. "We don't know that he hasn't doubled some other kind of watch. A secret one."

"Or..." I tap my fingers against my chin. "Could he be worried about getting on the wrong side of me before he knows what my skill is? After all, witches have been known to strike people dead."

Wei Wan is not up for my jokes. "The note in his chamber," he mutters. "That was freaky. How could he know your name? Someone must have betrayed us. Do you think it was the old lady? In the village?"

"How could she know my name? Anyway, if he doesn't connect me to Long Si, we'll be all right." I change the subject. "How was the wooden horse collection?"

He pulls a small object from his pocket. "Not bad."

I gasp, "You stole one!"

"I told you my new skill would come in handy," he grins.

"But a wooden horse, whatever for?"

A shrug. "The more tools, the better."

"Funny, I had the same thinking, which reminds me, can you handle supper on your own tonight? I have something I need to do."

"What will I tell him?"

"Say...that I was feeling too tired and I miss Uncle too much. Or...improvise." I rise from the bed. "There's still a couple of hours left; we should both be seen, but not together. They mustn't get too used to that."

Wei Wan agrees, and I take one of the two extra candles on the bedside table and pat my pocket. The white stones are still in there.

Wherever I go, I feel curious eyes on me. Nothing has changed, the watch is just less imposing. Different people at different times, making it harder to map.

Right now, there's a beefy man on my tail, hand on his

sword pommel. I decide to go to the kitchen to ask for a glass of water, but inside, the armada of workers is too busy to pay me any attention. Fires are going on, pumpkins are being steamed, and ducks are braised and roasted. Amid fires and tantalizing smells, I search for a second exit, but my eyes fall on a tray with glasses and a pitcher. I go over and pour myself a drink. That is when I see her.

In the corner, a girl discreetly cuts bitter melon, and she is so inconspicuous that I have to look twice. Is it magic? Or just long practice of not wanting to be seen? Stay out of trouble?

I say my silent *Seikhar,* closing my hands before they go red. After two more attempts, something flickers briefly in front of her. But just like when I tried in the courtyard at Long Si, I can't bring out her heart orb, just a weak feeling. It is... nothing? It takes a moment for my brain to click: Air Heart.

How far can my magic take me? This is no battle; there is no threat, so, can I still borrow a bit of her heart energy? I shoot out a tendril and snatch at the space where something flickered. Instantly, I feel my contours loosen, as though I am dissolving.

I hide my excitement as the beefy man appears. At the kitchen entrance he scans the area, so concentrated that even though I am still faintly visible, I walk right by him. He turns and continues along the corridor, then doubles back, looking nettled.

I loosen my hold on the Air Heart energy as I pass him. "Just returning the glass." He startles at my appearance. "I helped myself to some water. I hope that was all right?"

He mutters but looks visibly relieved.

And this game I play for hours.

I learn to keep the quality I have borrowed, and

economize. When I focus, I picture it in my heart as a small core of shimmering light, and I practise activating it and setting it to rest. Slowly I amble around, sometimes my normal me, sometimes my new shadow version. At one point, I walk right by Wei Wan, who's studying a stone carving on the wall. He tenses, turns his head, and looks twice and there I am.

"*Jie*," he hisses between his teeth. "Your stealth is amazing! I almost didn't know you were there."

"Not stealth," I whisper back. "Magic."

Out in the yard, I stretch my arms over my head and yawn, walking around some more, waiting for dusk to fall. I glance at the left side of the massive entrance: the small moon door, just like at Long Si.

Guards come to light fires, and soon the iron-wrought cauldrons filled with oil burn brightly.

Focusing on my pilfered quality, I glance casually sideways. There is not much left, but with dusk and shadows on my side, I should be near impossible to spot.

When I get close to the wall, I drop down, searching for some kind of handle. Nothing. I shoot another quick glance around and then whisper, "*Seikhar*."

Seikhar, seikhar seikhar. Nerve-wracking seconds. Then, faint red lines appear on my palms. I press a hand to the door. It opens. Quickly, I light my candle on the torch beside me and slide inside.

Holding the candle to my chest, I protect it as the huff of the door sends the flame sideways. Then, carefully, I stand and descend crumbling stairs into the cold, stale air. The ancient fortress is full of underground tunnels, likely not visited for centuries. Dusty and festooned with creepy crawlers and cobwebs, they extend in all directions and are, I soon discover, cleverly connected to above.

Every time I follow a staircase up, I find myself exiting at the fortress's ground level. So far, I have ended up in deserted walkways and rooms. Where am I? I try a fourth one. This time, I know right away that straight ahead are the kitchens. Down to the right are storage rooms and tools. The left way leads back to the halls and Laoban's meeting room.

Distant boots interrupt my mapping. But in my excitement, I accidentally let the door slip shut. All I see is an intricate wall carving. A big dragon holding a pearl of flame, surrounded by swirling patterns.

Fear grows in my blood as the thudding nears. Should I pretend I was here all along, admiring a wall carving? That will cost me my opportunity to explore. In sheer panic, I try the only thing I can think of: the pearl of flame. I press my hands against it, and the unseen door opens.

I step in, cup my hand and bend to shield the candle left inside, secured in a puddle of wax.

Still shivering from fright, I descend the stairs and continue my search, squinting to see in my meager light. Every time I turn a corner, I place one of the white stones on the ground so I will find my way back. I climb four more stairs, but each time I reach the top, noises outside prevent me from exiting, so I don't know where I am.

How many hours have I been here? I am cold and hungry, and I have had enough.

CHAPTER 32

"I TOLD HIM YOU HAD A HEADACHE," WEI WAN SAYS the next morning. "He fussed and asked if you needed anything, but secretly, I think he was annoyed. Are you going to tell me what you were doing?"

"Exploring underground tunnels."

"What—without me?"

"Shh," I hush him with a glare. I still don't know if this room has ears. "How could I bring you? Don't you think it was hard enough as it was?"

"Did you find out anything?"

"Not really."

I tell him about the small moon door and that it was locked with magic, which makes me wonder if it was locked long ago or recently. Does someone here have that kind of skill? Wei Wan shrugs; what does it matter? He only wants to know about my new magic.

"Your stealth, *jie*! I almost didn't see you, but yet I sort of did..."

287

I explain about the discreet girl, the Air Heart energy I managed to borrow for so long, probably because I didn't use it a great deal, just enhancing my stealth, and then the underground tunnels, which need exploring. Is this where Uncle is hidden? "It's a big network, cleverly connected to the fort's ground floor."

"So, there are several entrances?"

"In theory, yes, but in reality, no. Unless you know exactly where you'll never see them from this side, I almost didn't make it back."

"Now what?"

"I keep borrowing heart energy and go again."

"When?"

"I'm not sure. I need a lantern, candles go out too easily." I stand up in the dimness. Our room has only arrow slits for light, and it gives me an idea. "Let us go down and have breakfast with Laoban. I want to ask him."

Once again, I do my best to appear a mixture of polite and apprehensive, pining for my lost uncle and wishing my host would offer a morsel of hope, which he doesn't. I praise his oolong tea which he has with all meals, and then I ask my question.

"Laoban, do you think I could have a lantern?"

"You need such a thing?"

"Yes. You see, I have brought some things to read on our journey."

"Read? What things do you read?"

"Oh, you'd think I'm very silly," I giggle—which I think I have done maybe, like, never.

"Not at all. Please tell me."

"It's a story about someone who believes that plants have consciousness. I know, I know."

"Not at all. It sounds interesting. I shall get you your lantern."

Plants. I knew he would warm up to that. And later, as I am walking slowly around, a servant girl comes running with an oil lamp. Two guards pass me, swapping weary glances, but I thank her plenty and continue to the kitchens, where I light my lantern with a stick from the fires. The discreet girl is in her usual corner, and I quickly borrow a snippet of her energy. As I feel myself dissolve, she glances my way, and for a moment, I freeze. But then she continues chopping carrots with her long sharp knife. I quickly leave.

Minutes later, standing in front of the grand dragon carving, I press firmly against the pearl of flame. The unseen door opens. I slip inside and descend the stairs.

For orientation, I retrace my steps to where I came down from the moon door yesterday. This was where the pathways initially split. The one I didn't take feels like it could be leading out and away, but I ignore it and return to where I finished searching yesterday. Several times, I come upon new stairways, but the fort is teeming with midday activity, and I dare not exit to see where I am. The only thing I succeed in is getting annoyed. Three days without a hint of progress.

"Thank you. I'm starving."

Back in our room, I wolf down the *baozi* Wei Wan has brought. He moped around alone and befriended an old woman in the kitchens. Since it is now common knowledge that we are Laoban's honoured guests, she snuck him whatever he hinted at.

"Urg and Warg passed me once. I think they really hate us. At least you."

"Thanks. That's reassuring."

"No, I just mean they see you as more of a threat."

"They've wanted to kill me since they first set eyes on me. Maybe it's the girl thing."

"At least you're not a snake." He grins.

I finish the *baozi* and tell Wei Wan he must do all the talking at dinner. "I'm too exhausted."

I am letting the dungeons wait for now. Last night was uneventful; after an early dinner with Laoban, we went to bed, and now I am walking around in the fort's easternmost part. After a quick visit to the kitchens, where I equipped myself with some air qualities, it was easy enough to make my way to this quiet end. To conserve energy, I lessen my grip on the magic, quickly passing corridors and halls searching for anything irregular. My eyes instantly hone in on a sturdy door with iron fittings, but something alerts me. A shadow, or watchful steps, I don't know.

When I turn, there is Warg.

"You certainly find your way around," he says. "Where'd you learn to navigate an ancient fortress? The bazaar in Kashgar?"

"As good a maze as any."

For a moment, we just stand there, sizing each other up. He is more than twice my size with a sword at his side and doesn't need to assess anything. I have two throwing knives I am not supposed to have, and no womanly charm under the sun will work here.

"So, girl," he steps closer. "What's your skill?"

"Heavens, I'm popular. You're the third one that's been asking," I lie.

A quick frown touches his face. I can see him grappling. Others have asked? Who? *Let him wonder*.

"You know, we're really allies, you and I." As he narrows his eyes, I say, "Just think of it. Laoban rules your lives, Urg wants his place, and while the two of them squabble for the top position, what's left for you?"

Irritation pools like a dark cloud around his face. "Your *skill*?"

"Oh, I don't know. Maybe I've been known to strike people dead. From a distance. Perhaps I'm something in between a witch and a voodoo master." His frown deepens. "Only, you know, better-looking." I smile.

He looks ready to tear out my liver but is unsure if I am pulling his leg or not. I hear footsteps. And while I am Laoban's honoured guest, I'm not sure I want to be in a deserted part of the fort with only Warg or several muscle-pumped brutes at any time, really. I bid him a courteous good day and leave. Then I spend some time in the central areas, where people can see me. Best stay out of trouble. Two other guards tag me for as long as I let them, and it's already after lunch before I get a chance to explore the second floor. The west side, opposite end from where our bedroom is. I try a few doors, but they are all locked.

A voice alerts me.

"Oh, I like 'em feisty."

I sneak up to a side passage and glance around the corner. There is the beefy guard. He leans into the wall, looking like he is talking to himself. I draw closer and sharpen my gaze. My insides contract.

The discreet girl, he's cornered her. I see her clearly this time; she has a weird sandy hue to her hair—so she must be one of the ethnic minorities. But I have intruded on shady dealings and my alarm bells go off. *Not your business. Stay out of it.*

She squirms as he touches her waist. "Let me go."

"I don't think so. Know the best part about nobody noticing you?" He pushes her against the wall. "They also don't notice if you're gone."

His creepy voice scratches my skin like cold fingernails.

"I'll scream," the girl threatens. But her words are weak.

"Yeah? Who would hear you? Who would care?"

He yanks at her shirt, and terror washes across her face. The same kind of terror that washed over me on the Silk Road when I had escaped Master Li and found myself surrounded by men. When I was so afraid that my throat locked and I could not breathe.

I take three quick steps.

"Excuse me."

The beefy man startles, and the girl races.

"You just did *what?*" he hisses.

"I was looking for the privy—oh." I whisk my head in the direction of the fleeing girl. "Sorry, were you talking to someone?"

Cold rage ripples from his voice. "The privy?"

"Yes. You know, like when you drink too much, and it has to come out."

I weigh my size against his, calculating body mass versus speed. The time it will take me to close in and deliver a minimum of four hard strikes and kicks as opposed to the time it will take for him to squash my entire body like it was a fly's. Even though I am Laoban's honoured guest. Untouchable. Unless it's self-defence, of course. I can see him waiting for me to make the first move.

"What's your skill?"

"That's a hot topic around here." I should be frightened out of my wits by this girl-molesting brute, but hatred fuels courage.

"I don't think you have a skill."

"And you're willing to bet on that?"

"I could kill you and dump the body without anyone even knowing."

"Did you know that those versed in witchcraft are experts at haunting their killers? Long after."

He takes a step back. Ukko, this one was easy. The witch thing works. The fact is, I am glad everyone keeps pestering me about my skill because, from a witch triad perspective, I am not handling things very well. I must keep the mystique alive.

I make a gesture. "The privy?"

He takes me all the way, making a point of waiting outside. When I come out, I try to look as if I best be on my way then, but he watches me like a hawk. Anger still rolls off him, and I can't ditch him for hours. He may be wary of my skills, but I still interfered in matters that were not my concern. What will Laoban say? Urg and Warg are waiting to pounce on me like hungry lions. Did I just add another member to my death squad?

On day five, I am beset by fleeting panic. What if we don't find Uncle?

I spend hours exploring the underground walkways. Ukko knows it's a thin consolation after wasting all morning on Laoban: a never-ending meal and boring talks, since the Chinese are experts at dragging things out; it is called *tuo*. Then he said he had to go and work. But not until he had taken my hand to compliment my long, slender fingers. He twisted my wrist slightly, and I let him get a look at the tattoo. I felt his moment of weakness; he wanted to ask what my skill is, but if he does, then he must tell me something about Uncle. Give and take, that's how it works.

I am climbing a new stairway. But it doesn't have an exit, just a minuscule room that I can't see the point of. As I turn to leave, a faint light comes from somewhere. I put away my lantern and let darkness flood the space. In one spot, thin light beams penetrate the wall. Muffled voices reach me, and I realize what this is: a walk-in spy hole.

One of the bricks is only partly solid. It has been covered with a thin layer of mortar, so porous that light filters through. Little holes have been poked, and as I press my eye close, I can make out people and guards, all with metal trays. It's the canteen. The mortar blurs my vision, but I recognize the beefy one.

Suddenly someone comes so close on the other side that

I draw back in fright. But the scraping of chairs brings me back. Carefully, I peek again, but too close. I only see hair and leather.

"There *is* no Uncle," the man says. I snap to attention. "Why doesn't he just throw her in the cells?"

"Until he knows her skill, he doesn't dare."

I recognize their voices. The first one is Urg, and the other one is Warg.

"I'd beat it out of her," Urg spits. "I'm not afraid of silly witch talk. I'd make a better boss than that sissy. I deserve it. How many years have I served with no recognition?"

At once, I understand how they suddenly were so close. They are sitting on a dais, partitioned off for privacy, a spot denoting privilege. That is why they are speaking so freely, and that is why the spy hole is located at precisely this spot.

"That's his problem," Urg rants on. "Too meek."

"Some call it strength, maintaining order with minimum force. The Brothers trust him. That's what loyalty breeds."

"They're sworn to our cause!"

"They're sworn to *him*."

"Well, he killed his warlord."

"Which is why they worship him."

"But not because he killed Jiang Xie, all because of how he killed him," Urg snarls. "The so-called master move. What if our Brothers knew? His mind-blowing swordsmanship would be reduced to ashes."

"Aye," Warg grumbles. "Poisoned blade, the oldest trick in the book. Wouldn't they love to hear that?"

"But nobody knows. Only us, and so it will stay." Urg leans back, and I catch a glimpse of his face. "This," he mutters grimly, "is the ace up my sleeve. Enough to turn the Brothers against him."

CHAPTER 33

"So..." I begin, but Laoban senses where I am heading, and he doesn't want to go there. No Uncle. "Did you sleep well?" he asks.

"Very well, thank you," I say. "But—"

"Eat, you must eat. I had Cook make vegetarian dumplings for you. With vinegar, you must try."

So, I smile and praise the food. The guards are their usual, stone-faced. *Ayi* stands in one corner, and servants move in and out.

"More tea!" Laoban calls. Oolong. Every day, he drinks his oolong.

I raise my cup, "To sharpened thinking and improved alertness."

"Lu Mei Mei, *ni tai congming.*"

Beautiful and simply too clever, am I? Frustrated, I spend the rest of the morning walking around the fort while Wei Wan goes with *Ayi* to see the wooden horse collection again.

To shake off the beefy guard who's stalked me for the

past half hour, I have to flee to the second floor. But as I heave a sigh of relief, strong hands grip me from behind.

"So, everyone's been ordered to let you wander, huh? How convenient," Urg whispers in my ear. "And do you know exactly how much Laoban cannot protect you right now?"

My back is still toward him. "You wouldn't dare."

"Who says it's me? People trip. Things happen."

He yanks me around, grips a fistful of shirt at my throat and nearly throttles me.

I force calm into my voice. "You could kill me right now. But before that, know that I can help you."

"Between the sheets?"

"I can tell you things."

"I'm sure you can."

"Things about me."

He snorts derisively.

"Don't you want to know about my skill?" I glance briefly at the tattoo on my wrist. "Laoban doesn't know either; he's too craven to ask." I raise my gaze somewhat. "I know you wouldn't be that meek. Personally...I prefer strong men." His grip eases an inch. "Your Sworn Brothers would be better off with you as leader."

Surprise makes his face drop.

"Become Laoban yourself. Isn't that what you want, ever since he killed Jiang Xie and stole the prize in front of your eyes?"

"How do you know?" he asks sharply. "Who *are* you?"

"Laoban has no plan to change your duties. You're his second...for as long as he keeps you..."

"I don't need homemade girl prophecies."

"Not even the date of your own death?"

I see him vacillate between wanting to beat me senseless and know the answer. "What do you mean you know things?"

I raise my brows.

"You're psychic?"

"Perhaps."

His grip eases some more. "What is it you can tell me?"

"Now that you are touching me, a lot more than a few minutes ago."

He looks unsettled. "What about Laoban? Can you see his death?"

"I need more time. Matters of this nature require physical contact." I pull my arm loose and leave.

"I'll give you until tomorrow," he warns behind me.

"Laoban, I was thinking," I say at lunch the following day. "You've been very kind to us, but I feel that some of your men are a bit..." I smile uneasily. "Suspicious. I would like to suggest that we all meet and clear the air. Could we not share a meal with your second and third? Talk it out?"

If he's surprised, he doesn't show it. He nods consent. "*Keyi.*"

"How about lunch tomorrow?"

"If it pleases you."

"It would, very much, thank you."

"See you at dinner." His face is unreadable.

Laoban intends to play the game of *tuo;* dragging things out until its bitter end. He is not going to tell me anything until

I reveal my skill.

But I have a new plan. My first one, to use my heart magic to explore, worked well enough. I've borrowed energy from the discreet girl every morning. This one is riskier but with greater reward if it works.

I wander aimlessly, counting on Urg watching me. Out in the first yard, I lean against the wall and shut my eyes, enjoying the bleak sunbeams of the twelfth moon. It does not take long.

"Let us walk," a low voice snarls in my ear. Urg.

He jerks his head sideways and leaves.

I nonchalantly join him.

"Tell me," he demands.

"What is it that you want to know?"

"Laoban."

"His day of death is tomorrow."

He stops sharp. "*What?* Do you mean to..?"

"Of course not," I snap. "Who do you take me for, a murderer?"

"Then how come..." His brow furrows in tight creases. "There are no current threats. He's in good health."

"Things can shift in an instant."

"But he is born a dragon; this year is auspicious for dragons."

"Anyone can be unlucky."

He stares at me. "How will it happen?"

"That has not been revealed to me."

"How do I know I can trust you?"

I raise an eyebrow and walk away.

I still have hours until supper. Time to go back down.

I search the underground tunnels but Ukko take them. They don't lead to anything. I did overhear Urg and Warg, but that's it. Like previous times I wander until I'm cold, tired and hungry and lose track of time.

Suddenly, my mouth goes dry. *Supper!*

I scramble up the stairs to the nearest exit. I will have to enter straight into the dragon wall corridor; I can't risk Laoban wondering where I am and sending people to find me. As I reach the top, I blow out my lantern, press my ear to the stone and listen. Then I push up the door, take one swift step, and my brain locks. I never went by the kitchens this morning. I have no Air Heart.

In front of me stands the beefy guard.

"What the—" he begins.

He stomps forward, and I sense someone rush past. The discreet girl, I almost didn't see her. She scuttles along the corridor, throwing her head around for one fast glance. Big, terrified eyes flash through strands of sand-colored hair.

The guard grips my arm hard. "I knew you were a fake!"

"Lu Mei Mei, there you are." Laoban comes striding around the corner. "I've had people looking all over." He sees the guard and stops. "Kai Lan, what're you doing?"

"Laoban, she's a—"

"Guest," Laoban cuts him off. "Did I order you to manhandle my guests? Release her at once."

Despite Chinese hierarchy, the guard attempts a protest. "But, she...look! Why is she carrying a lantern?" he splutters.

They both look at me.

I shrug. "It needs refilling."

"Laoban, I *saw*."

"It can wait. Right now, it's dinner time." He looks at me. "I already have your brother waiting at the table." To the guard, he says, "Come to my meeting room in one hour. I will hear you out then." He points to my lantern. "See to it that it's refilled."

He takes me down the hallway, and I am shaking. I am so distracted during dinner that I can hardly make a proper conversation. As soon as Laoban looks the other way, Wei Wan bores his eyes into me. *What's going on?*

I don't know what to signal back. How can I tell him I blew it? In less than one hour, the beefy guard will knock on the door and tell Laoban he saw me emerging from a secret door. We will be taken prisoners, thrown into the dungeons—killed? I know Wei Wan can see the panic in my eyes.

"I sent Urg and Warg on a scouting mission this morning," Laoban is saying. "They should be back in time to hear what Kai Lan has to say. That's so important." He snorts.

I focus on breathing.

Laoban sees my plate. "Lu Mei Mei, you're not eating? Is the food not good?"

I assure him the food is delicious; I am just a bit tired, that's all.

Wei Wan makes a point of eating more. "*Hen haochi*," he praises. Very good.

Agonizing minutes drag the hour by. I feel myself turning glassy-eyed, my brain alternating between a thousand bad excuses and total surrender. Just as I feverishly wish I could sink through the floor, there is a scuffle outside. We all look up.

302

Then comes shuffling, a thud, and a loud clatter.

Everyone rushes from the table.

"Open the door," Laoban shouts. The guards yank one handle each.

They pull with such force that I imagine the air vibrating from the draft. The space in front of me ripples with minuscule waves, for a second distorting the pattern of the opposite wall. On the ground lies the beefy guard. A long, sharp knife sticks out from his chest. Beside him is my lantern, and now Urg and Warg appear at the other end of the corridor. They break into a run.

I stare in disbelief at the prone figure, gripped by terror, and then a vast relief washes over me. *My threat is gone.*

"What's going on?" Urg shouts. He drops to a crouch by the fallen man.

"What happened?" Warg demands. "Who did this?"

Yes, who did this? I bite my lip. *And why?* Can I turn it to my advantage? Pretend I worry Uncle has met the same fate and demand answers now that I've first-hand witnessed how unsafe it is here?

"No Sworn Brother," remarks one of Laoban's guards.

"They couldn't," says the other one. "Kai Lan was too strong."

Indeed. Who can overpower him?

"His sword is still in his sheath." Warg points to the slim leather piece. "He must have been taken by surprise."

"Impossible," Urg snaps. "Too experienced."

My brain works fast. What if I could find the killer and make him indebted to me by a threat of revelation? My *Seikhar* allowed me to call Hidden Eyes. What's to say it can't call other

303

unseen things like the spirit of Kai Lan? He must have seen who killed him. But how do I call a spirit? And is it still lingering here, or has it passed into the Netherworld already? I need to get back to my room.

It takes a minute before I realize that Urg has risen, a shrewd expression on his face. "If you ask my opinion...," he says slowly, drawing out the words. "I'd say it was sorcery."

Everyone turns to me.

"Yes," Warg shouts. "Of course. It's *her*. I know it. She can strike people dead; that's her skill!"

"What?" Urg scowls. "How do you know?"

"I asked," says Warg excitedly before he realizes his mistake. "She tried to. I mean, she threatened me, and I overpowered her and forced it out of her. I had to. For my own safety."

Urg looks furious. "That was not your task."

"You *what?*" says Laoban to me.

"No," I begin, but my throat dries up. My audience is frozen, hanging on my every word. I make big eyes. "There must be a mistake."

"You said it," Warg presses. "Strike people dead from a distance. Do you deny it?"

"I, no," I try again.

Urg stabs a finger in my face. "It was you."

"I knew it," says Warg triumphantly.

The other guards grip the pommels of their swords, and a completely new kind of fear splits my chest in half.

"Stop!" Laoban looks livid. "No one is accusing anyone of anything until we have proof." He turns to Urg and waves a hand at the dead guard. "Remove him."

CHAPTER 34

I WALK FAST BACK TO OUR ROOM, TOO DISTURBED TO notice that Wei Wan is no longer with me. I thought he was right behind, but now that I look, he is nowhere. Our dinner got interrupted, perhaps he went to find the woman in the kitchen, the one that sneaks him treats. I don't care, I just walk. A thousand heavy boots marching frantically through my head.

The only person who would have blown my cover turns up dead, and I am accused of killing him. In a warlord fort. Inside our room, I keep balling my sweaty fists and walk in circles until a knock on the door snaps me out of my alarm. Two massive guards stand outside, holding a bloody heap between them. Wei Wan.

They dump him unceremoniously on my threshold.

"Looks like your brother had an accident," one says.

I suppress the shriek that is halfway up my throat. This is a warning. Girl histrionics will not do. They clearly believe I killed Kai Lan, but how could Wei Wan become a target? Did he upset them? Which, I realize in the next few rushing seconds, is precisely what I would like to do. One man has shown up dead. Why not ride the wave fully? Pull the rug from under their feet?

"Yeah, looks like it," I say. I realize I have missed Sun Tzu's first rule; I haven't really gotten to know my opponents properly. It's not just Laoban. Urg and Warg are all in it together, they're a team, and now I finally see it. I also see Wei Wan and myself, and a new sort of confidence blooms because if our actions made big men beat up a thirteen-year-old, we must have hit a nerve.

And right now, that suits me perfectly.

"Best make sure he doesn't get into any more," says the guard on the right. "Old forts can be dangerous."

"Right," says the other. "High places. People fall."

I shrug. "Never thought of that."

I detect a faint surprise at my indifference. Oh, how I'd love to break the cold veneer of these cocksure thugs. Not to mention Laoban, who uses ridiculous, fake-friendly ways. He thinks I will fall for that? Really?

The right guard toes Wei Wan with his boot. "Next time, look after your brother better."

"Sure." I yawn.

The two muscle-creatures leave, and as soon as they are out of sight, I drop to my knees. "Wei Wan," I whisper hysterically. "What happened?" I pull him to his feet and help him inside. "Are you hurting?"

"Looks worse than it is," he mumbles, but he lets me sit him down on the bed and examine him. I fill the wash basin with water and use the towel to clean him up. He flinches as I come near the eye with my wet rag, and his lip is cracked, but soon enough, I have him looking better.

"They ambushed me," he carefully nudges the lip with his fingers. "I told them it wasn't you, but all they kept saying was, 'Do you know what happens to brotherhood killers?'"

"How badly did they hurt you?" I scrutinize his face. "Is anything broken?"

He shakes his head. "No, no, I'm fine. All I need is some sleep." But he looks miserable. "*Jie*, I was afraid they were going to kill me, and then who would help you?"

Oh, xiao didi. Always thinking of others first. I put down the blood-colored rag and clasp his hand in both of mine. "They wouldn't. This was just a warning."

"But why now?"

Because on the stage of warlord play, something has happened that cannot be undone. By worming ourselves in here, snooping around, asking questions and pitching Brother against Brother, we have stirred things up.

"But who killed Kai Lan?" Wei Wan's voice is urgent. "Who killed him?"

"I have no idea, but let them think I did it. He is not my main concern. We need to get out."

Back to my plan.

"Wei Wan," I whisper. "Time to bring out your healer's bag."

He reluctantly gets up and hobbles over to the corner where he keeps his bag. Once on the bed, he opens it and brings out bottles, vials, and small packages of powders.

"Tell me," I prompt.

Some are just part of the typical healer's kit. I learn: disinfectants, cream for bruising, something for a cough, a headache, stomach ache and heartburn, and six rolls of fresh gauze.

"Then there are these," he points at three small, neatly wrapped packages. "Water hemlock, deadly nightshade, and white snakeroot."

"I need one fast-moving poison and one slow-moving."

"Water hemlock can cause death in as little as fifteen minutes. The other two are slower, hours at least."

"And you have antidotes?"

"Only for snakeroot." He pulls out a tiny vial fastened to a long, thin looped leather string.

"Then we will use water hemlock and snakeroot."

He takes them out and, on my orders, anything else we might need. "Now give me the bag. I have preparations to do."

And with that, I take our things and the lantern and slip silently from the room. I still have no Air Heart in me. Thank Ukko stealth is my forte.

After carrying out my nightly task, I head back to our room, sneaking along the walls in the sheen of burning torches. The corridors lie deserted, yet the chill night air vibrates as I turn the second-to-last corner. It's that sense again, as though in one small spot, the world gets distorted and waves ripple into nothingness.

I stop.

"It was you," I say into thin air. I get no reply, but I speak anyway. "You killed him."

In front of me, the discreet girl materializes. Her faint

figure melts into the stone behind her. Strands of sand-colored hair frame a face that looks oddly soft and strong at the same time.

"How did you do it?" I say. "How could he not see you at all?"

"I know you've been borrowing my heart energy."

Shame invades me. "I'm sorry." I lower my gaze. "Honestly, I, I didn't mean to."

"No." She puts a finger to her lips to make me lower my voice. "Don't be sorry. This is all because of you. I've only ever been able to make myself invisible once. Now I've done it three times in six days. You taught me." At my confused look, she says, "I had been focusing on all the wrong things: blurry outline, unclear contours when I needed to focus all the time on the core of my density. Only by thinning my heart energy can I diminish my physicality. You did that when you borrowed it from me." She pauses gravely. "But remember, you could only keep using my energy for long stretches because I let you take it. Usually, that's not how it works."

It takes me a few seconds to grasp what she is implying. From me, she learnt how to become invisible, steal up on Kai Lan, and kill him. The long, sharp kitchen knife she could already handle.

"You saved me," she says.

"*You* saved *me,* twice. Kai Lan was evil. Now, he won't bother anyone."

There is something so special about this girl, I can't say what, but a strong impulse hits me. "Come with us," I plead. "Leave this place. They might realize it was you."

"No, I must stay. There are things to be taken care of."

I am not sure what she means by that, but her gaze goes distant for a second, and she mumbles, "Some are after your flesh, others just watch, but they're all just as bad." She gives a light head shake. "I will be all right. I have magic, as do you, sister." She grasps my hand and meets my gaze.

I ask her name, and she tells me it's Yi Qian Xing. A Thousand Stars? Yes, just so, she nods with a faint smile as though reminiscing something far away and precious.

"I was born under a dragon's wing. The first thing I set my eyes upon was a thousand shining stars."

Under a dragon's wing?

"I shall succeed," she says solemnly. I want to ask; succeed with what? But she waves me away. "Goodbye, Lu Mi La. Be brave. Be strong. Perhaps one day we will meet again."

Already, I do not see her.

CHAPTER 35

It is time for lunch. Last night, in whispering tones, I told Wei Wan about A Thousand Stars, that it was she who killed Kai Lan. That she was able to utilize her Air Heart energy fully and steal upon him unseen. I cannot use my magic in long stretches like that again. It only worked because she let me take it. I did not sleep much after that. And all morning, Urg and Warg have prowled like hungry predators, until we retired into our little lair.

Wei Wan doesn't look too bad. He's got a blue eye and a fat lip, but that's about it. He says he is sore but that sleep did him well. Now, he double-checks his packages for the umpteenth time. He pats the side of his ribs where throwing knives are fastened with the entire supply of gauze. Four throwing stars are tucked underneath on the opposite side.

I had stopped wearing my strap with Skyhawks and my dirk, but now I bring them out again. Six slim knives go into their pockets of dark, soft leather, this time on the outside of my thigh, and the dirk is already snugly nestled in my chest wrap.

Two throwing stars go in a strap on my other leg. I have cut my pant pockets on the inside so I can easily reach my weapons.

"Water hemlock?" I whisper. "Snakeroot?"

Wei Wan nods and nods again.

Our plan is simple. Laoban will not give us any leads on Uncle, so we have to take him out. Then we use poison to make Urg talk instead. Dangling the antidote in front of his nose should be encouraging enough.

"You think he will tell us?" Wei Wan asks.

"He will if he wants to live."

"What if he doesn't believe that is the serum?"

"A man bargains with what he has." I take the vial of antidote and loop it around my neck.

We are seated around the table, Wei Wan between Urg and Laoban. Warg on the other side of Urg, and me on the other side of Laoban. Laoban looked genuinely shocked when he saw Wei Wan and asked what had happened, but I know it was just an act. Obviously, it was either he or Urg who ordered those guards to beat Wei Wan up.

Wei Wan told him he'd gone for a snack late at night and fell down the stairs, which clearly no one believed. But Laoban left it at that, and even though I can tell both Urg and Warg are dying to jump up and rip me apart, he has them silenced. Did I murder Kai Lan? He probably doesn't know what to think.

It is a big table, but so full of food that it doesn't feel too big for five people. Urg and Warg look grimly at their plates, and I can feel Laoban staring at me from the side as though he wants to say something. *Too late.* I press my lips together. *You had your chance.* His intense gaze is surprising. Here in China, it has only been Yong Da who stares that boldly.

I look down and see the tattoo on his forearm. The water character. I dimly hear the ghost of a whisper inside, something about...element...and birthmark...

"Lu Mei Mei, may I serve you some tea?"

He waves at a servant who fills up everyone's tea while I am thinking of the best opening to this meeting. Never go straight to the point.

"Tell me about your famous wooden horse collection," I begin. "It's a fine tradition." I dare a smile. "And horses have such powerful symbolism. Strong yang, head of the six domestic animals," I chatter, recalling lessons from Long Si. "Crucial in transportation and war."

Warg and Urg look confused, probably wondering if I am entirely deranged or dropping sharp hints, which is perfect. I *want* to confuse, *want* to orchestrate this event that no one yet understands. "They represent speed and freedom, no?" I dip a dumpling in vinegar.

"Many animals represent speed and freedom," Laoban says.

I feel there is something to that statement. "Do you have a particular kind in mind?" I ask.

"I do. Birds."

"Which one?" Wei Wan slurps up his *liang pi*, cold noodles. "Crane?"

"And oh, Laoban," I interrupt as though I just thought of it. "I finished my book on plants. It was so wonderful. Now, I believe more than ever in the life of plants. Look, I can

313

demonstrate." I let my chopsticks clatter on my plate and jump up, heading for the potted Chinese firs. "You can learn to talk to them, and they will respond."

In my eagerness, I trip and crash into the second plant. The pot breaks, scattering earth and china all about. "Ouch!"

Laoban rushes over. "Lu *Mei Mei!*" I vaguely notice the funny intonation again. "Did you cut yourself?"

He helps me up, and servants scurry over to clean up the mess.

"I'm so sorry." I limp back to the table. "*Bu hao yisi.*" My lowered gaze and reddening cheeks accentuate the apology. "I really didn't mean to ruin our meal."

"Here, have some tea." Laoban motions at my cup and around the table, "Sit everyone, please sit."

"Thank you. I think we all need some tea. Oh, I feel like such an idiot." For just a split second, Wei Wan's eyes touch mine, and I know. He has done it, placed the poison in their cups. We're all set. "That was silly of me; I'm really sorry."

Laoban waves it away. "*Mei shi.*"

I take a sip of tea and rub the knee I banged into the pot. "So, anyway, where were we?"

"Birds." Wei Wan has moved on to sautéed spinach.

"Right," snaps Urg.

"Right," snaps Warg.

"I said that many animals represent speed and freedom," Laoban says. "I meant birds."

"And I asked what kind he had in mind," says Wei Wan. "Was it a crane?"

"No, it wasn't. It was falcons. Most interesting because they can be trained. Did you know that training a hunting falcon can take years?" Again, he eyes me. "It's a real battle of willpower."

I suppress a sneer. I can see where this is heading.

"To tame it, the master must spend days just staring into its eyes."

He wants to make a point, but I have had enough of this game. I am *Seikhar*. I come from north of the Polar Circle.

"But the Manchus are strong," Laoban drones.

I offer an arrogant look. I have bathed in glacial pools and eaten a reindeer's heart. *What things had you done before you turned six?*

"What did you say about the Manchus?" I show tepid interest in his attempt at conversation.

"That they are strong."

"Oh. Yes." I sound less than impressed.

"It was they who began training hunting falcons during the Qing Dynasty."

Inwardly, I frown. Didn't someone tell me that already? I get a strange sense of familiarity over something that should not be familiar at all.

"My family has a hunting falcon," he explains. "We've lost contact mostly, but sometimes they get in touch. I had a message only two moons ago."

Urg's lips make an involuntary twitch. "That's right, I saw it."

"What did they want?" Warg says.

Urg plasters on a smile, and I know Warg just overstepped, asking the highest boss about a private matter. Urg takes a sip of tea.

Laoban produces the same fake smile. "*Jiu shi ma;*" just

my mother. "I miss her. She's a really good cook."

Even though something whispers in my mind, I don't react.

Laoban again. "She is so good that sometimes we jokingly call her Cook Ma."

CHAPTER 36

I CE COLD SOBRIETY WASHES OVER ME. HE KNOWS COOK Ma! *He knows Long Si. He knows everything.* Like a seabird racing for shore, my mind flaps wildly. I work to control the shiver that races up my back.

"Tell me," I say. "Is it common for a falconer to name their falcon?"

He raises an eyebrow. "It is," he says slowly. "But in a name rests power. Sometimes, no name is as good as any name."

Cook Ma's exact words! Everything comes crashing like an avalanche. His leniency towards my break-in—I was meant to find that note, it came from Long Si, notifying him of our arrival, Lu *Mei Mei* with a strange pronunciation; in fourth tone, it means little sister, as someone would affectionately call me if we had a bond, from Long Si for example. The talk of water, his tattoo, dragons are caretakers of water, he is born in the year of the Dragon, as is Master Li, as am I. Manchus, hunting falcons, when I asked Cook Ma how the hunting falcon ended up at Long Si, she said, *It came with its master. A proud Manchu.*

My eyes fly wide, but he silences me with a look. I know it, then. *Laoban is Uncle.*

He reaches for his teacup, and I stare at Wei Wan, who makes the tiniest of nods. Yes, he confirms once more; the poison is in.

Every molecule in my body fires.

Laoban lifts the cup to his lips.

I leap up and strike it from his hands. "Watch out!"

The room freezes at the commotion and sound of smashing china. Servants, guards, Warg, Urg, everyone. They stare at me, the mess of shattered pottery and spilled tea.

"Careful." I stab my finger at Urg. "He wants your place!"

Urg shoots from his chair with a roar, but the two guards at the door are faster.

Laoban flicks up a hand and all stops. The guards double their grips on the struggling Urg.

"You bitch!" Urg shouts. "She's lying."

"Quiet," Laoban says.

"Filthy lying witch, I'm going to kill you."

"*Quiet.*" A nod and one of the guards punches their captive, who crumples. Laoban turns to me, keeping up the pretence. The others don't know who either he or I really are. "Is your skill to tell hidden substances?"

"What skill?" I snap. "Who says I have a skill?" I flare my fingers in a quick signal. This lets Wei Wan know that we need to get out.

A chair comes flying into Laoban's neck, sending him to

the floor. Wei Wan—he doesn't know that this is Uncle! He drops the chair just as the guards release Urg and rush for him. He roundhouse kicks one and leaves the other one for me. It all happens so fast that I don't even think of heart magic. I plant a foot in his ribs, kick, punch, and double-tap kick.

Warg rounds the table, but a Skyhawk flashes through the air. It lodges firmly in his chest, making Urg stare in shock as his underling slumps to the floor. The guards come again.

A hand grips my ankle so hard I fall, landing next to Laoban.

He motions me near. "You must leave," he wheezes. "Tunnels."

I nod.

"The pearl of flame...unlocked."

"I know."

"I've marked the way out."

We found our target, and now we are leaving without him.

"Next message," I whisper urgently, "say 'glad Ma's better.' If things are bad, say, 'Sorry to hear Ma's getting worse.'"

The guard is upon me. I bounce up, duck under his blow, and do a low sweep that sets him off balance.

Swiftly, I drop by Uncle. "Urg has already drunk his poison. Do you want him to live?" I pull the vial with the antidote over my head, press it into his palm and close his fingers around it. "He wants you dead, but it's your call."

I make to rise, but he grips my wrist. "Tell her," he begs. "Tell her I'm fine."

I squeeze his hand and see droplets seep out of the skin

on his wrist from his tattoo, the character for water. His soul is crying for Cook Ma.

Wei Wan throws a star, and one of the guards crashes into me with two of the six points buried in his forehead. I spring at the other one with a front kick and a parallel punch. He dodges, but my reversed fist strike finds him true. A joint kick at the knee and he drops.

The servants have long since fled, but Urg is left. Blocking our way, feet apart, knives palmed.

"You lying, conniving, blood-sucking little—"

"I would conserve my energy if I were you." I cross my arms and narrow my eyes. My confidence throws him. Doubt flashes across his face.

"What're you talking about?" he snaps.

"*Jie*," Wei Wan motions anxiously. The door. We have only seconds before new guards arrive.

"Did you really not taste anything funny with your tea?"

Urg stares at me. Then, his eyes bulge with terror.

"And *don't* run after us. It will only make it worse."

I spin around and join Wei Wan, who's snatched back the knife from Warg's chest and is already halfway out of the room.

We race to the eastern corridor by the kitchens. Twice we have to dodge oncoming guards, jumping in behind doors and stairwells. One more corner. We round it at full speed, but six guards are approaching.

Again, I act on reflex; grab knife, raise arm, swing from shoulder, forward, downward. Next knife, next knife. Stars. Only two, a light tensing of fingers and wrist, and I send the first one on its way. Then, the second.

The first two knives miss. And my first star. But my last

knife and my last star hit their targets. Two down. At my side, Wei Wan has already taken out the other four.

We sprint past. By the wall carving, I grip Wei Wan's wrist, and we come to a stuttering halt. I press my hand to the pearl of flame, and as the door opens we dive inside, and it clicks shut behind us. On the ground sits everything I left last night: knapsacks, a lantern, matches, the healer's bag, and harnesses. I retrieved them last night from behind a sleeping guard.

I also made a trip to the rookery and released one of our homing pigeons with a note tied to its leg. I dared not give them hope about Uncle, but at least they will know when to expect us if we make it out.

We catch our breaths for only seconds as guards rush by on the other side of the wall. I wriggle into harness and knapsack, light the lantern with trembling fingers, and descend.

Wei Wan follows. "Won't they come after us?" His voice sounds tense as it bounces off the walls.

"The tunnels haven't been used for centuries." I steer us back to the fork where I first came down eight days ago. Here, I turn left.

I raise my lantern. "The way out should be marked..." And yes, there. I point. "That thing, the arrow."

We half-run, and half-walk along the earthen tunnels for what seems an eternity. But the surface is smooth and sloping down. Leaving is a lot faster than arriving. When we finally exit into a set of caverns hidden in a deep valley, it is so dark we can barely make out the forested cliffs around us.

"That saved us a lot of time," I pant. "Cutting through the mountain."

We leave the burnt out lantern and stumble on, but we have

no idea where we are, and in the end, the terrain gets too difficult. We break for a few hours of sleep.

CHAPTER 37

A SINGING BIRD WAKES ME, AND FOR A MOMENT, I AM confused. Then my stiff and sore body reminds me: fight, escape. I sit up and try to move my shoulder. I must have landed on it when I slammed into the floor. Relief and worry flood me. How long before they come after us? Or will Laoban be able to stop them?

I wake Wei Wan and start gathering our belongings. Above us, the sky is thick with lumbering clouds that cast an ominous shade over the valley.

"Which way?" says Wei Wan.

I point downward. "It's got to be that way."

We press through rocks and dense vegetation. After a few hours of stumbling and cursing, we finally step out onto a rocky path.

"At last," I mutter.

"At last, what?" says a voice.

We jerk up our heads and my heart plummets. A Brother, I can tell from his leather garb and spiked gauntlets.

He rests both hands on a sword planted in the ground, carefully scrutinizing us. "And you two are headed where exactly?"

"To Ying Pei village," I point vaguely. "We got a little lost."

"That's one way of putting it. This is forbidden territory; no one walks here without permission. Where're you coming from?"

There is no point in lying. "From the fortress where we have stayed as Laoban's honoured guests."

"Honoured guests? I wouldn't think so." He crosses his arms. "As one of the Sworn Brothers, I know him very well. I find it unlikely that two children of whom I have never heard would come to stay as his honoured guests."

"Not children," I snap irritably. *Know how many ways I can kill a man?*

"How about this version: you're escaped prisoners that he would very much appreciate getting back?"

I feel tempted to go for my Skyhawks.

"I'm just returning from a challenging mission, which I handled with ease." He taps his fingers on the pommel.

I am a poor thrower; this man is undoubtedly an expert swordsman. We don't have the element of surprise, no one is poisoned out of their wits, and no one is going to come to our rescue.

"I'm sure you're very good at whatever it is you're doing," I say. "But we must be going."

In a flash, the sword tip is at my throat.

"Maybe you're going the wrong way, little girl. Laoban lives that way." He forces my head sideways with the tip of his sword. "And I like to surprise my boss."

"I said we were honoured guests."

"Leaving without an escort? Why should I believe you?"

"Why do you think he'd let us keep our weapons if we weren't guests?" I point at the swords on my back.

"Exactly," Wei Wan adds. "Do we look like we're running? We also became good friends with both Urg and Warg; we had tea with them every day."

A subtle frown.

"Oh, yes," says Wei Wan. "They're much friendlier than you think once you get to know them. Especially Urg. I think he doesn't dare show that he likes children."

The Brother's sword arm softens. He slips a grunt.

Oh *yes*, little brother, I could hug you. *More, more. Lies need to be convincing.*

Wei Wan goes on, "You don't get it. Laoban gave us gifts and treated us with courtesy."

"Gifts?" the Brother snorts. "What gifts?"

"This, for example." Wei Wan tosses him his wooden horse. "From his famous collection."

The man inspects, searching for the initials, then straightens. "This is from Laoban's collection." He pulls at his beard, looking a mixture of confused and embarrassed. "My apologies," he finally says. He sheathes his sword. "Well then, I shall be your escort as long as the road demands."

A day short of Ying Pei village, our guard bids a courteous goodbye. "Be careful of that horse, boy. It's worth good coin."

After one restless night in his company, we're pining to be free. "Thank you for your help." I offer an unnatural smile.

"*Bu yong xie*." Don't mention it. He turns and leaves, and we run the second he is out of sight.

The sun has come out, and under different circumstances, this could have been a story of trickling streams, fluttering butterflies, and chirping birds. But we are so exhausted and relieved we can't even speak. Wordlessly, we slow down to a walk and continue for a good many miles before we decide to stop and search for a well-hidden spot. There, we place our bedrolls on the ground, and for a long time, we listen to all the sounds in the falling dusk. Several times, I go around the copse of trees we've hidden behind to spy on the mountainside. The land looms above me, dipping and rising in craggy formations. I let the eye travel as far as I can see before finally looping back to where I am.

Only when I am sure that nothing will betray our position do I pull out whatever bits of food I can find in our packs. We eat in silence.

"Did you know it would end like this?" Wei Wan asks.

"Could never have imagined."

"Me neither, but I knew stealing would come in handy."

"You're right," I say. "The wooden horse."

"*Hetian* jade."

I am too tired to speak. He is too exhausted to smirk.

It is already mid-morning when we reach the village, and we buy scallion pancakes at the first stall we see. Plenty of bean paste with soy and rice vinegar, gobbling them down on the go. Still, my palate registers the softness of the pancake, the streaks of ginger. A subtle burst of scallions dances in my mouth, even though we're not supposed to have them.

As we pass the old woman in her yard, she pays us no mind.

"Was it her, do you think?" says Wei Wan in a low voice. "Who betrayed us?"

"No." I usher him down the road; I want to get as far away as possible. "No one betrayed us."

"What do you mean?"

"Later."

I cannot speak of it for a whole day and a night. The mere thought of how close we got to poisoning Uncle sets my heart racing. It was my decision. *I nearly killed him.* The Second Master of Long Si. I force it away. We did locate him, and he is all right, he is all right.

"So, did you get it?" I ask Wei Wan, who is on the back of a horse cart we've hitched a ride with. "Why I did what I did? Smashed the teacup?"

"Laoban is not who we thought he was?"

I stare at tilled fields in winter sleep. The growing season in Shaanxi is exceptionally short. Still, it feels like we've been gone for an eternity.

"He is Uncle?"

Why am I not surprised? "Clever you."

"How did that happen?"

Wei Wan looks so different with all this hair, as though he is morphing into a whole other person, the way I always imagined him, bangs and all.

"I guess he infiltrated the Syndicate, maybe too well. Killed the former warlord and won the Brothers' respect. Warg and Urg claim he used a poisoned blade, but regardless, he impressed enough of them to take up the mantle of their fallen leader. But those two are suspicious, and he is always watched, so never a chance to tell us directly. Nor send word to Long Si. The messages could get intercepted."

"When did you realize?"

"So many things I missed. He tried to drop hints from beginning to end. Then he uttered a phrase exactly the way Cook Ma once did. That's when it all clicked."

I want to say that he likes Cook Ma and that she likes him. But that is not my secret to tell.

Wei Wan picks at a chestnut that has fallen onto our wagon. "Did we fail?"

"No."

"We found our target, but we left without him."

"We had no choice. A faulty move would have blown his entire operation."

"He sacrifices himself."

"For a cause."

"I suppose."

"As have we," I remind him. "You can't say it's been easy."

"We made it, our pilgrimage, *Journey to the West*."

"North," I point out.

"The same. An adventure, scary, but with insights. Lessons, I guess."

"What did you learn?"

"If possible, always circumvent ancient warlord forts."

I laugh. "But we were true in our quest. Did we not journey toward enlightenment by the power of virtue and cooperation?"

"Absolutely. Like the legend said, it is a pilgrimage to find truth, peace and beauty."

"Peace and beauty," I snort. "How about surpassing oneself and overcoming difficulties?"

"Exactly my meaning."

I roll my eyes. "Let's settle for the ending: We're returning home after many trials and much suffering."

"That sounds good. Only one thing."

"Yeah, I know. The Monkey King, Yong Da."

"Not trapped under the mountain for five hundred years?"

"I wouldn't count on it."

I wake up with a funny feeling, as though someone has nudged me awake. But as I sit up and blink in the predawn, I see Wei Wan snug in his bedroll, fast asleep. I look around our small camp, but all is quiet.

Three weeks have passed since we escaped the fort, but something in me has changed. I infiltrated a warlord cartel, lived in fear and nearly murdered an innocent man. Now, something grows that I cannot stop, drawing me toward a destiny I cannot see.

"You are worried?"

Wei Wan's quiet voice startles me. "It's nothing."

"*Jie.*" He makes an impatient face. "Don't treat me like a child."

"But you are a child," I tease and duck as a plum comes flying.

He snaps, "Want a knife-throwing competition?"

"Ukko no." I raise my hands in mock defence. "*Kai wan xiao bale.*" Just joking.

"So then, tell me," he says with a petulant face. "I'm your *didi*, I deserve to know."

A pang of humbleness still shoots through me whenever he displays this candid affection. And once more, I think he resembles a little frog.

"To be honest, I'm not sure. It's just, ever since the mission, I feel different."

"I do, too." I can see emotion gushing up in him. Too much, too fast, and I know what's coming.

"*Wo sha ren,*" he struggles to keep his voice under control. He killed. "How can you ever go back to what you were after that?"

"You can't. But it's a part of life we must both get used to. This is what we are trained for." Death. More real as we progress towards our goal to crush the warlords.

"When I die, will Guan Yin take me in her lotus flower to the Pure Lands Beyond?" His lower lip trembles and my heart wants to burst. In one swift move, I am there, taking him in my arms.

"Of course she will." He cries so hard his whole body is shaking, and I cannot stop my own tears. He hugs me back, and we lock in an embrace so tight it is hard to breathe. I tell him not to worry, "*Bie danxin, xiao didi. Bie danxin.*"

I had not realized how tightly fear had snared us. Or how good it feels to hug another. The closest I have come to it in eight years was two distressed half-hugs, one before the tournament and one in the fort when they had separated us the first night. Cook Ma's quick embrace before we left. My body hungers for human touch. Beneath our skins, we begin to dismantle our emotions, big ugly constructs full of dark shafts and broken angles. To bare everything, even just to myself, I feel vulnerable, more exposed than I ever did on the wide-open mountains in Sápmi.

"I killed," Wei Wan repeats as he pulls away, and we both dry our soaked faces with our sleeves. "You didn't."

He is right. At least, from what I saw, I did not kill anyone. Thus, I cannot fully understand his new burden. Again, he breaks down in uncontrolled sobbing, and I stare at a tear in his shirt, thinking of how long it is and frayed, how Cook Ma would have a fit if she saw us in this state.

"I understand how you must feel," I say quietly.

"How can you? You didn't do it."

"You're my brother. I see myself in you, I see your pain. I don't know...just...makes it tangible somehow."

I want to stop myself from saying more. My words are just a flawed attempt to open the gate into his well of emotions and feel what he is feeling. Instead, I am filled with shallow silence.

"Really, I do. I know what you're going through."

"That's good," he snivels, but I know he's just being kind.

We make our way, trying to devise a quicker route, and mull over how old-fashioned Laoban and his followers are.

"Maybe they have firearms hidden somewhere," Wei Wan speculates.

"Yeah, maybe."

"But where'd they get the money to buy them?"

"Threats and corruption, I guess, same as in the olden days."

"But why do they cling to the past?" Wei Wan goes on.

"I don't know. There must be a reason."

CHAPTER 38

THE REST OF THE TRIP IS UNEVENTFUL. ON THE LAST LEG of our journey we ride another horse cart, and I settle into sacks of grain. Wei Wan falls asleep whilst I ponder my glimmering hands. The northern lights can set them off, it shows I belong to that tribe Mother spoke about. And in the underworld of Long Si, Hidden Eyes played his part as it was he who awoke my powers. I can open doors locked by magic, and I can borrow people's strength. Anything else? Or are the red lines in my palms just a trade mark for the Tribe?

Does the Tribe really exist?

We are almost home, but something nags me. The note from Long Si to Uncle. What could be so important that they felt the need to inform Uncle that they had found me? *Me?*

At the edge of my mind, faint shadows dance; the change I have been sensing, like tendrils nestling into my very core, rooting themselves, yet hankering for answers. *We found her. We found her.* The words play dreamlike in my head, all the way until I spot the curved rooftops of Long Si.

My thoughts are abruptly cut.

"*Tamen laile!*" They're here!

The words remind me of the first time I arrived with Master Li over eight years ago. And just like then, everyone rushes out to meet us, staring in a mixture of awe and trepidation.

Perhaps we look foreign. We have been gone for moons. Wei Wan has long hair, we are dusty, tired and dishevelled. For a moment, everyone stops.

Then Ming Pi pushes through, and I see Yong Da bump his shoulder, but Ming Pi doesn't care. He stops right in front of us. "You're back," he breathes. "How did it go? Where were you?"

The spell is broken. Questions burst from everywhere.

"Tell us what happened!"

"You were fighting somewhere, weren't you?"

Everyone flocks around us, and I feel strangely touched. Ming Pi looks like he is going to burst any minute, and several boys from Group Four look at me with a new eagerness. Yong Da keeps his distance, together with Wicked and Ugly Bulldog, and turns his back on us.

I remember Habllek and suddenly realize: The person he was so jealous of when I surprised him and Steel Master, that day I was chasing after her, and Yong Da said, "Why don't they let *me* go?"—was me. He was talking about this mission, and he wanted to be sent. He must have planned it for years and that's why he was so well-read on Sun Tzu and the art of espionage, gloating in Master Li's history class. And it must have been Steel Master who told him. Clearly, he would be privy to this kind of information. I trap my fury and smooth my face. *Not now, not here.*

Cook Ma comes running. "Everyone, back to your chores!" she commands and rushes at me with open arms. I have never seen her gait so light, and I swallow a lump in my throat.

San Dun's chubby legs propel his ample shape forward, and even Master Li strides with determined steps, leaving his colleagues behind.

"Lu Mi La," he calls. "Wei Wan, you're back."

We're ushered away to Master Li's office, but I catch a glance from Apple. He smiles, and I smile back.

A warmth coats my chest.

"Your message said you would try to escape. Heavens, I've been worried sick!" Ma blurts.

"Yeah," I smile. "Sorry we couldn't bring the second pigeon."

But she hurries off to fetch tea while San Dun looks excited. I am surprised he's allowed in here, but Master Li says that Head Archivist has not been well, and San Dun has kindly stood in for him when they needed information. San Dun flushes slightly, embarrassed at the praise.

"Here, sit." Li pulls out chairs. "Tell us everything."

Cook Ma returns, a tray of steaming green tea before her. With measured calm, she hands us a mug each, but as soon as she sits, her fingers twiddle.

"We found Uncle," I say, and Ma draws a breath.

Master Li tenses. San Dun's eyes bulge and Ma's hands keep curling into balls. I tell them he is all right and detect a collective sigh of relief. "I am sorry we could not rescue him," I begin, but Master Li waves a hand.

"No, my mistake. I realize it was too hard a mission. I should not have given the order. I am afraid my personal interests may have clouded my judgement."

San Dun edges forward on his seat. "Did you actually meet him?"

"How is he?" Cook Ma arrests herself. "Sorry, I didn't mean to..."

"We could not rescue him because he doesn't want to be rescued."

I get three blank looks. "Uncle is not a prisoner."

"He is Laoban," says Wei Wan.

"What?" Master Li blinks. Cook Ma and San Dun drop their jaws in unison.

"He killed the former warlord, proved his strength, and impressed the Sworn Brothers."

Cook Ma's mouth is still an *o-shape*. "He's not a prisoner? He, he is...free? But...why hasn't he sent word."

"He is not really free." I take a sip of tea. "Surrounded by people and never alone. You were right when you thought he could not send messages for fear of interception. And not all are in favor of him. His second and third guard him like hawks."

I see their anxiety return and assures them he is fine. Ma relaxes a thread, then a flash of awkwardness. She thought she had hidden her feelings better. "And I designed a way to at least keep some contact, using his falcon."

"So, what you're saying is," Master Li clarifies, "he is doing well and the resistance work is progressing as planned?"

"Even better, I imagine. You have your own man inside

and at the highest level."

"Right," says Dun. "Brilliant."

"How he got out of sending guards after us, I have no idea. Perhaps the search was slowed by nobody realizing where we'd gone. I don't think they know about the secret tunnels." I take another sip from my mug. "Or at least not that they could still be used."

"Good," Master Li nods, "good. Now we can really get to work."

"Yes," San Dun exclaims. "Restore the Three Masters of Long Si and vanquish the warlords." He goes abruptly silent, as though he just took up too much space.

"The three—?" My thinking slows to glacial speed, groping for something implausible. Silence fills the room, and now my throat burns. My next breath rattles all the way to the bottom of my lungs. "The third brother," I manage.

"Is you," Cook Ma says.

"You see, don't you?" Master Li asks.

But I don't. Or...somehow, I think maybe I knew, deep down, but I don't see. I really don't. "I... I am...the third Master of Long Si?"

"Mi La," San Dun smiles. "You are aware that a soul can take any gender in each lifetime?"

"Yes, but how can it be?"

"You are Hidden Eyes' twin spirit," says Master Li.

"Anyone could be that," I say dismissively.

"The second criterion," Dun says. "You are born in the year of the Dragon."

"Many are."

"But they are not *Seikhar*," Cook Ma finishes, and my

grip on the mug tightens. "You are a Child of the Northern Lights. That's why Hidden Eyes could awaken your powers, and you have a birthmark on your right shoulder blade. I saw it when I asked to see your injuries after the tournament. The one that tells us your element is water."

My mind stumbles down a tunnel of memories so long I end up all the way back in my cradleboard as a baby in Sápmi. The portable carrier of birch wood and reindeer hide is padded with linings of sphagnum moss and cattail down. And right now, that is what I smell. My mind has broken through the amnesia that besets every child at babyhood, erasing all memory of the soul's existence before birth and the early stages of life in this body.

I feel hands lifting me out of my cradleboard. Cold air touches my skin as clothes are being peeled away. A finger presses a spot on my right shoulder blade.

"The mark I dreamt of." It is the *noaidi's* voice. "Her element is water. I am sorry to disturb you, *Beaivi*," mother of humankind. "But I had to confirm. The inception rite must take place this evening. You need not be present."

"But, she must be initiated, no?" my mother says, confused.

"Later. She will be later, *Beaivi*."

I recall something else: Mother and Father discussed my element when I was several years older. It should be earth, they reasoned, as I, the oldest of their children, was to tramp the earth and lead the flock once they were gone. In my birthplace, the oldest child can never leave. Water, however, symbolizes flow and movement.

"The *noaidi* must be wrong," said Father.

"The mark speaks for itself," said Mother.

I jolt back from my buried past, clanking down my tea mug a little too hard. "A mark. That's what the legend spoke of." I recite from memory, " 'They will all bear marks pointing to flowing bodies.' "

"That's right," San Dun nods eagerly. "The rest went something like, 'inspired by their leader and lodestar,' but there was a blotch of wax; it was impossible to read."

"Their leader and lodestar," Master Li cuts in. "Who do you think it speaks of?"

Bits and pieces of *The Water God's Chronicles* drift in my mind. *In many belief systems, dragons are connected to water...rulers of fluid bodies such as lakes, rivers, waterfalls, or seas...*

"Hidden Eyes." I breathe. "The spirit dragon of Long Si."

"Exactly. The Three Masters of Long Si are all born in the year of the Dragon, and all bear marks that point to water." He holds up his arm. "For me, three wavy scars for a flowing river. For my brother, the water tattoo that unseen forces guided him to get. And for you, a special birthmark."

"But, wait." I squint in perplexity. "How did you know I was *Seikhar?* That's got nothing to do with Masters of Long Si."

Cook Ma folds her hands. "Something else gave you away."

"The Nefarious," says Master Li. "They hunt anyone with magic, but seldom all the way from north of the Polar Circle."

"You see?" San Dun counts on his fingers, "Heart magic, water element, born a dragon, the only one able to call Hidden Eyes, stemming from the glaciers of the true north *and* wanted by the Nefarious. We couldn't get more signs."

Three heads bob in confirmation.

"So," Wei Wan finally speaks. "We have Uncle and the Three Masters of Long Si, and we have a spirit dragon and his twin spirit. Not bad." He looks at us under his bangs. "Now what?"

"Now our work begins." Master Li rubs his chin. "Two thousand years of imperial rule may have ended, but the warlords still exist."

"Guerrilla warfare." Cook Ma looks at us each in turn. "A hidden threat that grows with time."

But for now, Master Li tells us, we must return to our routines. "And, both of you, well done," he says with a curt nod. "This is good news."

Cook Ma rises. She looks unable to choose between angst and peace. I want to tell her more, but my mouth is dry as dust, and all I do is stare mutely. *I am a Master of Long Si.*

Li sends us off to eat and rest.

On the way out, I nudge Ma aside and whisper, "He wants you to know he is well." She squeezes my hand, and for a second, she tears up. Then she turns away, and I leave, but as I glance back, I see that Master Li puts a hand on her shoulder. So then, he, too, knows.

Uncle has been gone for nine years. That is a very long time. Cook Ma is near forty now, maybe too old even to have children.

Outside, Wei Wan says. "Cook Ma likes Uncle."

"How did you become so clever, little frog?" I smile and put an arm around his back.

"I have an older sister," he grins back. "She is really

clever."

"No, *xiao didi*, it's you."

"And she's a master."

"Don't get me started, or I won't be able to sleep a wink tonight."

We head up to the river to wash and change into clean clothes. Then we eat a hearty meal, just the two of us. Cook Ma lets us have as many *baozi* as we want, and Wei Wan manages four before slowing down.

"I've missed Ma's cooking." He gobbles down the stinky tofu, his favorite.

"I can't believe we did it."

"We'll end up in the chronicles in First Archive."

"Huh," I snort. "Not."

"Who else here undertook a *Journey to the West?*"

"North."

"Same thing. True or untrue: We infiltrated the fort, located Uncle and escaped?"

"True," I concede.

"We used all the skills we have learnt in Long Si."

"And some more." We both grin.

"We are better than we were?"

I stop and think. "Definitely." My *gong fu* has progressed. Then there's knife throwing, stars, and heart magic. *And womanly charms.*

"What're you grinning at?"

"Nothing."

Wei Wan gives an eye roll. "On a scale, how much have you bettered yourself? I think I'm an eight."

"Why do you need a number?"

"I'm trying to simplify."

"Well, I'm not." I chow down my rice. "Too plain." I understand this moment. I have been plain all my life.

"Okay, no number then. A statement."

"What kind of statement?"

"That tells of your advancement."

I think, dropping a piece of tofu in the process. It falls into the sauce ramekin with a splash. "Right, I have a sentence."

"Trick is, you have to say it out loud. Otherwise, it doesn't count."

I pick up the tofu. "I am Lu Mi La, versed in the perplexing arts of magic and conquest."

"Whoa, *jie*. That's like a ten."

CHAPTER 39

I AM BACK BY THE RIVER, ALONE. MASTER OF LONG SI? MY
entire body still buzzes at the mere thought. I can tell of my
new knife-throwing skills if I wish to share it with someone, and
the mission. But, Master Li says, I must keep Hidden Eyes a secret,
as I must my heart magic. Except for Wei Wan, himself, Cook Ma,
and San Dun, nobody knows. There isn't a single soul here who
practices magic. Yong Da would get the ultimate reason to crush
me, *nüwu*. Witch.

"Master of Long Si. No easy thing." Startled, I turn.
Master Li taps his hands on the front of his thighs. "Nor is
obeying the oracle bones."

"Because?"

"Because what fate has in store for a person might not be
what that person wants. And so, you have to...play god." He
takes a step closer. "Override."

The word flashes unpleasantly in my mind. As in taking
a child scared witless and abducting her instead of bringing her
home? I spend a few seconds restraining an old burning pain

that suddenly flares. Years have passed, I tell myself, and things have changed.

"Have to," he repeats, with such an earnest look of sorrow that something finally clicks in me.

How did I not figure this out earlier?

One: He had no choice. To save Long Si and the whole nation, I have to do my duty as fate predicts. Master Li was presented with only one option: to bring me here.

Two: It was not easy. Master Gang, for one, was firmly against it. So, he could not help or praise me; it would've been seen as favoritism.

Three: That look of disappointment that I picked up when I refused to walk on the Silk Road, that I have picked up countless times since; it was him, not me. *He* was disappointed in himself because *he* betrayed *me*.

Why has this never connected in my brain before?

"Mi La?"

My eyes fall on his nostrils. They are slightly tensed. As though I can only focus on details, unable to take in the whole of his face. "Later, Master."

I turn and walk fast back to my pavilion in the dusk of early evening. But upstairs in my room I am too wound up. The epiphany that Master Li never had a choice hit me like a ton of bricks. He was right. I had to come here. There was never any choice for him or for me.

When silence has deepened to its midnight pitch, I sneak downstairs and take a lantern. Finally, I understand the feeling of something growing inside. Tendrils. I *am* changing. I am a Master of Long Si. Nothing will be the same.

Hidden Eyes lies before me, glimmering like hot coals. His gaze penetrates me, and a glow flares around the fin-like spikes on his cheeks. But I am not afraid.

No, I can see that.

I had forgotten the mind reading. *What now?*

You have completed your mission. It means you have taken the first step to becoming a Dragon Mayster. I suppress my impulse to ask, and he says, *Well, at least if you can accomplish the next step. But for that, you must conquer your hardest opponent.*

Who?

Yourself.

I can do it.

Oh? Rows of sharp teeth glisten. *Can you now?*

I outwitted the warlords. I am a Brotherhood killer.

Not really, he says with a sly grin. *But let them think that you are.*

When I exit from my secret trapdoor, a wild energy gushes through me. We completed the mission, we returned. I get a sudden urge to release it, now. Knife throwing, empty hand, sword—anything. No one will know if I go for a nightly session. It's not like I haven't broken rules with Wei Wan a thousand times.

In the armory, I blow out the lantern and put it down, sneaking cat-like. As I'm about to draw a sword, a sound stops me.

I freeze, gaze darting in all directions. I step back, turn sideways and press my back to the wall. Softly, I shuffle sideways, advancing toward the practice room.

I peek in.

A person is kneeling in the furthest corner. I see hands tracing circles in the air around a glowing blue light. For a second, I am dumbstruck. *Magic?*

I can only pick out bits and pieces in the dark, but I would know that hard, steely frame anywhere.

Yong Da.

Learn more about Mila's world
at www.lilliehookbooks.com

Since centuries back, acolytes have been trained in the Dragon Temple. The monastery was established in the Year of the Rooster, 625 AD, seven years into the Tang Dynasty. Despite following the omens, the founders still succumbed to terrible afflictions. But according to an old prophecy...

On a snowy night far above the Polar Circle, reindeer herder Mila was born. She had an idyllic childhood playing in nature with her beloved reindeer, until one day, eight years later, her life shattered overnight. Mila was brutally abducted and an icy fear gripped the village. It had been long since any such child were born. No wonder they weren't prepared...

Throughout history, reindeer have played an important role as a source of food and clothing to the Sámi—Indigenous People of the Arctic. They live in an area called Sápmi, and still today the animals constitute a pillar of their livelihood. In Mila's animal kingdom, reindeer are beings of magic and grace and she will always, always be connected to them.

THANK YOU

My most heartfelt thanks goes to Authors At Large and their amazing crew of instructors. I specifically wish to mention Xu Xi, Chantelle Aimée Osman, Kim Echlin, Rachel Kadish and Ira Sukrungruang. Crafting a book is a group effort, and I would not be where I am today without your endless rounds of edits, critique, encouragement, brain storming, tips, advice and truly sincere teachings— sometimes in such exotic settings as Iceland or by a beach in Thailand. This journey is not for the faint-hearted, and to not give up halfway that extra push can sometimes be crucial. It can come in different ways. By ignoring for example.

Me: "Just so you know, after this retreat I'm quitting."

Xu Xi: "So this bit here, it needs some more work."

Me: "So," clearing my throat—she obviously did not hear me, "uhm, just so you know, after this retreat I will not be writing anymore."

Xu Xi: "Yes, yes. Now, this character is not developed enough. See, this is exactly what you need to do…"

That was eight years ago. And guess what? I'm still here.

The fantastic troupe at ShadowScript Publications; my deepest and most sincere gratitude for help with *everything*. I especially wish to name Niall Mac Giolla Bhui and Conor Mac Giolla Bhui for amazing work and never-ending support in every area. You guys are true pros with solid skill sets and a brutal eye for details. I could never have done this without you—what a dream team!

Indescribable appreciation goes to Dorothy Dreyer for gob-smacking cover art that surely hails all dragons of all times. Also, in the leviathan area; special thanks to Josefine Thelin for creating the most amazing website the world has ever seen. Keep flying high, Dragon Girls!

My husband Michael Thorneman—for being the most encouraging and supporting partner I could ever dream of. You are my heart of hearts.

And last but maybe most, those close friends who are always *there*, new or old, who are with me every step of the way, cheering loudly from the sidelines and truly believing. You know who you are. I love you guys. In this life and the next.

Finally, everlasting gratitude to you, the reader. For what would all my efforts be worth without you?

www.ingramcontent.com/pod-product-compliance
Lightning Source LLC
Chambersburg PA
CBHW020257120726
47904CB00001B/241